A STOLEN KNIGHT'S KISS

Melissa Oliver

MILLS & BOON

First published in Great Britain 2022
by Mills & Boon, an imprint of HarperCollins*Publishers* Ltd,
1 London Bridge Street, London, SE1 9GF

www.harpercollins.co.uk

HarperCollins*Publishers*
1st Floor, Watermarque Building,
Ringsend Road, Dublin 4, Ireland

A Stolen Knight's Kiss © 2022 Maryam Oliver

ISBN: 978-0-263-30198-4

10/22

MIX
Paper | Supporting
responsible forestry
FSC™ C007454

This book is produced from independently certified FSC™ paper
to ensure responsible forest management.
For more information visit: www.harpercollins.co.uk/green.

Printed and Bound in Spain using 100% Renewable Electricity
at CPI Black Print, Barcelona

To my three beautiful daughters—
all so different and special in their own way.

Chapter One

❧❧❧❧❧

Southwark, London 1227

Nicholas D'Amberly was born a sinner and he would no doubt end his days a sinner, heaven save his soul. But at this very moment it was another soul that had captivated his attention. One who stood just a short distance away on the other side of the damnable busy tavern in London's Southwark. In truth the young woman seemed rather out of place in this ramshackle place filled with many unsavoury characters, but the demure glances she threw in his direction surprised him.

He concluded matters with the informant he had been meeting, Brother Michael of St Albans—a self-righteous, pious monk who snatched the proffered coin while he looked down his bulbous nose at Nicholas, expostulating on the dangers of vice and licentious sin. The execrable churl! But then the man did have his uses since he was part of the Bishop of Winchester's retinue, and happily provided valuable information for said coin. Which was just as well, when London was still rife with conspiracy, rumour and whispers of treachery.

It was *this* that Nicholas needed to uncover, using the secret contents of the missive that the man had just passed to him. It was with this that Nicholas would be able to determine whether there was treachery afoot with the Bishop and his retinue, or whether he was innocent of any involvement with The Duo Dracones, a notorious shadowy group bent on traitorous, subversive action against the Crown. And with the Bishop of Winchester being one of the most powerful men in the realm, he had to tread with caution.

Indeed Nicholas, along with his brethren of a secret group, The Knights Fortitude, were duty-bound to untangle and quash all of it. For King Henry. For the Crown of England. And for his lord liege, Hubert de Burgh, Regent of England until very recently.

In truth it was a good thing then that anyone could be bought for a price, especially obnoxious greedy monks, but Nicholas could hardly complain. They had only just exchanged hands, with a swift flick of his wrist as they passed one another, when Nicholas looked up and noticed the young woman from afar. With flame-red hair tucked beneath a sheer veil and exquisite features, she was indeed a beauty but carried an air of vulnerability about her that alarmed him decidedly.

Deftly he tucked the compact rolled vellum that the man had provided inside the leather pouch dangling from his belt, his movements quick, nimble and under the cover of his cloak. And all without breaking eye contact with the young woman. He took a sip of ale, wiping his mouth on the edge of his sleeve, watching in amazement as she began to weave her way slowly towards him. Well, now, this was a surprise. Yet there was something in the manner in which she moved and the way in which she carried herself that did not ring true. Her fixed smile, for one, was far too sweet and far too innocent for a dirty, unsavoury place such as this.

Oh, God, but the more the maid moved towards him, the more he realised that she seemed just as innocent and just as naïve as her smile. What on earth was she doing in this busy, stinking tavern crammed full of scoundrels and sinners alike? His mind whirled at the endless possibilities that might befall this young woman and none of them were particularly good. Unless, of course, she was a working moll. Nicholas might be on friendly terms with most of London's prostitutes, especially since he paid good coin for information they might glean from their wealthy customers, but this woman did not seem to be one of them—not yet anyway.

His chest clenched with a sudden unexpected sadness. There were many things he might not be proud of in his life but hell would have to freeze before he would venture anywhere close to someone this innocent and naive. Mayhap he would talk to her and try to assist in some way. Coin usually settled a situation such as this. And, with any luck, the young maid would leave and put this behind her. He hoped she would, not that she was his problem.

Nicholas watched as she continued to make her way through the throng of people, when an old codger grabbed her around her waist and pulled her onto his lap. She gasped and tried to break free as the man clamped his hands around her, to whoops and cheers around them.

Nicholas ground his teeth together, knowing that this was something that he could hardly ignore. Reluctant to draw attention to himself and understanding the need for caution, he nevertheless had to offer help to the maid and intervene. He strode towards the group, who sat around a small table, and leant over, glowering at the old man.

'Let the maid go.' His voice was quiet but held enough determined steeliness to make the man swallow uncomfortably, loosening his hold.

'It was only a jest. No 'arm done, sir.'

But Nicholas ignored him and the pathetic excuses often made when a woman was groped and mauled against her wishes. His eyes flicked to the woman who stood before him, biting down on her lip and nodding her thanks with a mixture of relief, gratitude and guilt before turning and taking a step back. His eyes followed her, ensuring that she moved safely through the tavern.

And it was then that it happened. A sudden shift, a sudden stirring movement in just the blink of an eye. Nicholas might have missed the slight pull, had it not been for the fact that *this* was precisely what he did. He was trained to notice everything—every small detail, every single facet of every single person—and yet he had missed this.

Nicholas knew with a sinking feeling as he

fumbled beneath his cloak that the pouch had been cut loose and taken. He looked all around the tavern but nothing seemed amiss. Damn, but he had been lax, his attention solely fixed on the maid... The maid! He now understood perfectly the look of shame and guilt that had flashed across her eyes quickly before being shrouded.

His head snapped up as he searched, his eyes darting around the tavern. But she was nowhere to be seen.

His heart pounded in his chest as Nicholas once again felt beneath his cloak, even though he knew it was futile. This could not be happening. The pouch had indeed been taken while he had been fooled into acting the knight, ensuring the maid came to no harm. But whom, he now realised, had been used solely for that reason—to distract him. Which meant that she must have had an accomplice.

His head darted in every direction, searching for her. Nicholas pushed through the groups of people and made his way to the door.

'Have you seen a young woman with red hair beneath a veil and wearing a grey cloak, about this height?' he asked a man who looked less drunk than the one beside him.

'Who wants to know?'

He grabbed the man by the scruff of his neck, glaring at him. 'I do, friend. With so few maidens in this damn hole, and pretty young ones at that, it cannot be too difficult to remember. Now, again—did you happen to see such a woman? Think!' Nicholas was not one to use such a menacing tone in his voice, but in this instance he was forced to and used it with great effect. It was a matter of urgency and he needed answers quickly.

'Yes…yes, I did, sir. She left just moments ago…with a young lad. Please do not hurt me.'

A young lad? Well, of course. Who but a lad would otherwise have the opportunity to cut the strings from the pouch attached to his belt? A person beneath his notice. And in this case a boy—one probably carrying a tray, giving the appearance of a serving boy in the tavern.

What an unmitigated fool he had been.

He ran out into the misty London road, looking in desperation, hoping that he might catch up with the culprits.

He knew with a sense of foreboding that the stolen pouch not only contained the missive with a possibility of damning treasonous information, but also his mother's ring. It was all he had left from the only woman he had ever truly loved, made from hessonite and entwined with pearl—a token he always had on his person as a reminder of the past. The irony was not lost on Nicholas that he had deliberately placed the ring in the pouch for safe keeping before entering this unsavoury tavern, for fear of having it filched.

What a damn mess!

His chest tightened, knowing the huge mistake he had made on this night. He could not believe how easily he had fallen for a ruse designed to divert and distract him, as he went headlong into assisting a distressed maiden like the veritable dolt that he evidently was. He should have trusted his instincts, but then he never could walk away from someone, least of all a woman, in trouble.

Nicholas cursed under his breath, looking desperately in both directions, knowing he had to make it right somehow. And then he heard it in the distance. Fading footsteps echoing on the deserted cobblestones. Thank God, there was hardly anyone outside along these pathways in this part of London.

He stopped, turned and listened. Two pairs of footsteps walking in haste, practically running. There was only one thing for it and that was to give chase. Nicholas knew that he would be faster than a mere slip of a maid and her young accomplice. He sprinted towards the pair, who had now come into the periphery of his vision, as they jumped into the shadows down a narrow lane. They crisscrossed from one to another, up, down and across the empty winding lanes. And although he was mildly surprised by the duo's stamina, it was nothing on his. He would have them in his clutches before long. Of that he was damn well certain.

He turned the next corner and saw them just ahead. They had hit a dead-end and had nowhere to go.

Good.

As he rushed forward, the young lad laced his fingers together and helped the maid jump over and to the other side of the stone wall.

'Hell and damnation! Stop!' he bellowed at the boy.

'No. Let her go, sir. It is me you want.' The lad wore a mask over his eyes, and a hood over his head for some strange reason. And he held his hand, dangling a pouch—*his* pouch—between his nimble fingers. 'Now, you are better than most, and I had not expected that. Impressive and fast too!'

'Why, you little miscreant knave!' he spat out as he took a step forward. Too late! The boy tossed him a wry smile, a mock salute and jumped over the wall. And all without any assistance. Now *that* was impressive, but Nicholas was in no mood to reflect on such talent. Instead, he was seething at his own ineptitude and lack of foresight. The eventide had brought one calamitous situation after another. And the moment that he'd get his hands on the damn impudent boy could not come quickly enough. God help him but he had to get that pouch back one way or another. He ran and scaled the wall.

Eva Siward looked behind her, knowing that the man she had been forced to steal from would soon climb the stone wall and continue his pursuit of them. Only this time they would no longer be in such a desolate and deserted area of Southwark. No, they would, as she had known, be much closer to the busy riverbank with its muck, its toil and its veil of cloudy fog that hugged the marshy terrain. She smiled to herself, knowing that she would not even need to venture that far.

With her mission nearing its end, relief flooded her senses. Not that it was over yet. Nearly there, she reminded herself. Nearly... yet there was still much to do. Much to negotiate. And mayhap, when this was all over and she had avenged the murder of the only man she had ever cared about—Simon the Rook—at the hands of a Crown Knight, she might finally find some semblance of peace. God, but she hoped that would be so.

Simon's death was still so raw and still so recent that Eva wanted to scream and rage at the world for taking him away and leaving her to fend for herself again. He had been the only one who had come to her rescue and looked after her when she had nowhere else to go, after she had run away. And he had been more of a father to her than the man who was her flesh and blood.

She fought back the tears that inevitably came whenever she thought of Simon and her loss. This had been for him, she reminded herself. She had done this in part for revenge and for retribution. The other reason: for silver. And although she knew that this man was not the one responsible for Simon's death, it mattered not. They were one and the same. Besides, with the success of this theft, she would gain enough coin to leave London for good. Start again, somewhere new and far from the dangers it posed. Especially the strange man who had hired her to steal from this Crown Knight in the first instance and who had made her feel as though she had little choice in the matter. And, in truth, Eva doubtless did. She shuddered and fixed her mind on the coin she would receive for services rendered. It would do—it would be enough. It had to be.

Eva turned a corner and walked through an archway and took off the mask she had fashioned to conceal and protect her identity as a woman.

'Marguerite?' she whispered into the cool night air. 'Are you here, Marguerite?'

'Yes, I'm here and I have done exactly as you requested. I've taken off the kirtle I wore earlier and changed it for the boy's clothing you left behind.'

She had left Simon's leather saddlebag—the only item she had left of him—with a change of clothing in a deep opening between three large stones in the wall.

'Thank you. You did very well earlier, by the by, and performed your part precisely as we had discussed.'

'I did. Was it not exciting? Everything went exactly as you planned it would—except for the disgusting old man. In truth, I was thankful, if a little surprised, that the Crown Knight came to my aid.'

Eva frowned as she glanced at her young

friend. Yes, she too had been surprised at the turn of events. She had not expected Sir Nicholas D'Amberly to intervene in that manner. It certainly marked him as a man of integrity and even honour, but she did not want to dwell on that. No, she had not anticipated that. It had been far too disconcerting and for a moment she had been stumped, before she'd pushed away the twinge of remorse and played her own part. Indeed, everything had gone to plan and far better than she had ever envisaged. And yet the feeling of apprehension remained with her.

'Indeed, but it is not over yet. Not by any stretch of the imagination, Marguerite.' She began fumbling inside the leather saddlebag, where she had placed female clothing to change into. 'We still have to get away from here, as the man whom we stole from, Sir Nicholas D'Amberly, is still on the hunt for us. There is still much danger to avert. Do you think you are up to the task?'

'I believe so, yes. You know I shall provide aid in any way I can.'

'And I thank you. You are a good friend to me.'

'As you are to me, Eva. I doubt I would have survived the streets of London without you.'

Eva nodded her thanks and removed the pouch that she had stolen and held it up in the air.

'And it was all for *this*,' she murmured absently, turning it in her fingers.

'Shall we see what is inside?'

'No, best not.' The less her friend knew the better.

'What will you do with it, Eva?'

'Leave it here for safekeeping...for now. Until the time is nigh.' And that moment could not come quick enough, so that she could be done with this business. When the man who'd hired her would arrange to collect it and give her the money he owed. Not that she needed to explain any of her trepidation to Marguerite and her reasons why she needed to hide the pouch. Eva knew instinctively that it might somehow provide her with a small measure of security. But from what, precisely? It was too soon to tell. Yet the man who had hired her might attempt to employ underhand methods to procure it, especially if he wanted to renege on the exorbitant amount of silver that he had offered. No, it was prudent to employ caution.

She pushed the pouch inside the clothing she had been wearing while resembling a young boy and placed it all neatly into the saddlebag.

She then shoved it back inside the secret opening in the wall and covered it with three large loose stones, concealing the gap to the eye. She turned and smiled, pulling on the kirtle over her tunic and tying the laces at the front, turning her back into a maid.

'You look very well as a boy, Marguerite,' Eva said as her friend hid most of her red hair beneath a coif cap before covering her head under a large scallop-edged hooded cloak. This somehow managed to drown her diminutive petite figure in so much material, but there was very little to do about it now. It would simply have to do.

'Do you think so?'

'I do... Well, mayhap a small boy. Now, are we ready to leave?'

'Yes, I suppose we are. Shall we?'

They ambled out of the shadows which had concealed them and back through the archway, stepping out on the road. Eva held out her hand to her friend, their roles completely reversed now. Although, in truth, she always felt far more comfortable in a boy's attire than the burdensome layers worn by her own sex. And, if Eva was honest with herself, it was more to do with the fact that she felt so awkward and ungainly wearing women's clothing. For as long as she could remember, she had disguised herself as a boy for her own protection, the streets of London being a dangerous place for a young maiden, alone as she had been.

That had been Simon's idea, and one that she had been happy to abide by as it not only protected her but offered her the freedom that few maidens could hope to experience. In truth, he had encouraged her to act and behave as a young boy, and in exchange he had taught her all of the skills and tricks that he knew, from wielding a dagger to the clever ploys used to steal. From the moment Simon had encountered Eva as she had tumbled out from the back of a wagon making its way into London, he had taken her under his wing. He must have seen something in her that he knew he could use— something that made an impression on him, standing out from the other waifs who found themselves lost and bewildered in London.

Indeed, they had made a good pair, thieving their way to survive. And for Eva it had been a choice between learning to thieve beside Simon, dressed as a boy, or the inevitability of becoming a prostitute as a maiden, alone and friendless in London. No, there had never been a choice in the matter.

She gave Marguerite's hand a gentle squeeze

as they hurried along the busy thoroughfare, hoping that her friend had remembered to keep her head down low. They could hardly risk Nicholas D'Amberly somehow stumbling upon them now.

Nicholas D'Amberly… Now, there was a fine-looking example of sinewy yet beautiful masculinity. Eva had never encountered anyone like him before. His presence in the tavern had both irritated and fascinated her in equal measure. He'd seemed so self-assured, so supremely confident, exuding an inner steely resolve that made Eva suddenly doubt herself and question whether she should be stealing from such a man. She had felt a jolt of something that she'd never experienced before, especially when she had ventured close enough to take the pouch from his person. Whatever it was had arrested her then, in that very moment the blasted man had gone to the aid of her friend, challenging her preconceptions. And it frightened her. The reality of the man, her confusing reaction to him, not to mention what she had agreed to do, had made her feel as though she could no longer breathe.

But then she had shaken herself out of it. She had not given into the restless unease that had suddenly crept under her skin. And while this whole commission had come at a high cost, Eva hoped that it would in some way go towards avenging the murder of Simon at the hands of a Crown Knight. A faceless coward and mayhap not Nicholas D'Amberly, but they were all the same arrogant bastards after all. Every single one.

Chapter Two

Eva and Marguerite continued to make their way back through the narrow, winding lanes until they reached the quayside, with London Bridge coming into view. Her agitated heartbeat would settle once they were safely back on the other side of the river and within the hustle and bustle of the City's gates. And back where she belonged—*home*.

Home in the heart of the city. Home in the dirt, the filth and the squalor, not that Eva allowed any of that to encroach on her small but neat and comfortable abode above an inn near Queenhithe wharf. It served her purpose well. Besides, it was only one flight of the stairs for her to get to the daily grind of working at the busy inn itself, as well as helping to brew the ale she took particular pride in. And yet without

Simon the Rook's influence and protection the uncertainty of her situation still loomed large.

Eva had believed that she could continue to remain at the inn and work for her board and lodgings. And yet she knew that it did not mean that she could remain safe there indefinitely. One mistake and she could be tossed out onto the street with nowhere to go. As a woman without any means, it was precarious. Which was why, when she had been approached by a stranger and offered a commission to steal from a Crown Knight for silver, she'd jumped at the opportunity. This was her chance to make a new start—and, with any luck, get away from London.

Hopefully, she would take her guileless young friend with her. She had pledged to look out for her safety—Marguerite, who so reminded Eva of her younger self when she had found her on the streets a few years ago, running away from her troubles, just as Eva had once done. It did not bear considering what would become of the maid, had Eva not been there to support and watch out for her.

In truth, they had to look after one another, as there was no one else now. If Eva hadn't come to Marguerite's aid she would no doubt have been swallowed up whole by London's dangerous seedy side and been forced to sell her body down the notorious Popkirtle Lane. It made Eva shudder to contemplate such a fate for her friend, knowing perversely that it would inevitably have been hers too, had Simon not taken her in and provided shelter for her. Fate had smiled kindly on her the day that she'd been thrown in his path and he'd seen something promising in her that would one day make her his apprentice thief! She would choose that fate every single day rather than be forced to do what those poor souls down Popkirtle and other notorious alleys were made to do for coin.

'Ah, London Bridge is upon us.' And mercifully without a certain knight ready to intercept their movements.

'Oh, thank goodness,' Marguerite mumbled. 'My feet are beginning to ache.'

'And yet there is still awhile to go before we get back.'

'I do know.' Her friend chuckled softly. 'But the bridge signifies that we shall be back at the inn before long.'

'Do not count on it being as quick as that,' Eva scoffed. 'You know how busy it becomes, even at this time of night.'

They paid the toll at the gatehouse and as Eva predicted the bridge proved a trifle difficult to

cross with so many people hustling to get ahead.
They made their way through the formidable
stone gatehouse and onto the bridge itself, passing many merchants selling their wares, from
vintners, cutlers, fletchers and bowyers as well
as haberdashers and their haggling customers,
even at this late hour. They passed the Chapel of
Thomas à Becket and the tavern on the bridge,
known locally as The Three Choughs, so named
in honour of the martyred saint. Which was a
shocking name, but not particularly for pious
reasons. No, Eva had it on good authority that
the establishment served wholly inferior quality ale, far too watery and more expensive than
her own excellent brew.

Eva flicked her head up and almost collided
with a man with a dark complexion and golden
eyes standing before them like a huge impen-
etrable wall. She heard Marguerite gasp beside
her.

God, but if her friend raised her head any
further the man might see that she was anything
but a boy and they would do well not to draw
unwanted attention to themselves. Eva jabbed
her elbow into her side, reminding Marguerite of what was at stake here. The man smiled
slowly as he removed his hat gracefully and

then moved aside, allowing them to pass. Thank goodness!

Eva expelled a big puff of breath that she had not realised she'd been holding. It was the Crown Knight from earlier, Sir Nicholas D'Amberly—the whole damnable commission had rattled her. The sooner they were back home, the safer she would feel. She grabbed Marguerite's hand and rushed on, weaving their way through the throng of people, her head darting around in anticipation of some unexpected obstacle that might impede their journey back. Or rather the sudden appearance of a man with a wicked glint in his blue eyes in pursuit of them. But nothing happened. No one was there. It was simply her own imagination playing tricks on her. And what in heaven had she been doing noticing the colour of Nicholas D'Amberly's eyes anyway? It mattered not.

'Are you well, Marguerite?' Eva mumbled from the side of her mouth.

'Yes.'

'Was it that man back yonder?' It had been surprising, her friend's reaction.

'The one with the extraordinary eyes?' Marguerite muttered. 'No, of course not. But it seems that *you* are the one perturbed by everything that has occurred tonight.'

'No, I assure you.' Eva smiled, shaking her head. 'It is exceedingly hot here with so many people. I admit to feeling a little stifled.'

'Then it is fortunate that we are almost here at the end of the bridge. Come.' It was Marguerite's turn to tug her by the hand as they approached the northern gatehouse.

They went through and finally stepped down onto the cobbled pathway, turning left swiftly to continue the last leg of the journey. Almost there... Almost. And yet Eva could not shake off the feeling of trepidation. It was like an unwelcome chill that danced across her skin, making the hairs on the back of her neck stand up.

They walked to the other side of the road and picked up their pace, even though they were both now weary of the night's activities. Her bones ached, her muscles felt fatigued and yet she had to remain vigilant. She had to remain alert.

'You feel the same as I, do you not?' Marguerite hissed from beside her.

'And what feeling is that?' She flicked her head from side to side, trying to chase the shadows lurking at every turn.

'That we are being watched, Eva. That we are being followed.'

'For goodness' sake, don't be ridiculous.' She

gripped Marguerite's hand tighter, giving it a reassuring squeeze. 'It is late and we are both tired after a very arduous evening. What we both need is our pallets to right everything, I promise.'

The mist rose from the nearby wharf and swirled around their feet and in the distance Eva saw two huge men on either side of the road, walking slowly towards them. She stopped suddenly, looking around her, her heartbeat stuttering in her chest.

'We best run. I, for one, need my pallet now.' She dragged Marguerite down the narrow lane on the right, practically sprinting down the road before crossing to the other side and zigzagging their way through. Her breath was ragged, her chest in pain. God, but why did she feel so untried, so lacking in experience? This was not like her.

Eva had done this many times, for as long as she could remember. Running, hiding, surviving. But never had she felt anything quite like this. Indeed, this whole situation was entirely different and for the second time that evening she was keenly aware that she might be out of her depth.

They ran down a narrow winding pathway with Marguerite panting beside her, evidently also wanting this night to be over and to be safely ensconced within the walls of her chamber. They crossed the road and there—the inn was within reach.

Eva exhaled deeply and felt the palpable feeling of unease drain from her bones as they stepped inside the courtyard of the inn.

'Oh, thank God, Eva. We are back.' Marguerite threw her a weak smile. 'And I, for one, could no longer continue to run in that manner.'

'Thank the heavens we no longer have to. Come, let's go.'

'I shall follow you in a moment, after fetching a tray of food and ale. We need some repast after this evening's efforts.'

Eva nodded and ambled to the wooden doorway to the rear of the timber-clad building and climbed the stairs to the large chamber she shared with Marguerite. She pushed the door open, hurried through and slid the bolt across, closing it behind her, sighing deeply, her shoulders sagging in relief. She glanced around the room, noting that everything was exactly as they had left it. Two pallet beds adjacent to one another covered with crisp coverlets, clean rushes on the floor and a welcoming fire flickering in the hearth, casting a low glimmer of light in an otherwise dark chamber. And yet in that moment she knew. She instinctively knew that she was not alone.

Her eyes widened, her breath coming in short bursts. It was the stillness in the shadows of the room that somehow raised her suspicion. The unyielding presence that she had felt prowling, following them at every turn from the moment they had left Southwark was now here. And, whoever it was, it lingered still, shrouded in the darkness of her chamber.

'I know you are here,' she whispered. 'Who are you?'

Nothing but an eerie silence wrapped around her. 'I will ask again—who are you? What is it you want from me?'

Her eyes darted around the room as icy-cold dread prickled down her spine. And yet still there was no sound. But then a slight shift. A small movement. Her heart tripped over itself, thudding wildly in anticipation. She carefully removed her dagger from its sheath, her hand clammy.

'I... I know that you are here.' She raised her voice, hoping that it held an even tone. 'Show yourself.'

And the stranger did just that. He stepped out of the darkness, large and casting shadows in his wake. Even with the low discernible light she could see the high slash of cheekbones, the sardonic gleam in his eyes and the hard planes of his jaw with a shadow of stubble and those lips twisted with mild irritation. As though he'd been forced to capture an errant horse.

Sir Nicholas D'Amberly—the man who had relentlessly pursued them from the moment she had cut his pouch from his belt.

'You!' she stammered, hating that her voice was suddenly so breathless.

'Yes, *me*.' He prowled towards her. 'Who else did you expect?'

She frowned, needing to say something to halt his movement. She needed time to think. 'But how? How did you manage it?'

'It seems I am as *impressive* and *fast* as you believed me to be,' the man drawled, shrugging his shoulder. 'Does it not, my little thief?'

Eva remembered then that she was clutching a dagger, which she turned in her hand, tilting it higher in front of her, trying in vain to hang onto her composure. 'You might congratulate yourself with your impressive stealth, but this is what we shall do, Sir Nicholas. You will allow me to open this door and leave the chamber, while you shall remain here.'

She took a step back and then another and then a deep breath to steady her nerves, before groping for the bolt behind her. But, before she knew what had happened, a strong hand had wrapped itself around her wrist, twisting it and making the dagger slip from her fingers. And in a flash he had caught her other wrist. He turned her slightly, pushing her back and pinning her against the stone wall, raising both wrists now in only one hand and holding them both firmly above her head.

'No, I do not think so.'

Nicholas gazed at the damnable woman with a certain satisfaction, even though she had caused him endless trouble this evening. He knew that his friend, and fellow Knights Fortitude brethren, Savaric Fitz Leonard—he with the *extraordinary eyes*—whose services he had secured outside The Three Choughs, would have at that very moment snatched Mistress Marguerite, while he was now stuck in this chamber with this hoyden. A hoyden who nevertheless stirred his blood and made him feel the unexpected sparks of something akin to desire. Or mayhap it was vexation.

It had been a shock, of course, to discover that the thief he was ready to throttle was not in fact a *he* but a *she*. And she was just as lush and delectable as her friend, if in an entirely different way. He wanted to touch the lock of russet hair that spilled from under the veil she wore, if not the skin along her neck. Mayhap then brush the pad of his thumb across her lips… No. He must remember what he had come to this god-forsaken inn for—his pouch. Which she had stolen from under his nose.

Nicholas had followed the little wench and her flame-haired friend the moment he had spotted them, dressed quite the opposite from when he had first encountered them, making their way towards London Bridge, as he'd assumed they would do. He could have easily reprimanded them then and there but was unwilling to attract more attention in Southwark, a ward that belonged to the Bishop of Winchester, Peter des Roches. Besides, he'd needed to discover where the two maidens would go and whom they might meet. Indeed, he had to ascertain why *he* had been chosen as a victim of their petty crime, especially since the maid evidently knew his name. Yet he somehow could not quite believe that tonight had been mere coincidence. No, he needed to find out more. And he needed to get the pouch back. It was imperative to decipher the coded message the informant monk had scribed in the missive and whether there was the possibility of a link between the Bishop of Winchester and The Duo Dracones, with the threat that this might pose to the Crown.

'No, this is what we shall do. You shall return what you have taken from me. And you shall do it immediately.'

He watched as the maid tilted her head before answering. 'I am afraid that will not be possible.'

'Oh, everything is quite possible, my thief. Anything and everything.'

'I am certain you are right, sir.' She managed to coat her words with such sardonic inflection that he had to swallow down his sudden burst of amusement. No, he would not be charmed by this thief.

Instead, he smiled. 'Indeed, so I shall ask you again—return what you have stolen.'

'I believe your ears were not deceiving you when you heard me the first time, sir.'

'Why, you impudent wench.' He chuckled softly, unable to contain his bemusement, despite the inconvenience the maid had caused. 'Such foolhardy words seem to flow freely from that mouth of yours, when I have your person restrained in my grip.'

This woman needed to know that her fate was now in his hands. Indeed, if she proved uncooperative he could always confine her in the bowels of the Knights Fortitude's donjon. But he hoped that would not be necessary.

'And pray what would you do to my person, restrained, I might add, a little too tightly?'

Nicholas raised a brow and loosened his grip on her slender wrists a little, moving her arms down to her sides. But he kept her in his grasp. He could not afford to take any chances with this woman and he decidedly would not be taken in by her smart mouth. Not when he had to get that damn missive back, as well as his mother's ring.

Even so, her assured manner as she held her head high did surprise him.

'You really wish for me to answer that?'

'Yes.' Her eyes dropped to his lips briefly before she realised what she had done. Before she realised that he had noticed. Interesting...

The maid looked away, her confident façade seemingly slipping a little as a look of mild irritation crossed her face. At him or at herself for letting herself be distracted, Nicholas didn't know. Mayhap she was more guileless than she had attempted to appear. The uneasy look that she had tried to conceal behind the bold words and sly glances could vouch for that. Unless it was a clever ruse, a contrivance used to manipulate, lie and cheat. And he had known many people who had done that to great effect. Who could, with the bat of an eye, upend a young man's whole world. It mattered not either way. Nicholas needed answers. He needed her to understand her predicament. That this was a dangerous situation in which she had embroiled herself.

'Yes,' she said again, clearing her throat. 'I wish to ascertain whether you mean to intimidate me.'

The young thief was spirited if a little foolhardy, which Nicholas could not help but admire. He wondered for a moment about this maid's past and what had led her to thievery.

Desperation, no doubt, something which Nicholas knew all too well. Such were the lengths people would go to when hungry and destitute. And all manner of ill-advised deeds and crimes they would commit when they were desperate.

He blinked, pushing away any twinges of regret he might have for this young woman. This whole situation could quite easily be remedied if the thief handed back his pouch and answered a few pertinent questions.

'You believe that I cannot?'

'I… I believe that you are being deliberately vexatious, Sir Nicholas.'

'My apology.' He tilted his head to one side. 'I was not informed of the courtesy I should afford thieves such as yourself. I suppose you also believe that I should let you go and wish you merry on your way?'

She lifted her head higher. 'Have I not already expressed it so?'

'In truth you have, and I have denied it.'

'Well, then, we must be at an impasse.'

'I think not, my young thief. Since I am in good spirits, despite all that you have put me through this night, I shall endeavour to give you what you want and let you go. But only in exchange. I want you to return what you took from me and to answer a few questions.'

'Ah, I would like to be obliging, especially since I realise that I should take advantage of your good spirits, but I cannot in good faith promise you that.'

'And do you have good faith attached to your name? In fact, what is your given name? You seem to have full knowledge of mine.'

She frowned. 'Why should that signify in any way?'

'You know, my little thief, you have answered nary a question that I have put to you and I begin to grow weary. Answer me. Your name, if you please.'

'I applaud your manners, sir. It makes me inclined to say that my given name can be whatever you wish it to be.'

The maid was beginning to be tiresome. 'Coyness does not suit you. Your name.'

'Eva.' She exhaled. 'Eva Siward.'

'Well, Mistress Eva, that was not so difficult, was it? Shall we try another?'

'On the condition you let go of me.'

'You do not set the conditions, mistress.' He shook his head, knowing that he could not afford to let go of her wrists. 'I am afraid I cannot do that. Not until I have some satisfaction.'

'But must you restrain me?'

'Oh, I must, just in case you attempt to bolt out of this chamber or draw out another dagger, which I have little time for. And if you wish to avoid being handled in such a manner then I would advise you to think twice about stealing.' He leaned in. 'As I have been told it is a terrible sin.'

She looked away, so he used the crook of his finger under her chin to bring her gaze back to him.

'Now, listen carefully, Mistress Thief. I want

you to hand me the pouch you stole. And I want it now.'

'I am afraid I cannot do that.'

'I have humoured this nonsense long enough. Now, I will you ask once again—where is it?'

His jaw hardened as he pierced her with a penetrating gaze and continued to hold her in place with one hand, while using the other to skim her waist, looking for a belt, wondering whether she might have tied the pouch to one since it did not seem to be on her person. Frowning, Nicholas knew that she could not have had time to hide it somewhere at the inn before she'd burst into this chamber, otherwise Savaric would have come up to inform him.

'It is not here,' she murmured, holding his gaze.

'Then where?' The woman remained silent. 'Hell's teeth, I asked: where?'

'I had the foresight to…to hide it first before I ventured back. Far away from here.'

He exhaled through his teeth. *'You did what?'*

'I believe you heard.'

'And you believe I should congratulate you?' he retorted sardonically.

'Vous ne pouvez pas entendre ce que vous refusez de croire, mais ce sont de vraies paroles prononcées,' she hissed under her breath.

How could this have happened? How could he not have considered this to be a possibility? Surely Nicholas could not have misjudged her. He studied her again through his narrowed gaze, and realised something then that he had overlooked. She was not the usual kind of woman that he would find on the streets of London, working in a tavern or elsewhere. And not because the maid had an obvious proclivity for dressing as a boy, and not for the first time, judging from the length of her hair. Those glorious russet locks spilled only to her shoulders— far shorter than most women would willingly wear. No, it was her voice, which was cultured, refined and held an intonation that whispered of another time and place.

Vous ne pouvez pas entendre ce que vous refusez de croire, mais ce sont de vraies paroles prononcées. She spoke a language that was ordinarily used at Court. Interesting. And she evidently believed him incapable of listening to what she believed to be the truth? Either way, the maid, this Eva Siward, was educated and in possession of skills far beyond those of a tavern maid.

Yes, very interesting…

'Oh I assure you that I am indeed listening,

but your words have only served to make me more exasperated and irascible.'

'Then the solution is easily resolved, Sir Nicholas. You could offer to pay more coin and I shall grant you your wish to be reunited with your precious pouch.' She lifted her head and smiled, clearly happy with her ingenuity.

'Pay more than whom?' He glared at her. 'Who paid you to steal from me? Tell me.'

'I cannot say.' Her lips twisted in discomfort.

'I demand satisfaction,' he said in a low voice. 'Listen to me, Eva Siward, if that is even your true given name. I want you to fetch what you have stolen and I want you to do it now. Do you comprehend?'

'Indeed I do, sir. But what would you do to me, I wonder, if I cannot fetch it? Grip my wrists tighter?'

'Oh, no, my little thief.' He flashed a quick smile. 'I too have foresight and a measure of a contingency, should plans go awry. After all, it might be too fraught and difficult to take *you* out of here as well.'

He waited until realisation struck her with the full force that he had expected.

'Marguerite…' she whispered absently, as all colour drained from her face. 'What do you mean to do to her?'

'Consider it already done.'

'No!' she cried, trying to pull free for the first time since he had pinned her to the wall. 'She is innocent in all of this.'

'But you are not.' Interesting that she would fight for her friend and not for herself. 'I shall tell you what you are to do, mistress. You will meet me at The Three Choughs tavern on the Bridge at the witching hour tomorrow night and you will bring what you stole from me. In exchange, I shall release your flame-haired friend and we shall all part ways.'

The look she threw at him would easily have curdled milk. And yet Nicholas cared not one jot. He must have the pouch back. And by any means.

'You would let us go. And then we part ways?' she murmured, lifting her head to meet his gaze. There was a resolute steeliness in her manner that he could not help but admire in that moment. She had courage, this thief. And her obvious distress and apprehension for the sake of her friend showed a modicum of honour that was as unexpected as it was commendable.

'Naturally.'

'As easy as that?'

'Of course.'

'Of course…' she repeated wryly.

'You doubt me?' He raised a brow. 'And you a thief?'

'Ah, so thieves cannot have misgivings about men who prowl after them.' Her voice rose a notch. 'They cannot feel or care or become concerned for their young abducted friend.'

'What a moving, impassioned speech. Cease or I shall expire in despair.'

'You mock?' Her eyes flashed with indignation.

He lifted one shoulder. 'I merely observe the incongruity of your situation, Mistress Eva.'

'How fortuitous then that I too am reminded of my woeful lack of judgment by someone as discerning as you,' she retorted, her words dripping with derision. Ah, she was good, she was very good indeed. 'Pray, Sir Nicholas, is there something further for me to acknowledge?'

God, but she would dare to taunt him? When it was *she* who was being held against the wall. When it was *she* who had hurled them into this situation in the first instance. When it was *she* who had stolen from him.

'Yes. You should not steal.' He stepped closer, pinning her with his gaze. 'Not from a man like me.'

'Ah, but I have met many a man like you, Sir Nicholas D'Amberly.' Her voice was but a soft whisper but he could still detect the disdain in her tone.

'I rather doubt that, Eva Siward,' he growled as she lifted her head.

Their gazes locked and the air between them fairly crackled with a different and inexplicable kind of tension as they stared at each other, waiting for the other to blink first. Her gaze dropped to his lips once more before straying back to his eyes, a flash of unbidden desire echoed in them. Before Nicholas knew what he was doing he dropped his head and pressed his lips to hers. And it was then, at that very moment when the disconcerting woman arched closer with a small moan escaping her lips, that he was lost. Everything changed. *He* was the one who was suddenly inflamed. *He* was the one who was bewildered when she kissed him back with a ferocity that frankly shocked him to his very bones. But then everything about this woman was different. Everything about her had confounded and surprised him.

He softened the kiss as he slanted his lips over hers again and again, licking into her mouth wanting to taste, wanting to savour her sweetness. The kiss started to shift and change and he could feel himself falling deeper and deeper into her as Eva Siward boldly followed his lead. He had not expected this; he had not expected that he would lose himself so utterly and completely.

God's breath!

He tore his mouth from hers in shock, muttering an oath, and took a step back. He watched her for a moment as she also tried to tamp down and master the untapped passion that he had roused in her. Just as she had done to him. At least she had not been immune to him, even though, from the look on her face, she had surprised herself. Eva Siward might be indignant but Nicholas was relieved that the woman had failed to notice the damnable effect she had on *him*. That would be far too lowering to consider.

'The Three Choughs at the witching hour. Do not be late,' he ground out, and with that he turned and left in the same manner in which he had entered the chamber—by pulling back the shutters, climbing out of the narrow arched window and down the side of the timber-clad building, before jumping down to the ground below.

Chapter Three

After a particularly fretful night's slumber, where Eva tossed, turned and eventually abandoned her pallet altogether, she rose and readied herself for the difficult day, and even more arduous night ahead. Guilt flooded through her as she reflected on the night that Marguerite must have endured while in the clutches of Nicholas D'Amberly and his wretched friend. Even though Eva somehow instinctively knew the man who had stalked into her chamber last night would not hurt her friend, it still worried her nonetheless.

As well as this, the man who had hired her to steal from Nicholas D'Amberly would now seek her at the inn today, expecting the spoils he had demanded. He would want satisfaction and there was no telling what he would do once he learnt of the failure of the previous evening.

There had been something so indelibly menacing and cruel in *that* particular man's demeanour that made Eva think twice about crossing him, even if she had been dissembling as a boy and worn her mask to conceal her identity when he had initially approached to parley with 'Simon the Rook's apprentice'.

She was not willing to chance it. Nor was she prepared to risk anything happening to Marguerite. No, there was only one thing for it. She would return to Southwark, fetch the pouch and meet Nicholas D'Amberly as arranged. Her gambit was that the insufferable man would also pay coin for her trouble. And once they had made their exchange she would grab Marguerite and leave London for good, hoping to make a new start far away from the city. And with the coin she could still hope to make, Eva could put together a plan to open her own tavern, her own inn, and brew the ale she had become known for. All of which was another reason why she had risen at this ridiculous hour—so that she could pack her belongings and small keepsakes, as well as Marguerite's, and leave the inn before anyone happened upon her.

At sunrise, when glimmers of light streamed inside, she glanced around the chamber that had been home during her formative years and sighed deeply. With a deep sense of resignation, she gathered up her belongings and turned to look over her shoulder one last time before leaving the chamber to venture south of the river on foot. Even at this hour the bridge was once again getting busy, with the hustle and bustle of traders and vendors, just as it had the night before.

Before long Eva was going back along the deserted alleyway and through the archway, reaching her special hideaway, tucked away as it was. She carefully dragged the three large loose stones away and thrust her arm inside, fumbling for the pouch in the darkness, finding it in the far recess of the hole. She pulled out the contents and examined them properly for the first time, surprised to find a ring at the bottom of the pouch which was exquisite and seemed to be of value. But the innocuous roll of vellum seemed hardly something to go to all this trouble for. Which meant, of course, that what it pertained to and the message it imparted would likely be of some significance.

With her curiosity roused, Eva unravelled the small roll, opening it up to see if she could discern much, but was surprised to find very little that she recognised. Instead, many strange shapes were scribed between letters and numbers that seemed familiar from the long-ago memory of her childhood. She brought down the shutters immediately, unwilling to retread those painful memories. She pulled her mind back to the vellum and frowned. None of it made any sense, but mayhap that was the point. Mayhap it was by design.

Eva shoved the ring into Simon's saddlebag and put it back into the hiding place, as far as she could reach in the darkness, knowing that retaining the jewel was a wise course of action. It would force the aggravating Nicholas D'Amberly to pay a good measure of silver just to obtain it back from her.

'Oh, yes,' she muttered, smiling to herself. 'I too have foresight with a plan and a contingency, should plans go awry, Sir Knight of the Crown.'

Eva made a deep mocking curtsy to no one and nothing in particular and settled herself in the alleyway, knowing it concealed her well, since few wandered down this dirt path that led nowhere. She had decided to remain there until it would be time for the rendezvous, to avoid any unwanted or hazardous encounters, but of course that meant that Eva had much time on her hands. It meant too that her mind could once again travel where she had refused until now—back to the previous night and Nicholas D'Amberly.

The whole encounter had been disconcerting and highly unnerving. There had been a part of her that could not help but rise to his challenging, provoking manner.

How infuriating he had been. How reprehensible, how annoyingly handsome and wickedly attractive. How insistent he had been in making his demands, putting all her plans into disarray by forcing the situation, leaving her with very little choice.

Then she recalled the kiss.

God, how mortifying. Even now, alone with only her thoughts to torment her, she blushed furiously at her shameful response to the man. He had penetrated her senses and awoken an emotion inside her that thrilled and confused her at the same time. She remembered how his kiss had softened and become something unfathomable. Even his hold of her wrists had eased as his fingers moved to caress her skin, shooting a prickly sensation up her arm and down to the pit of her belly. But an awareness of the situation and the inevitable awkwardness had soon seeped through her. At least the experience had been just as bewildering for him as it was for her. The man had seemed just as shocked and dismayed at his reaction to her.

Good, she welcomed his discomfort, even if it had meant that she shared the sentiment. It mattered not. After this night there would be little need to think of the man again. Soon she would be far away from London and the dangerous men whom inhabited it, men like Nicholas D'Amberly. For now, Eva would turn her mind to furthering her endeavours. She would consider closely the vellum in her hands and attempt to decipher the strange message it carried.

Daylight had dissipated and merged into night by the time Eva woke from slumber, momentarily befuddling her. She took a sip of ale from her flagon to wake her senses and rose, smoothing out her skirts before tying the pouch to her belt and gathering her meagre belongings together. She would come back for the valuable ring and Simon's saddlebag after this meeting was concluded and Marguerite was safe and back by her side. The rest they would procure along the way. Once they were free from London and onto new beginnings.

Taking a deep breath and exhaling the frigid night air from her chest, she began to amble her way back to London Bridge and its damnable tavern, The Three Choughs.

Pulling her hood over her head, she picked up her pace and before long she was paying the toll on the bridge before walking through the gatehouse and weaving through, making her way to the tavern.

Eva stopped just inside the entrance, darting her gaze around the place, which seemed surprisingly busy at this time of night. But then the bridge, with all its merchants and tradesmen, was always teeming, as people made their way back and forth at all hours. Day and night. Night and day. Every day at every hour. She meandered through and there, at the furthest recess in the corner, sat Nicholas D'Amberly with a hood covering his head, leaning back against the stone wall, watching her.

Eva took a deep breath before she made her way towards him, and sat down hesitantly at the proffered stool on the other side of the wooden table.

'Good evening, Mistress Eva,' he drawled. 'I am glad to see that you have come exactly as we arranged.'

'I believe in such matters it is prudent to do so.'

He smiled and tilted his head in approval.

'That is a very astute and wise approach, and one I wholeheartedly commend for tonight's proceedings.

In truth, I am certain that we should conclude this…er meeting and part ways.'

'Once we both get satisfaction?'

He raised a brow. 'Precisely.'

'Then where is Marguerite? I do not see her here.'

'That can wait for just one moment,' he muttered, taking a sip from his drink, his eyes never leaving hers. 'Here, allow me to fetch you a mug of ale.'

'Thank you. I believe I am quite parched.'

The man clicked his fingers and it wasn't long before a voluptuous tavern maid brought more mugs and a small jug of ale.

'Allow me.' He sloshed a measure into a mug and handed it to her.

'Well…' she raised the mug in mock salute '…now that we have the pleasantries out of the way, Sir Nicholas D'Amberly, would you care to inform me where Marguerite is then?'

'Of course.'

'Since she does not seem to be here presently.'

'That is because she is not at the tavern.'

Eva was immediately suspicious. What in heaven's name was the man talking about?

'Then where is she?' Her voice rose a notch but Eva could not help herself. Her heart thumped against her chest as she worried her bottom lip. 'You vowed that you would bring her here, if I were to fetch the pouch.'

'No.' He smiled, shaking his head. 'No, I rather think you have forgotten our agreement, mistress. Our agreement was to meet here but I said nothing about making the exchange here.'

'You have purposely misled me.'

'Come now, let's not descend into recriminations. And surely you can comprehend that it would be unwise for either of us to do an exchange here, in such a public place.'

She shrugged. 'I would have thought it a perfect place to accomplish our arrangement.'

'Would you?' he murmured, tracing his finger around the rim of the mug absently. 'Interesting.'

'I fail to see how, when you have broken your promise.'

'I made no promises to you, mistress.'

'And why would you. I am just a petty thief.'

'Just so.' He tipped his head. 'Besides, you cannot expect me to bring forth my only means of bargaining, when you could have arrived with the same people who hired your services in the first instance.'

'But I have not.' She lifted her head and threw him a look dripping with indignation. 'Are you satisfied, sir, that I have come alone?'

He watched her for a long moment before blinking. 'I suppose I am, as much as I can be.'

Eva had had enough of this conversation. She had complied with the man's edict—well, as far as she could. Now it was his turn to honour his promise. 'Good, then please would you do the courtesy of taking me to Marguerite, so that we can finish this and go our separate ways?'

'Certainly.' The man stood and held out his hand to her, which she ignored, rising from the stool without the need for any assistance—or, rather, *his* assistance. 'Come with me, if you will.'

Nicholas swallowed down his amusement as the woman mustered all the dignity and poise befitting a lady rather than a conniving thief— his eyes skimmed her from her head down to her toes—albeit an inelegant lady at that. And while he could understand her apprehension at his coming alone, it had been a necessity to protect both himself and the secret work he and The Knights Fortitude did for the Crown. And it had been imperative that the woman had come alone and without any accomplices who might have scuppered his aim to regain the pouch, with not just the important missive it contained but also his mother's ring.

After all, Eva Siward had gone to great lengths to steal it from him in the first instance so, in truth, it was not outside the realm of possibility for her to use underhand methods to renege on their agreement. Besides, he wanted more from her. He needed answers regarding the men who had hired her. But the only way to achieve his aims was to put his questions to her in a place out of earshot. Somewhere safe.

'Where are we going?' she mumbled as he led her through the narrow hall at the back of the tavern.

'All shall become clear very soon.'

'I can hardly wait,' she said wryly.

'Good, I do aim to please.' He chuckled softly despite himself as he grabbed a flaming torch from the rusty sconce on the wall. 'In fact, I had hoped to engage your anticipation.'

'Indeed, I am all agog, Sir Nicholas.'

He watched her from behind as they made their way down a dozen steps that led to a damp, dark narrow hallway and bit back a smile. Eva Siward was indeed as inelegant and ungainly as he had initially observed, dressed as she was in a long flowing woollen kirtle flapping about her feet and a short cloak draped over the shoulder. Yet it was more than her attire but the way she fidgeted with her veil, the long strides she took when walking and the way the woman had slurped and tossed the ale back in the tavern that amused and surprised him most. Once again, he wagered that it had not been the first time that the young woman had dressed as a boy when he had first encountered her. But then as a London thief it was evidently useful and prudent to disguise herself as she evidently did.

They reached the dead-end of the hallway, moisture skimming the surface of the walls.

'Where to now, then?' she muttered, turning to face him.

'Now we venture below.' He nodded to the trapdoor beneath the rushes on the floor as he passed her the flaming torch. He knelt and pulled open the square wooden door with the metal ring handle, revealing the River Thames lapping and surging around a waiting skiff far below them. Under London Bridge itself, concealing their descent, this was a highly effective means for The Knights Fortitude to get in and out of the city without arousing any notice. Nicholas could take no chances with this woman, in case she had other accomplices, or even the man who had hired her, ready in wait for him outside the tavern.

She snapped her head around and then shook her head. 'I am not going down that…that ladder. And I am not going on that thing. Not with you.'

'It does not seem as though you have much of a choice, mistress,' he sighed. 'It's either that or terminate our agreement here and now.'

'You are despicable and dishonourable, Sir Nicholas.'

He forced himself to grin, hiding a spark of irritation at being described as such. 'So I have been told by many a good woman. Not that I would put you in their esteemed company, Mistress Eva.'

Her eyes flashed. 'I would never expect anything less, sir. We thieves would never dream of being likened to real ladies. After all, we are nothing but the lowest of the low, after all.'

'Whatever you say, mistress.' He chuckled. 'But they're your words, not mine.'

'I do not even know whether this is a highly inventive ruse to entrap me for whatever nefarious reason you exalted Knights of the Crown might have.'

'What an extraordinary imagination you

have, mistress.' He raised a brow, crossing his arms over his chest. 'And the only entrapment I have in mind is to get you on that skiff, so that we can be away. In fact, the sooner you board it, the sooner you shall be reunited with your friend.'

'Do you swear to it?'

'Solemnly. Now, shall we?'

Eva Siward clenched her teeth tightly and released an exasperated sigh. 'Very well, let us get this miserable night over with.'

'I shall pretend I did not hear that. After all, we Knights of the Crown do have a reputation to keep. Now, grab the metal pole. Just so, and take care as you climb down the steps as they can be a little slippery.'

With a deep breath, the maid grasped her skirts in one hand and the metal pole with the other, taking a step on the long rope and timber ladder suspended from the trapdoor that descended down to the choppy river below.

Nicholas followed her down, keeping his eyes firmly locked on her progress. 'Take each step slowly, mistress. There is no rush.'

'If that is so, then I cannot understand why we did not board a skiff in the usual way, by the wharf or even the quayside.'

'But surely this is far more thrilling, would

you not say?' Not to mention that he could not risk anything more going awry with this woman.

'Ha! And you mention my penchant for the extraordinary.'

'Well, you must admit this is a novel way to jump onto a skiff, mistress. And far from any inquisitive gaze.'

'I would rather we had embarked on it differently,' she bellowed into the night as she carefully made her way down.

'Just keep your eyes on what you are doing at all times and we shall be aboard the vessel before long.'

She continued to tentatively make her way down. 'For your sake, I hope you are right. I would hate for this night to end disastrously.'

'Believe me when I say, mistress, that, withstanding your charming company, I hope this miserable night, as you call it, will go as smoothly as possible. Then we can all part ways as swiftly as possible.'

'Good, because…' She screamed. It all happened so quickly as her foot slipped, missing the next rung of the ladder, making her fall, and dangle from the pole. 'Oh, God. Help me!' She shrieked again. 'I'm falling.'

Nicholas swore an oath as he clambered

down to get to her. 'Hold on, Eva. I am coming. Hold onto the pole as tightly as you can.'

'I can't,' she shouted. 'My fingers are sliding and...oh, God!'

'Hang on tightly, I'm nearly upon you. Just hold on.'

Nicholas made his way down the wooden ladder as she cried out again. 'I can't hold on much longer. I'm slipping.'

One more step and he would be there, ready to grab the maid's hand and pull her up. Just one more and he would have her.

Eva Siward's eyes widened with a look of fear as she shook her head. 'I can't...cannot hold on...'

'Mistress, wait!'

Her hands slipped off the pole just as Nicholas was about to catch her. He watched in horror as she fell, plunging deep into the murky waters of the river beneath. He let go of the pole and followed in after her, diving into the frigid waters of the Thames, which hit him like a punch to his chest. But he ignored the sudden pain. He had to find the woman—he must. Swimming to the surface, Nicholas could see very little in the darkened hollow under the bridge. He desperately looked in every direction and there—he could just about see a figure in the distance, flapping in the river and frantically swinging their arms before sinking back in. They bobbed up and sank down a few times before they no longer resurfaced.

His heart plummeted. God! It must be her.

Nicholas dived back under the water and swam as fast as he had ever done in his life in the direction that the maid had disappeared within the swell and perilous current of the river and knew with certainty that once she had gone down within a certain distance there would be no way to find her. She would be lost for ever.

He pushed further down and opened his eyes under the murky water, unable to see much, but there, close by, he could just about detect a small desperate movement. Descending further, he somehow managed to grab onto the body that was floating away into oblivion. Thank God, he had her! Thank God. All he had to do now was to somehow get both of them back to the skiff in these choppy, hostile waters.

Nicholas dragged her back to the surface, taking in a huge gulp of air as he coughed and spluttered, while holding onto the woman for dear life. He gripped her from behind, tilting her head back onto his shoulder so that she would be able to catch her breath, but she was heavy and lifeless.

He began to swim towards the skiff but his legs were trapped by the swathes of material from the maid's skirts. He reached below the surface and yanked at the material, tearing it off her body, feeling the surplus weight fall away from them and allowing easier movement back to the skiff. His squire, who had been waiting anxiously, helped them on board.

Once Eva Siward was also on the skiff safely, he fell to his knees for a moment, his limbs feeling heavy, before he scrambled back towards her. She was breathing faintly. Without another thought, Nicholas pushed her on her back and tipped her head onto his lap, gently tapping and stroking her face and pressing her mouth open.

'Breathe, Eva. For the love of God, breathe.'

Her chest suddenly heaved as she took a deep unsteady breath and began to cough violently, bringing up a little of the river water. Her eyes flew open as she continued to cough, curling to her side.

God's breath, what a relief.

Nicholas exhaled as he rubbed and patted her on the back.

'It is all well, mistress,' he muttered in soothing tones.

'Th...thank...y...you,' she said in a small voice as she shivered violently.

He grabbed the blanket that he always kept aboard the skiff and covered the maid's legs before lifting her wet form and depositing her on his lap. They might both be wet and cold but at least they could draw some heat from one another's bodies as they huddled close together.

'You are safe, mistress, I have you,' he murmured, feeling the tremors from her body. 'Hush, you are safe.'

'You…you…you,' she mumbled breathlessly.

'Yes, me, mistress. Your terrible tormentor.' He attempted to make light of the situation when, in truth, he had been exceedingly shaken himself. He lifted his head and gave the signal to his squire to begin rowing, wanting to be away from the river and out of these damn sodden clothes.

'You…you saved me.'

'I did, but rest assured that the enmity between you and I can still stand if you are so inclined?'

'You saved my life,' she repeated, making Nicholas feel a little awkward, especially because of the maid's proximity and the close manner in which he held her.

'Come now, I need you, mistress. After all, how could I possibly get the pouch back without you?'

The woman blinked a few times as a small gasp escaped her lips.

'My clothes… What has happened to my skirts?' Her eyes widened in shock as she tried to sit up, her hands searching beneath the blanket.

'Calm yourself, Eva,' he muttered gently. 'I had to tear them off you, I'm afraid. The material had wrapped itself around my legs and was impeding my ability to swim away with you in my arms.'

'But you do not understand,' she mumbled breathlessly. 'The pouch! It was secured to my belt.' *Oh, God, no…* 'And the belt—it was tied around my skirts. It's gone!'

Chapter Four

Nicholas directed all his pent-up energy into rowing the skiff furiously alongside his squire. He could not believe the extent of the failure of this night—and it had been as *miserable* as it could possibly have been. All the time that he, along with his Knights brethren, had spent, carefully planning, organising and considering with a view to obtaining the secret findings from their informant, as well as regaining the damn missive once it had been snatched—and all for nothing. But worse than that was the loss of his mother's ring. Shutting his eyes, Nicholas rubbed his brow, feeling the cold bitterness cut through him.

How had this happened?

He could not help but feel responsible for how the events of the evening had transpired. After all, it was he who had pushed the maid into the situation. It was he who had teased, who had provoked and challenged her to go down the rope ladder when she had clearly been wary of it. All because he had thought she would be well versed in the demands of such exertion, when clearly she was not. Eva Siward might be a thief, but that did not mean that she was confident in every situation. And now, because of this oversight, his mother's ring—the only thing he had left of her—was gone. Nicholas felt numb with its loss, bereft.

He exhaled through his teeth and looked out into the distance at the first glimmers of light peeping through the grey clouds.

What the hell did it matter anyway? It was only an object, a jewel, and while it might fetch some coin, it was only a bit of metal and stone. Nothing more. And his mother had left this world a long time ago, despite it. Nevertheless, he felt the loss of the ring like a punch in the gut, knowing well that it was the very last earthly item he had left of his beloved mother and his connection with her.

Nicholas's eyes flicked to the maid huddled in the corner, with the blanket covering her legs, her head dropped, her arms wrapped around her knees, and sighed. At least he had managed to make one good decision tonight when he had grabbed the woman to safety. For now, that would do. He would deal with the repercussions and consequences of this night later.

'We're nearly there, Sir Nicholas,' his young squire said.

'Good, and thank you, John.' He stood, passing his oar to the lad.

'Sir, wait. I shall wade in and grab the mooring rope.'

'Sit, John. Besides, I am wet already.' Nicholas jumped into the shallow water at the riverbank and fetched the rope, catching a pair of eyes watching him from the skiff.

What was he to do with the thief now?

Eva could not remember the last time she had felt this wretchedly cold, wet and shaken. It had been so close, so dreadfully close. Her life had almost expired, had almost been forfeited, as she had slipped away into the depths of darkness. Had it not been for him—Nicholas D'Amberly. It might have been for the reasons he had dismissively given, but she was thankful all the same. So very thankful.

She was wrapped in more blankets, trying to coax some warmth into her body as they travelled on a rickety old wagon to God knew where. All she needed at this moment was a proper fire, shelter and a pallet to rest her head and somehow get more heat into her body, which was so cold she could barely feel her fingers and toes.

Above all, it was sleep that she wanted. She did not care that her hair and body smelt of the fetid river water. Sleep and warmth was all she needed. And with those thoughts running through her head, she closed her eyes. Just for a short time.

When Eva next opened her eyes she was alone in a small, well-appointed chamber with all the things she had hoped for—a hearth with a fire crackling, a roof over her head and a warm, dry pallet. Her hair and skin were somehow washed clean, and she was no longer wearing the sodden clothing she had been wearing—well, what was left of them. Indeed, someone must have cleaned her skin of the debris and muck from the river, since she had been incapacitated to do it herself... Lord, but had it been the man who had brought her here? The one who had saved her and torn off her skirts and held her close to him. Her face scorched just thinking about *him*. She looked down and realised that she was wearing a long clean tunic. A man's tunic.

Eva sat up, stretching her arms out, and wondered where she was. From the dappled light peeping through the shuttered window, it was much later than dawn. She staggered to her unsteady feet and tentatively made her way to the window, opening the plain wooden shutters. Her lips curved into a small smile as she looked in every direction, surprised to find a pretty courtyard and, from what she could see beyond, thickets, open green fields and woodland. Far from the stench of London. She breathed in the clean air and tilted her head back, welcoming the slight breeze against her skin.

The heavy curtain that separated the sleeping area from presumably the main chamber opened and Nicholas D'Amberly strode in, carrying a tray with provisions.

'Ah, good, you are awake.' He nodded. 'How are you feeling this morn, mistress?'

'Well, I thank you. If mayhap a little disorientated. Where are we?'

'Somewhere that provides a little safety, a little solace away from the hustle and bustle of London, and yet still within easy reach of the city.' He placed the tray down on the pallet. 'Here, it isn't much but I thought you might want to break your fast.'

She smiled and nodded. 'Thank you for everything, especially for last night, after...after I fell.'

He waved his hand and shook his head. 'Please, there's no need. Think nothing of it.'

She noticed that the man had deep rings around his eyes, obviously from lack of slumber. 'I do hope that you managed some rest yourself, Sir Nicholas.'

'Some, yes.' He turned towards the door. 'There is someone who would like to see you before they...before she leaves. She has been waiting quite anxiously.'

'Marguerite?' She smiled. 'Oh, yes, of course.' Before Eva had even uttered the words, her friend rushed in and pulled her into a hug.

'Oh, my goodness, Eva. I cannot tell you how happy I am to see that you are well.'

'And I, you.' She returned the hug, suddenly feeling a weight that she did not know she was carrying slip off her shoulders. 'Tell me, have you been well? How have you been treated? I hope you have been eating? Oh, God, Marguerite, I have been so worried.'

Her friend chuckled softly and shook her head. 'I am well. I have been treated with respect and I have been well nourished. If anything, it is you, Eva, who had me worried, especially when you were brought here last night and after I attended you.'

'You attended me?' she muttered, a little touched that Nicholas D'Amberly had the foresight to think of her needs.

'Yes, and I am glad that you are safe and well.'

'I am, thank you, my friend. And as soon as I am back on my feet we shall leave here, you and I. We shall venture back to London, which by all accounts is not too far. We shall fetch the coin that I have put aside and we shall…'

Marguerite pulled away and shook her head, her ready smile slipping away.

'Oh, Eva,' her friend whispered in hushed tones. 'You must know that they will not allow us to leave.'

'They?' Oh, God, she did not like the sound of this.

'Yes, Sir Nicholas and the man who brought me here—Sir Savaric Fitz Leonard.' Was it her imagining, or had Marguerite flushed? 'They won't allow us to just walk away, Eva. Not now, after what happened.'

'But the loss of the pouch was through no fault of mine.'

'I believe that they acknowledge that. But until matters are resolved we cannot go back to London.'

'But I…'

'Listen.' Marguerite lowered her voice even more. 'Have you thought about what the man who hired you to steal from Sir Nicholas would do if he were to discover that you reneged on your agreement? That you meant to trade the missive for me, for which I am eternally grateful, mind, but it does put you in a dangerous predicament.'

'He will never find us, I assure you.' She covered Marguerite's hand and gave it a squeeze.

'How can you be certain? And I do not worry about myself but you, Eva.'

'The man and whoever he represented were only ever interested that the contents of that missive would not reach Nicholas D'Amberly, for whatever reason. And that has inadvertently been achieved now, since it is at the bottom of the Thames.'

'And do you think this man would believe you?' Marguerite sat on her pallet and wrung her hands together. 'You would take that risk?'

Eva opened her mouth to reply and then shut it again. 'That I cannot answer, but we shall find a way. And how is it that you are suddenly so worldly and knowledgeable?'

She shrugged. 'I have been listening behind curtains and when they believed I was asleep, just as you have taught me.'

'That was well done of you, Marguerite.' Her lips quirked. 'But we shall have to make a plan now. Or come up with some sort of bargain.'

'What do you propose?'

This was indeed a good question, not that Eva had an answer, especially at that particular moment, when her head was still a little dazed and bewildered from the night before. She desperately wanted to extricate herself from this obscure, dark world that she had somehow found herself in. Darkness that was not too dissimilar to the waters in which she had almost drowned. Yet she knew Marguerite had the right of it, despite the fact that she wanted to run away from it all.

'I do not know, but I shall think of something anon,' she mumbled unconvincingly.

'I am not certain that anything can be done. Not now. And not until those men out there have what they want.'

Eva felt the truth in those words. She had only agreed to the scheme of stealing from Nicholas D'Amberly because the coin was considerable and the opportunity to gain a measure of vengeance for the death of Simon the Rook at the hands of another Crown Knight incentive enough. Not that she'd believed she actually had much choice, but she had heartily acquiesced nonetheless.

There lay her mistake. As though Knights of the Crown such as Nicholas D'Amberly were easy to cross. As though someone who possessed as much ruthlessness and guile as he evidently did would ever be taken in by the likes of her. God, how mortifying.

She wondered again about the nature of their work, since it was certainly more than mere Crown Knight.

'Did you, by any chance, glean a little more about them while you were listening behind the curtain?'

'Not enough to be of any import. They are very good at saying what needs to be said without revealing anything more of real substance. Yet I know enough to realise that as long as they believe that we might have some use, or rather you, Eva, they will continue to keep hold of us. And possibly offer a measure of protection in return.' Why had none of this alarmed Marguerite?

It was those words, *'we might have some*

use', that unsettled her. What if she simply did not possess the information they sought? What then?

Something else suddenly occurred to her. 'It has already been arranged then?'

Her friend simply nodded in discomfort.

'Before they...before she leaves', Nicholas D'Amberly had said. Where was Marguerite going? And with whom? She knew instantly their plan—to separate the two friends, so that it would make them—or, rather, *her* comply. And it was so easily arranged, with the aim to manipulate Eva and extort information as well as anything else they so wished.

'What have you agreed to, Marguerite?'

Before her friend could answer, the curtain once again drew back and Nicholas D'Amberly stood before them. 'If you would like to join us?'

Nervous apprehension rippled through her. With her heart racing to an alarming beat, she followed the man out into the living area.

She noted the large central hearth with a pot crane and a large iron pot dangling from it in one corner, a livery cupboard against the wall, stacked with pots and kitchen utensils, and a wooden trestle table with a few stools around it at another corner. And there sat the man they had passed on London Bridge only a few short days ago. God, had it been only that short time ago, when everything had changed since?

The man dwarfed the furniture with his huge stature and long limbs, as he sat tapping his fingers on the table with an air of insouciance. And Eva had considered Nicholas D'Amberly large. Good Lord, who were these men?

He stood slowly when they entered the chamber and smiled at them, showing pearly white teeth set against his dark complexion. 'Ah, mistress, it is good to see you back on your feet again,' the man drawled.

'You must be Sir Savaric Fitz Leonard. I have heard much about you.'

'At your service.' He inclined his head and flicked his gaze to Marguerite. 'And I hope that I meet with approval from…er…what you have heard.'

'Indeed, sir, it is a pleasure.'

'The pleasure is all mine.'

'Now that we have got the pleasantries out of the way, shall we conclude our discussion regarding our next course of action?' Nicholas D'Amberly sat on a stool opposite and gestured for both the maids to follow suit, but Eva declined.

'I think I should stand, if you don't mind. Especially if the discourse is to decide any such thing. As we have established from last night's disaster, I am not suited to all types of action.'

'Just so, and trust me, Mistress Eva, there will be no repeat of any such activity.'

Trust him?

How could she trust Nicholas D'Amberly— or any of them? Lord above, but the only man she had ever trusted was dead. There would be no trusting of this man—not by her. Not by any means.

'Good, well, let us hear this plan then, Sir Nicholas, or do you intend to keep us all in suspense?' Eva knew that after this man had saved her life she ought not be this churlish, but she could not help herself. She hated that she felt powerless in having to acquiesce to him. Yet in truth she had little choice in the matter.

'Mistress Marguerite will travel with me to join Sir Thomas Lovent's household and tend to his wife and their young son, for a brief amount of time.' Savaric Fitz Leonard nodded at Nicholas D'Amberly, slapping him on the back. 'While you, along with my friend, shall stay here for a short time to…er…recoup your health before being reunited with your friend. Nothing simpler.'

'Thank you, sir, for your concise if not brief

explanation. And without prevarication.' She turned to the other man. 'But would you care to fill in the details, Sir Nicholas?'

'If you wish. What more did you need clarification on?'

Was there something here that Eva could not comprehend? It was as though they had all been party to a secret that she had no notion of.

'Just more would suffice, I am sure,' she said sweetly.

'After what happened last night, I need your counsel, mistress, to help provide more information.' He must have seen some concern on her face as he quickly added, 'But we shall not be alone, mistress. Another Crown Knight, Warin de Talmont, will arrive shortly with his bride. You cannot see it from here, but behind this building there is a larger cottage that provides more accommodation.'

Well, excellent. More Knights of the Crown to tarry with, but at least another woman would soon join their midst. Not that Eva was certain whether this newly married woman would have much to do with the likes of her.

'I see,' she uttered, a little relieved. 'However, I still cannot think in what way I can provide any information that might be of use to you.'

He raised a brow. 'Can you not?'

'No. And I assure you, sir, that we are not involved with any of this.' Eva knew that her protestations were futile but she still had to speak.

He leant forward and shook his head. 'Ah, but it's too late for that, and you *are* involved, whether you wish to be or not, mistress.'

His gaze locked onto hers, relentless, unyielding.

Heavens above, what had she got them involved with here?

The other man cleared his throat and turned to Marguerite. 'Mistress, can I show you the vegetable patch and herb garden that I was telling you about?'

Marguerite looked to her and then to Nicholas D'Amberly, before Eva gave her a small nod.

'By all means, sir.' She then smiled at Savaric Fitz Leonard and followed him out of the small timber abode.

Good, now Eva could turn her attention to the man who sat on the other side of the trestle table. She grabbed the stool, the legs scraping on the wooden floor, scattering some of the rushes, as she sat down, facing him directly. 'As I understand it, if I am to assist you, as you put it, and provide the information you seek, we can then still part ways?'

Nicholas D'Amberly rubbed his jawline and nodded. 'Although the terms of our original agreement have now changed, we can still part ways when the time comes.'

She exhaled in relief.

'And once I have satisfaction.'

She snapped her head to meet his watchful gaze.

'Would you care for a mug of ale?' he muttered.

'Yes, I thank you,' Eva replied without taking her eyes off the infuriating man, remembering the last time he had offered her ale in the tavern, as well as its aftermath.

He poured a measure into a wooden mug and handed it to Eva, his fingertips skimming across hers. The touch was incidental and brief but a bolt of awareness shot through her, making her breath trip a little. But then Nicholas D'Amberly must know what he was doing somehow. He sat back, his eyes fixed on her, and took a sip.

Eventually he spoke. 'Something has been bothering me about last night. Tell me, what was it that frightened you?'

She nearly spat out the ale that she had been drinking. Of all the things Eva had expected Nicholas D'Amberly to say, this was not it. He had quite effectively changed the presumed line of questioning, putting her immediately on her guard.

'Was it the water,' he continued as he assessed her, 'the river itself that made you uneasy? Was that the reason for your reluctance to use the trapdoor and the rope ladder?'

Eva blinked at him, startled at where this curiosity was leading. 'No, not the water.'

'Then what?'

'Does it matter?'

'Not especially.' His eyes were so very blue, so very intense at that moment that it unnerved her. 'But I would like to comprehend what happened, if you would be so obliging.'

She shrugged. 'I fell. You saved me. There is nothing more to it and there is no sense in revisiting what happened last night.' *When she had almost drowned.* Eva left that unsaid.

'As you wish, mistress, but there is no shame in what happened. I only wish to ascertain the reason.'

'It was not the water and not because I could not swim.' She smoothed the creases from the long tunic, wishing that she too had gone out to inspect the vegetable patch and herb garden. 'It was before all that came to be.'

He nodded, taking in her answer before speaking again.

'After the dexterous way you removed the pouch from my person and the agility you displayed when you scaled the wall in Southwark, I believed that climbing down a rope ladder would be nothing to you. In truth, I had not anticipated it.' He shook his head. 'I could not fathom how it "all came to be", as you put it. And hence my concern.'

Eva felt a torrent of heat seeping through her cheeks and spreading down the column of her neck. She swallowed. 'You mean your curiosity?'

'That too.'

'It was the height. I had no notion that it would have such an effect on me until the moment you demanded I walk down the rope ladder.'

'Did you not think you should have made it known to me? This newly found fear?'

'I assumed most people hold such fears, common as they must be. Besides, are you saying that you might have considered a different route to the skiff had I done so?'

He shrugged. 'Mayhap.'

'How generous of you to bestow a "mayhap"

in regard to such a fear. I am glad that I did not disclose it after all.'

'Yet I still maintain that you should have mentioned it nonetheless, mistress,' he said softly.

She took another sip of ale and considered him over the rim of the mug.

'But I could not admit to it and have you think even less of me than you did.'

Eva realised her mistake as soon as the words left her lips. As soon as his mouth curled into a small knowing smile. God, how disconcerting to reveal such a thing. As if his opinion of her mattered. As if she cared. She swallowed, looking away.

'Il vaut mieux prévenir que guérir.' She shrugged.

'Yes, I agree. One should never take unnecessary risks. And yet you continued to step down on that ladder despite your fears?'

'I did.'

'Une coeur vaillante...'

No, Eva was not valiant but did what she believed she must. And her heart was indeed beating ferociously in her chest. They descended into an uncomfortable silence until Eva spoke again. 'I still do not know what you want from

me, sir.' All she did know was why she had
been separated from Marguerite. In order that
she was not afforded the opportunity to devise
a plan to flee. And yes—the temptation to do
just that would be there if her friend was here.
It would pose yet another possible problem for
Nicholas D'Amberly to contain. And by sepa-
rating them he could fix all his attention solely
on Eva. God, but the time that they could part
ways could not come soon enough.

'That will become clear eventually, but we
can wait until later for questions, mistress. Once
you have regained your health.'

Eva had a good idea about what Nicholas's
questions might entail—mainly regarding the
man who had hired her. But then he would want
to learn more than that from her. About the life
she led, about Simon, about everything. Nicholas D'Amberly must be aware that he did seemingly need to disarm her. She instantly thought
of the kiss they'd shared in her chamber and
how much it had disconcerted her. How easily
she had fallen into that, just as expediently as
she had tumbled into the Thames. Oh, yes, she
felt that she could easily have drowned in that
damned kiss.

'What was it that frightened you?' the man
had asked her earlier and she understood then

that it was far more than merely the events from the previous evening, but also her visceral reaction to him. Oh, yes, that frightened her just as much. But it could never happen again. Eva must somehow build her defences against this man and find a way to bring this interlude to an expedient end. She had to.

Chapter Five

‿‿‿⧜‿‿‿

It had not been long after, when Marguerite had left with Sir Savaric Fitz Leonard as arranged and Eva had found herself alone, unsettled and strangely disorientated, standing in the main living area of the timber dwelling, her body still sore from the ordeal of the previous night.

Nicholas D'Amberley had also departed to fetch provisions needed, for the friends he had mentioned who were due to arrive at this remote little sanctuary. However, with every passing moment, her sense of apprehension grew. It was niggling doubt and a sense of guilt about all that had come to pass that caused this restlessness within her. She had misjudged him and for the first time in her life Eva felt shame for her actions. For taking from someone. For taking from Nicholas D'Amberly.

Despite whatever reservations she had about

the man, she could not deny the fact that he had honour and fortitude. He had stepped into the fray for her friend in the tavern without a thought for himself. And before considering his own safety he had jumped into those icy perilous waters after her. It had shown his mettle, yet it did not take away from the fact that Nicholas D'Amberly was still a Crown Knight. He was still damnably vexatious.

Just then the very man himself strode into the room and stopped abruptly, giving her a slow smile as he raised a brow.

Oh, yes, he was very vexatious indeed.

Nicholas did not know what to do with the maid. He had left her to rest awhile before his friend and fellow Knights Fortitude brethren Warin de Talmont and his bride, Joan, arrived, but it seemed they were delayed, as newlyweds were inclined to, not that he knew much regarding that blessed state. He intended to wait awhile until he took Eva Siward to task about the events leading to the theft of the missive, hoping that a little time might restore her spirits as well as her health.

He had walked into the dwelling presuming that she might be abed but no, the woman was there, standing in the middle of the chamber, startled, abashed and just as unsettled as this morn. Nicholas took in her appearance properly, noting her pale face, her delicate features, the curve of her graceful neck, down to her shoulders and the tension emanating from her body. She had changed back into her own clothing, which had dried now after last night. And she had pinned her dark russet locks loosely at the back of her head but had forgone the addition of a veil, which somehow made her appear far younger than he had initially believed her to be.

'May I fetch you something, mistress? A repast? I believe these apples from the small orchard yonder are quite sweet,' he said, holding up a small sack.

'Thank you, but no. I need nothing further, I assure you.'

'In that case, may I enquire if you are well?'

'Quite well.'

'Then is there something amiss, because you seem unduly anxious?'

'Can you blame me, Sir Nicholas? I'm here, in the middle of nowhere.' With *you*. She had left that unsaid but he had heard the resounding whisper all the same.

Ah, so it was that which was troubling the maid. That she presumably felt vulnerable being alone with him. Eva Siward seemed nervous around him. Him! This woman who had, from the very moment he had met her, stolen from him, given chase through Southwark, scaled a wall and sparred with him in her chamber and kissed him back, measure for measure. Mayhap she was still shaken after her fall into the river. Or mayhap it was the kiss.

'Mistress Eva, I hope you are comfortable while you are here and know that until the moment you leave you are under my protection.'

She looked astounded as her eyes widened in surprise. He frowned, realising his mistake, and spoke again in haste to clarify his meaning. 'No, not that type of protection, mistress. On my honour.'

She raised a brow, giving him a baleful look. 'Your honour is commendable, but truly, would you have me believe that after you stole a kiss?'

'You have my word as a Crown Knight that you will come to no harm under my protection.' Strange, but the woman seemed to bristle on hearing words that he hoped would alleviate her concern. 'And we are not in the middle of nowhere but on land that belongs to the Justiciar of England, Hubert de Burgh.'

She arched her brow. 'Your honour and your word as a *Crown Knight*? It seems that I am fortunate, indeed.'

Her derision surprised Nicholas. His assumption about this maid seemed to be true. She was just as different to what he had initially thought her to be. But Eva Siward was as interesting as he had first believed. 'It would appear so.'

'I have been taught never to trust anything based on appearances.'

'Wise counsel.' He narrowed his eyes at her. 'But who taught you that?'

She hesitated a little too long before she answered. 'The streets.'

'I see.'

'Do you? Because I do not.' She marched to the entrance of the dwelling and opened the wooden door, stepping outside. He followed her and came to stand beside her, waiting for the maid to say her piece. Eventually she did. 'I look on all of this in disbelief, Sir Nicholas. This secluded dwelling, the comfortable pallet, the fire in the hearth back inside. The green fields and even the blasted vegetable patch and herb garden out there.' She turned slowly to meet his gaze.

'If I had not planned to take liberties with you, seduce you or mayhap steal another kiss as well?' He raised a sardonic brow. 'It would be quite an elaborate ruse, do you not think?' Her assumption of his purpose in bringing her here nettled as well as irritated him. 'Eva, I have never done anything so reprehensible and, on my oath, I never will. Believe it or not, some women actually desire my company and seek a dalliance. In truth, they…er…take liberties with *me*.' Her blush from earlier bloomed and intensified even more. 'My intentions with you are quite different, however. I was not lying earlier when I said I needed you, mistress. Strictly for the purpose of finding out more.'

'More?'

He nodded. 'I need to know about how you came to steal from me. How you came to know my name and who hired you. If my suspicions are true, then you have embroiled yourself with some very dangerous men, Eva.'

Nicholas believed it to be the work of The Duo Dracones. It could not have been mere coincidence that had brought her to that specific tavern on that singular night when Nicholas was meeting his informant, where that particular missive was stolen. No, there were simply far too many coincidences wrapped around that one theft.

Once more, Nicholas thought about his mother's ring, which he had managed to lose through his carelessness. It was gone and there was no point in dwelling on it. He ignored the stab of pain in the pit of his stomach and turned his mind back to the more pertinent issue at hand.

The Duo Dracones... God, but they made his blood run cold. And so called because their emblem depicted two entwined serpents. The damn group had thwarted Nicholas and The Knights Fortitude ever since they had discovered them, more than three years ago. And since then, every time the Knights had drawn close to finding more about them, they had managed to elude them, largely because their members chose death rather than having their group or leader exposed.

But Nicholas did not tell the maid any of this. He did not tell her that his informant, the monk, Brother Michael of St Albans, had been found, just hours before he was due to meet her at the tavern, with his throat slit. And he did not tell her that with the loss of the missive and the possible information it contained, *she* was now the only possible link to them that they had left. In just one short day Eva Siward had become extremely valuable to him and The Knights Fortitude. For her sake, Nicholas hoped that she had not been hired by the treacherous group. Then she could put all of this behind her and they could part ways as she so evidently wanted to.

And with the loss of the missive and also the

murder of the monk The Duo Dracones had once again cleaved together. Once again the trail had gone dry, with Nicholas and his fellow Knights Fortitude no closer to the bastards than before.

'I suppose he did seem dangerous.' She shuddered a little.

From the stiff manner in which she was standing and the way her throat worked, Nicholas knew the rest could wait. The maid looked tired and weary from it all.

'Come, let us take a stroll. Apparently the vegetable patch and herb garden are quite the attraction in these parts.'

He held out his hand to her and waited as she assessed him, just as he had done earlier. Nicholas understood well that it would be best if he were to be taken into Eva Siward's confidence. He needed to gain her trust somehow and he would achieve far more with such an approach, even though he knew he must tread carefully with the woman.

Yet there was something about her manner that he could not help but admire. An inner strength and an astute intelligence, underlined with a vulnerability that was as intriguing as it was captivating. A potent mix. Dangerously potent. He sighed, pulling his mind back to matters at hand and earning Eva Siward's trust, which was not going to be easy.

Besides, Nicholas held the loss of the pouch to be just as much his fault as it was hers. Yes, the woman might have initially filched it, but his shoulders were wide enough to take the blame for what had happened at the tavern, leading to the near-death disaster in the river.

'Well, mistress? Shall we take a walk together?' he said softly.

She blinked several times and a small smile curled her lips as she nodded. The effect was quite endearing and far more dazzling than he could ever have imagined. And all from such an innocuous smile. Her tongue darted out to lick her lower lip as she lifted her eyes to meet his, her smile widening.

God, but everything about Eva Siward was strangely beguiling. And without her even being aware of her allure.

His eyes dropped to her lips and then back up again. No, he would not allow his thoughts to wander where they should not. He had given his word, as well as his oath—such as it was. Indeed, it would be good for him to remember the reason why she was there in the first instance. These stirrings were dangerous and ones he could ill afford. Not with so much at stake.

* * *

Eva strolled beside Nicholas D'Amberly, taking in the beautiful surroundings that she had only been able to peek at before, with a lovely cottage adjacent to the one she had been staying in as well as a small pasture for a handful of livestock, a chicken coop and indeed a vegetable patch at the rear of the dwelling as well as a herb garden near the small building that housed more provisions and a stable. And, further along the path, the woods that hugged the terrain and a small stream that ran through it.

The man beside her continued to explain how this smallholding was run by the farmhand who saw to its upkeep and the fact it was part of land that belonged to Hubert de Burgh, Justiciar of England. Naturally, Crown Knights did move in exalted circles.

And yet, throughout all of his chat, Nicholas D'Amberly's words from earlier were spinning around Eva's head.

'Some women actually desire my company and seek a dalliance. In truth they...take liberties with me.'

She had stood beside him trying to appear composed, when in truth she had felt quite the opposite. Her skin had prickled and heat had suffused every part of her body as she listened to the man talking so nonchalantly about how it was nothing to him that women took liberties with him, since so many desired his company after all.

As much as Eva hated to admit it, she could well imagine the truth in that. Nicholas D'Amberly was so shockingly attractive that her breath hitched every time he was nearby. As he currently was. And those lips… God save her, but when the man smiled at her in that knowing manner Eva could not help herself from thinking on that kiss in her chamber a few nights ago. The one that had scattered all thought and reasoning. In truth, it was meaningless and she should be indifferent to it, as though the kiss had never happened at all.

Yet the way in which Nicholas D'Amberly had held her in the skiff, and later in the wagon last night, had been nothing but tender and warm. She felt frustrated that all of this awareness of the man was making her feel quite unlike herself. And after slighting him regarding his intentions it seemed churlish to think on the man's kisses now, or even his powerful arms wrapped around her. Her gaze followed his languid movements and she swallowed. Mayhap after her ordeal in the water her head was addled. Yes, it must be that. It would pass soon enough.

'Of course, you need not reply, mistress.'

Oh, God, what had he asked her?

'Apologies, sir, I was not attending.'

'No matter.' He smiled congenially at her. 'I was pondering on how it is that you are so well-spoken, mistress. Your voice is not one that is usually found residing in the dark, seedy side of London.'

'Or presumably working there either?'

'That too.' He threw her a glance as they meandered towards the pig pen. 'Especially one who speaks French tolerably well, as I've noticed you do from time to time, especially when you are vexed. That is certainly not something the common folk toiling away in London's streets would know.'

Eva knew that to be true. 'What if I were to tell you that I could change de ways I speaks just like dis, fer a fine fella like yerself to fink na'fin of me? Bin speakin' like dis to fits right in fer a long time now.'

That made him smile. 'I would think nothing less and can well believe that you could easily change your voice *to fits right in*, as you put it. It does beg the question of the need to fit in a place like that when you evidently do not belong there.'

She knew what he was implying and what he was attempting to comprehend—by putting all the small pieces about her together. But Eva was not certain that she was comfortable with such close scrutiny. Which was ridiculous since that was the main reason she was there.

'Of course you do not need to feel obliged to answer,' he continued to say. 'It was merely an observation. That is all.'

For a long moment Eva continued to stroll beside him, contemplating whether it would be prudent to disclose more about herself. In truth, her past, such as it was, was nothing out of the ordinary. There were many like Eva who had been drawn to London, only to find it wanting and far more precarious than they had ever envisaged.

'You are quite correct, Sir Nicholas. I was not originally from that side of London. I was not from London at all.'

'But it swallowed you up all the same?'

'Indeed.' Eva knew that the man was waiting for her to elaborate further. 'I ran away, for reasons I have no wish to revisit, but my family…we were…we lived quite comfortably— my father was a mercer and, as a merchant in wool, he met my mother at the port of Le Havre, where trade was exceedingly good. In time, I believe my mother birthed me there. But soon afterwards they returned to England and set about expanding both my father's trade and also our family.'

'Quite an idyll.'

'It was, and it was my mother who taught me French and who always expressed her annoyance in that particular language. So I suppose I must take after her.' She smiled a faraway smile. 'We were very happy. But then…then my mother, my father and all my siblings, became sick and perished one after the other. Only I was spared.'

He frowned. 'What happened to you, mistress?'

'I went to live with my father's sister and her husband. They had a young family, so the belief was that I would be made to feel welcome with them—but that was very far from the case. Then I realised one day that I could no longer stay there. So I gathered up my belongings and the silver that I had amassed and left. I was but twelve in years at the time.' She shuddered.

'You were alone? Unprotected?' He stilled. 'God above, mistress, life must have been decidedly bad with your aunt and her husband for you to take such a desperate decision to leave the safety of their home.'

Yes... Yes, it had been the most desperate of decisions warranted by the most desperate of times. She would never forget the night when her aunt's husband had come upon her as she'd slept, with darkness and dread filling her veins as she'd watched his approach from under the coverlet. Somehow, she had known. Somehow, she had guessed that the man had meant her ill. He had meant to touch her as a man should never touch a child. God have mercy but, young as she was, Eva had known his intent when he had deviated into the chamber that she had shared with his own young slumbering children. She had seen that look on his face before. And she had acted quickly and without hesitation, instinctively knowing that she had to flee. Knowing she had to get far away from her uncle's bold and disgusting appraisal of her. So she did, after first surprising him as he'd advanced towards her, kicking him in the stomach and winding him. She had managed to gain enough time to get away as expediently as possible that very night, running and running until her legs hurt. Until she had felt her lungs might burst.

'Sadly, it was.' She sighed deeply. 'Their dwelling was in a small hamlet in Kent and so

London really did not seem far. Thus I made the journey and until last night remained there, ever since. And that concludes my pitiful, yet unremarkable story.'

'Unremarkable?'

'There is really nothing that happened to me that does not happen all the time, Sir Nicholas. It is a common occurrence, unfortunately, although I wish that was not so. Indeed, I found Marguerite alone and friendless in much the same way and decided to take her in.'

'Admirable, and I assume that the reason why she came to be in London was similar to yours?'

She nodded. 'I suppose, but that is her story to tell.'

He stopped and gazed around the verdant vista of the soft rolling hills, before turning around to face her. 'You have the right of it. Sadly, there are many who find themselves in a predicament akin to yours. But tell me, mistress, who was it that found you when *you* were equally alone and friendless?'

She blinked, momentarily stumped by his keen observation. Eva realised that very little escaped Nicholas D'Amberly's attention. 'I too was fortunate to have someone who took me in. Who clothed me, fed me and gave me shelter.'

'And presumably taught you how to steal?'

She flicked her gaze to him and lifted her head. 'Yes, and taught me how to steal.' She was not going to allow this man to reproach her behaviour. 'And more besides. We did all we could to survive.'

'You misunderstand. I do not sit in judgement of you, mistress. In fact, I can well understand your reasons. My only complaint is that you stole from *me*.'

'A mistake I am sure I will always regret.'

'Never say that you regret our short but wonderful time together.' He smiled wryly, instantly lightening the mood. And for once Eva was relieved that he had, not wanting to dwell further on the darkness of her past.

'Never that.'

Dusk had almost settled by the time Eva awoke from a restorative slumber. And this time she was well rested and felt far more like herself than before. It was as though a veritable weight had dropped off her shoulders after all that she had revealed to Nicholas D'Amberly. But it was also the oath that he'd made on his honour earlier, putting an end to the doubts she had about his motives for keeping her here.

She felt strangely at peace. And safe. All that was left to do was to suppress this absurd attraction she seemed to have inadvertently developed for the man and all would be well again. It should be easy to do now that she no longer felt the aftershocks of what had happened the previous night at the river. Indeed, the more she pondered on it, the more convinced she was that it was prompted by gratitude for what he had done. After all, it was not every day when a relative stranger, a foe, risked their own life to save another's. To save her life. Not that she felt the man to be a foe now. But neither was he a friend. He did want to gain information from her, after all.

Eva rose and pushed back the curtain, stepping into the main chamber, and darted her eyes around the room. Strange…the man was nowhere to be found. She wrapped a blanket around her shoulders and walked outside, breathing in the sweet-smelling air of the outdoors. God, but she did not think that it mattered how long she stayed here, she would never fail to be amazed by this air, this scenery, this serenity. Perfect. Everything about these small self-sufficient dwellings and their environs was perfect. She could not think of a place more happily situated than this, but it begged the question of how Nicholas D'Amberly and his friends had become so closely associated with such a powerful man as Hubert de Burgh. Knights of the Crown or no, she suspected that this was not the usual way of it. Indeed, from her limited understanding, there was more afoot here than she'd first believed.

A dull noise alerted her from the side of the timber building, piercing her musings. She meandered towards it, following the sound, which seemed to suggest a flurry of toil and sweat, coming from around the corner of the building. And there indeed was the source himself—Nicholas D'Amberly wielding an axe.

A small gasp escaped her lips as she took in the sight of him, stripped naked to the waist, his hands clasped around an axe as he effortlessly chopped planks of wood into more manageable logs…for some reason presumably. Some reason that she could not think on presently. Her mind had gone blank as she froze, unable to move, unable to breathe.

Eva watched the working of his whipcord muscles stretch and ripple as he swung the axe forward, over his head, mesmerised by his endeavours. His skin was gleaming, taut, the fading light casting golden hues of burnished umber, light and shade dancing across his skin. Of their own volition, her eyes skimmed over the expanse of wide shoulders, across his muscular chest and light smattering of hair that trailed across his chest and down his abdomen, vanishing beneath a pair of hose clinging to his narrow hips. She watched in fascination at the series of powerful movements of his body, slick and sinewy, as he wielded the tool. And scars—slashes, dents and old wounds—a reminder of who and what this man was—a warrior.

It was not as though Eva had never seen a half-dressed man, but invariably they were bedraggled and drunk. Never like this. Heavens above, but this man was unlike anything she had ever seen.

She should look away, turn back quietly and leave, but her feet would not move. Her gaze remained fixed on him—Nicholas D'Amberly. She stood rooted to the spot, her pulse racing wildly, confused by this visceral reaction to him.

The man wiped the back of his hand over his brow and lifted his head. And it was then that he caught her staring at him. Her skin burned with mortification, especially after their earlier discourse. What must the man think of her wanton behaviour, standing there gawping at him? Eva could only assume that he would find her wanting, believing that she was fickle, faithless, and her words hollow. Or, like the women he had described earlier, she now desired his attentions. She wondered whether he would say anything. But he had stilled, dropping his arm to his side, the axe falling away from his fingers and onto the ground. And he did not move—he stared back.

His gaze bored into her before a faint smile touched his lips. Her cheeks flamed and, as if waking from a spell, she inhaled sharply, turned on her heel and made her way back inside. How could she have ever thought that she was safe? It was not possible. Not with a man like Nicholas D'Amberly.

Chapter Six

Nicholas had a cooling wash at the stream and made his way back to the dwelling, carrying with him a couple of speared fish that he had caught, skinned and gutted. It would do nicely for the eventide meal, with a few herbs grown nearby and some bread rolls that Savaric Fitz Leonard had procured earlier before he had left.

His thoughts meandered back to the sight of Eva Siward, standing watching him from afar as he'd chopped a few dried planks of wood to be used in the hearth. It had seemed disconcerting to be so openly scrutinised by the woman and if it had been anyone else he could have sworn that he had caught a flash of something akin to desire flare in her eyes, but he could not tell with her. It must have been the twilight hour that had winked and played tricks on him—and it said more about his wholly inappropriate fascination with Eva Siward than anything else.

Yet there was something about her that made Nicholas want her to succeed. Mayhap it was the impassive, detached manner in which she had recounted her altogether familiar story. Indeed, her candour had been surprising, especially for a woman who made her way in the world by stealing. Not that she had much choice. But she had disclosed it all without showing any trace of emotion about her reduced circumstances, making his chest ache surprisingly. And as well as that was the unseemly attraction to the woman, which was as perplexing as it was disconcerting.

It was best to leave well alone, especially when he considered that she would soon be departing, taken far away, once The Knights Fortitude had extracted the information they needed from her. They would ensure that they bought her silence with enough silver so that she could start anew elsewhere. And even if the information was of little use, Nicholas would still ensure she was settled tolerably well. Not that he owed her anything. The young woman had brought this situation on her own head. Yet he felt a responsibility for her nevertheless.

All that was needed now was for Warin de

Talmont and his wife Joan to finally arrive and this could all commence as it needed to. For the longer he spent in Eva Siward's company alone, the more his fascination with her grew. Which was something that he could not allow.

He crossed the entrance and stepped inside the chamber to find her huddled over the hearth. She was dressed as before, in a long simple tunic that he had acquired from his squire and her kirtle that had been washed and dried by Marguerite after falling into the river the previous evening. Yet there was something different about her. Mayhap it was the rest she'd had, or something entirely different, but Eva Siward had colour in her cheeks and a glow in her eyes.

'Ah, good, you are back, Sir Nicholas. We are in dire need of some kindling to feed the fire.'

Naturally the woman would not actually mention the moment she had caught him chopping firewood. 'Then it is a good thing that I swung my axe in anticipation of the need for… er…kindling.'

Nicholas knew he was deliberately provoking her but he just could not help himself. After all, she had been staring at him. Openly. Intently.

He watched her throat work as she swallowed uncomfortably. 'Yes, a good thing. Where might I find it?'

'Allow me. I shall fetch it presently.'

He left momentarily, returning with some firewood, and together they stoked the fire in the hearth, adding much-needed warmth to the chamber. He then set about preparing the meal, with the trout he had caught, stuffing it with borage and dill, cooking it in the iron pot, stirring it now and again.

'I never thought that you'd do such menial tasks as this, Sir Nicholas,' she muttered from the other side of the hearth. 'In truth, you are not what I expected either… I mean that you seem extremely competent and resourceful.'

'And why would that surprise you? I am all but a soldier, used to doing many tasks, including setting up camp and, believe it or not, hunting for food and even preparing it.'

'I would have thought esteemed knights who are used to being in the company of ennobled men such as Hubert de Burgh would have squires to see to such tasks.'

'They would invariably, but I have sent John, my squire, to see to other more important matters.' The boy in question was more a squire for The Knights Fortitude and was at that moment patrolling the demesne and beyond to make certain there were no unwanted visitors lurking nearby, not that Nicholas believed there would be, but it was prudent to be cautious. He added a touch of mace and a little salt, some verjuice pilfered from de Burgh's kitchens months ago and lastly a knob of salt bought from a local farmer. He continued to stir and coat the liquid sauce that had oozed out over the fish. 'Besides, I am a better cook than he.'

'I can well believe that.' She lifted her head and met his eyes. 'It looks and smells quite delicious.'

'Then you should sample it, to be certain.'

He tore a chunk of bread and dipped some in the sauce from the serving spoon and held it out to her. She flicked her eyes from his hand holding the morsel and then back to him before deciding to accept it. Keeping her gaze fixed onto his, she reached out and took the offered food from his fingers, nodding her thanks. Nicholas licked the remnants of the sauce from his fingers and watched in fascination as she took a bite, closing her eyes, savouring the taste.

'Yes, that is most delicious,' she murmured, licking her lips and taking another bite, her obvious enjoyment sending a jolt of heat through his body, pooling in his groin.

Dear God...

'Would you care for more?' His voice was low and husky even to his own ears. He could easily plate some of the food onto the serving trencher but for some inexplicable reason decided to feed her again. Mayhap he wanted to see the burst of pleasure in her eyes as she sampled the food he had prepared. Mayhap he wanted the brief touch of her fingers as she took the offering. Or mayhap he was an inimitable fool. He held out another chunk of bread dipped in the delicious buttery fish and herb juices and again she tentatively took it.

'My thanks.'

'My pleasure.' His voice was gruff as he continued to stare at her, reaching out to brush away a drop of the sauce from her chin with the pad of his thumb. God, he should not have done that. He should not have touched her, however fleeting it was. It made him want more. More of something he could not have. He took a step back and swallowed uncomfortably.

They stood there a moment with neither moving, neither uttering a word, just staring intently at one another as though there were some inexplicable spell that bound them together. Nicholas did not know how long he stood there gazing at Eva Siward, watching the different shades of brown, green and flecks of gold dance in her expressive eyes that tipped upwards and were rimmed with long dark lashes. But he was exceptionally relieved a moment later when he heard the sound of horses pounding the ground, otherwise he might have done something he might later regret. Just thinking about kissing Eva made his gaze drop to her lips.

He blinked and looked away, the spell broken. Thankfully. Taking a step back, he turned and strode towards the entrance of the dwelling, needing to distance himself from the woman. God, but he also needed to fill his chest with a huge breath of air. Mayhap that might cool his blood, his head, his body. He snapped his head up to find Warin de Talmont helping his wife Joan dismount their destrier. And behind them a couple of Knights Fortitude squires. Thank the heavens, as the man could not have come soon enough. His friend turned and gave him a nod.

'Where the hell have you been?' Nicholas had not meant to sound so irritable but could not help it.

'Ah, D'Amberly,' Warin de Talmont muttered wryly. 'I see that you have left your manners back in London, but I sincerely hope that it has not been too trying for you to…' His friend looked behind his shoulder and must have seen Eva Siward standing behind him, and whatever he saw made him give a quizzical look as he raised a brow. Nicholas let out an exasperated sigh and tried again, ignoring his friend's curiosity.

'De Talmont, your lateness knows no bounds. Joan, lovely as always. Come, you must be weary after a journey with my oaf of a friend.'

He held out his hand to Joan. 'Here, you take my hand instead of using a walking staff.'

Joan, whose eyesight was exceedingly poor and diminishing year by year, smiled up at him. 'Oh, Nicholas, I have missed you, and you must not blame Warin since the fault was mine why we have arrived later than expected.'

'Then in that case I shall cease to complain. Come, you must be hungry.'

The introductions, such as they were between Eva and Warin de Talmont and his wife, were made. And although the atmosphere was pleasant and congenial, she had never felt so conspicuous as a thief and evidently an interloper than she did at that moment. Indeed, neither Sir Warin nor his wife made her feel inferior and yet Eva felt it all the same.

They soon settled around the table, sharing the large trencher of the food that Nicholas D'Amberly had prepared earlier. Food that only moments ago he had been feeding her, and then stood gazing at her afterwards. Food that was delicious, with tender, succulent pieces of trout cooked in butter and flavoured with verjuice and herbs. She could not remember ever tasting anything so deliciously decadent and yet at that moment Eva had lost her appetite, each mouthful difficult to swallow. It was because of *him*—Nicholas D'Amberly and the way that he had been staring at her…in fact, the manner in which they had both been staring at one another. She flushed, pushing the memory out of her head.

'Tell me, Mistress Eva, for I have been desperate to know, but what is it like to be a lady thief?' Joan de Talmont muttered without a hint of malice. Nevertheless, the awkwardness and tension that she felt hummed in the air.

Eva coughed, clearing her throat before answering. 'The truth is that it was never a chosen path for me but sadly a necessity, my lady.'

'I do understand.' The young woman chuckled. 'Oh, I am far from being a lady and also the last person to cast judgement on how one is forced to survive.'

Eva smiled, instantly warming to Joan, with some of the tension that she had carried easing. 'Thank you. Not many would have the insight, or even the kindness, to look past my misdeeds and lack of rectitude.'

'Ah, but my spirited wife is all benevolence, Mistress Eva,' Sir Warin said as he lifted his wife's hand and kissed the centre of her palm. 'Amongst her many charitable works, Joan is a patron at All Hallows Church in the City and takes a personal interest in the plight of those less fortunate, especially young children.'

'Very commendable.' Eva could not help but admire a woman who, despite her obvious limitations, managed to put her efforts into meaningful endeavours.

'And brave,' Nicholas D'Amberly added.

'Oh, I do not know about that, since bravery has many guises.' Joan de Talmont waved her hand, dismissing the notion. 'In any case, I would rather hear about *you,* mistress.'

'Please call me Eva.'

'As long as you call me Joan.'

Eva smiled. 'Very well, Joan, what would you like to know?'

'Oh, apart from how you became a thief, which must have been as exciting as it was dangerous, what I would most like to learn is how you managed to do it.'

'How I managed to do what?'

'How on earth did you manage to best Nicholas?'

'Oh, quite. Joan and I have been wondering

how D'Amberly was so easily fooled,' Warin de Talmont added. 'For my friend here is not a man who is taken for one…not usually, at any rate.'

His wife smiled slowly. 'No, not usually.'

'So glad I can be the source of your amusement,' Nicholas D'Amberly added sardonically.

Eva's chest clenched a little at their easy friendship and camaraderie, making her feel a little pensive, wondering where Marguerite was and hoping that her friend was safe.

'But you are not so easily fooled, Sir Nicholas, for I am here after all. Ready for your questioning.' She smiled tightly.

That caused the convivial repartee to stutter, as they all stopped chatting and resumed eating in silence. Eva, for one, was glad. She felt weary and wanted this all to be over. Especially this absurd, inconvenient attraction for Nicholas D'Amberly.

It was not long afterwards that Eva found herself alone in the small adjoining chamber, tucked up under the coverlet, trying to fall asleep, while the man himself was sleeping in the main chamber with a rolled-out flock mattress, which surely could not be comfortable. She felt guilty for having been allotted not just a chamber to herself but a proper pallet as well.

It was she who, after all, was detained here to aid these men in their endeavours. Not that she wasn't treated with courtesy. It was disconcerting to be treated so well by all of these people, even though she might have once been respectable, coming from a family who took pride in what they achieved. But she was no longer that maid. And that family no longer existed.

Eva's life had taken such a drastic turn that all she had been fit for now was a life on the streets. But mayhap, with the silver that she might extract from these men in exchange for the information she had, Eva might now have the opportunity to alter her situation for good. And with just a little good fortune she might escape the need to ever have to steal again, along with that part of her life.

The following morn the reprieve that Eva had been granted following her near-death experience had come to an end. After waking at dawn to help feed the chickens and other livestock, as well as other menial tasks which, in truth, she enjoyed, she broke her fast alone. It was not long before Nicholas D'Amberly and Warin de Talmont reconvened with her in the living chamber where they had shared a meal only the night before. This time, however, without the presence of Mistress Joan.

She took a big gulp of ale from her mug and wiped her mouth with the back of her hand and nodded at the men.

'Thank you for agreeing to confer with us.' Nicholas gave her faint smile. 'All we need is your help, mistress, for you are one of the few that might provide the information we seek.'

'I am glad to be of help,' she said, glancing at them as they both took a seat.

'Good. In that case, we would like to commence with the man who hired you to steal from my friend here,' Warin de Talmont added.

'Where would you like me to begin?'

'At the very start, mistress.'

Eva nodded. 'Well, about a sennight ago, I was told that a man had specifically asked to have an audience with me, at the inn I resided in.'

'Very good. And you met with him?'

Eva nodded. 'I did… I met the man who had summoned me in the small privy chamber at the inn, whereupon he informed me of his plans. He set these out and made an offer which was difficult to refuse. Indeed, he did not seem to be a man one should cross, or whom one could ever decline. Besides, the silver he promised was significant. All I had to do was steal from you, Sir Nicholas. I was instructed to watch you, and the moment you were handed a pouch, a satchel, or a package or some such I was to steal that very item from you. I was made aware how imperative it was that you were not to familiarise yourself with the contents. In fact, the theft had to be done the moment you were given the item.'

'And you never knew what was inside the pouch when you took it?'

'No, I was only ever hired for the theft itself and nothing more. The man gave me the specific time and place when this was to be done, but left me to devise the plan myself.'

'I see.' Nicholas D'Amberly's gaze was inscrutable. 'And how did you know who I was?'

She shrugged. 'I asked around within the city and eventually found those who know of you, Sir Nicholas, and once I discovered who you were I followed you on the day of the theft. And that night, with everything in place, I lay in wait for you in the tavern in Southwark, with Marguerite, as you well know.'

'And when were you to meet the man who hired you again? Did he leave his name?'

'No…no names. But the following morning, after the theft, I was to meet him again at the privy chamber at the inn to hand over the spoils from the previous night…but of course that never occurred.'

Warin de Talmont leant forward. 'And do you by any chance know why the man who hired you had gone to so much trouble to get that missive back?'

'No, Sir Warin, I did not, but I presume it was to prevent you from knowing the contents of this missive.' Eva shook her head. 'But, as I said, I had no notion that the pouch even contained such an item until I went to retrieve it before I was to meet Sir Nicholas at The Three Choughs on London Bridge.'

'Ah, so you looked at it then before you came to the tavern?'

'Yes.' She nodded, slouching forward and leaning on her elbows. 'I did, while I waited until it was the appointed time for the meeting.'

'And the man who hired you…can you describe him?'

'Indeed. He is unremarkable really, and I would say he was decidedly average. He was of average height, average weight, with greying hair at his temples. His eyes, though, they were distinctive—pale blue, as though he had frost in them. Quite peculiar, unsettling even.'

'Then not so average after all.'

'Not when you really looked on him. Properly looked on him.' Eva shuddered just thinking about the man. 'But otherwise he was not someone you would particularly notice when passing him on the street.'

'That is most helpful, mistress.' Nicholas flashed a brief smile before he opened out his hand and revealed a gold ring. Placing it on the table, he pushed it forward towards her. 'Can you see the emblem on this ring here? There are two serpents intertwined, with the heads facing one another. Have you by any chance seen this emblem before?'

Eva picked up the ring, turning it around, studying it, before placing it back on the table and shaking her head. 'No, I have never seen anything like this before.'

Both men looked disappointed by her answer, seemingly wishing that they could tie the theft in with whatever that emblem represented.

'Never mind, mistress, you have been most helpful. Thank you.'

'I am happy to be of use.' And for once Eva actually meant it.

'There is, however, one matter that still bewilders me about all of this.' Nicholas D'Amberly's brow furrowed. 'Why did he seek *you* in the first instance? How did he know of your…er… skills in thievery?'

'Did I not say?' She blinked, darting a brief look from one man to the other. 'He sought me directly because of who I was—Simon the Rook's apprentice.'

Nicholas D'Amberly stared at her in disbelief as his friend beside him raised a brow, muttering an oath. 'I do not believe I heard correctly. Did you just reveal that you are, or rather you were, the apprentice of one of London's most notorious thieves?'

'I did, yes.' Eva was not altogether surprised that these men had heard of Simon. Many in London had heard of, or had known, him personally, especially on the streets where Simon had been something of a champion and hero of the poor and destitute.

'You never said any of this before, Eva,' Nicholas D'Amberly hissed.

'You never asked.'

'And was this man not surprised to encounter a…a maid as the Rook's apprentice?'

'Oh, no. You see I never went to the meeting undisguised. God, no. I learned a long time ago that would not be prudent. Besides, Simon would never have considered a maid as an apprentice, as he did not believe they were fast enough to escape when need be. He made the exception with me, but always had me in the guise of a young lad.'

'Are you saying that you *always* dressed as…er…a young lad when you worked for the Rook?'

Eva found it difficult to explain the life she had led with Simon the Rook. It might seem odd to outsiders, peculiar even, that the man had always insisted that she not only dressed as a young lad but behaved as one too, even when they were not thieving. But Eva had understood even from the start that it was a way to protect her from any unwanted attention. Her name too had been changed to a masculine one—Evrard, and it was the only way in which she had known to live until recently. She had learned since the age of twelve that she had to hide herself and who she was in every way imaginable. From tying down her female parts once they became too obvious to changing her way of speaking and walking, to adopting far more masculine mannerisms. In fact, it was only on his death that she had allowed herself to grow into the maid she had always been. And even dress as one. Not that Eva felt entirely comfortable in such cumbersome attire or knew how to truly behave as a maid. Nevertheless, she was still a woman. One who no longer had to hide who she was.

'Yes. Always. And at this particular privy meeting I was disguised, as on the night you met me, Sir Nicholas, as a boy. I even wore the same mask to hide my identity.'

'That was very clever of you, Eva.'

She shrugged. 'I endeavoured to protect myself as much as I could.' But who could say in truth whether the man who had hired her did not already know who she was? He had been most perceptive, as though those pale eyes could see right into her soul.

Sir Warin frowned, rubbing his chin. 'You said you looked at the missive. Did you, by any chance, understand much?'

'I can read, sir, and write but no, it contained such strange looped shapes with intermittent letters and numbers. None of it made much sense, actually.'

'Shame, but no matter.'

This was the moment that she had been waiting for. To make a bargain with these men for the real information she had. 'Oh, I would not say that, Sir Nicholas.'

The man narrowed his eyes. 'What do you mean, mistress?'

'What would you say if I were to tell you that

because I had much time on my hands while I waited for our rendezvous at the tavern I engaged in something that might be of great value to you…to you both.'

'I would inform you that I'd be very interested to learn of this, Eva.'

'That is what I hoped you would say.' She nodded, smiling. 'As I said, I did not understand anything that had been scribed on the missive. But I did, however, do something that I hoped would be of use later.'

'And what is that?'

'I memorised it.'

Chapter Seven

Nicholas felt his jaw drop as he stared at Eva Siward, not quite believing the words that had just come out of her mouth. 'Apologies, I must have misheard you, mistress, but did you just disclose that you committed the contents of the missive to memory?'

'Yes,' the damn infuriating woman replied, 'I did, and you heard quite correctly, sir. It was something that I was taught how to do and became extremely proficient at.'

'I see. And you did not see fit to mention this—*all of this*—beforehand?'

Hell's teeth, but the knowledge that Eva Siward had also been Simon the damn Rook's apprentice and that she had always disguised herself as a young boy was making his head reel. Oh, Lord, but the Rook, of all people? How could he not have seen this? It must have been the Rook who had taken her in when she had been alone and friendless when she had run away to London, as she had mentioned before. Indeed, her association with the man explained why she had managed to pilfer his pouch so expertly. Yet the woman had chosen to keep all this to herself until now. Which meant, of course, that she wanted something in return for this information. Naturally she did.

'I did not mention it beforehand until I was certain of the knowledge, sir. Especially after the ordeal a couple of nights ago. I did not, as you must imagine, deceive you.'

Mayhap not intentionally, but Nicholas knew that this was what she hoped to bargain with. Lord knew, she owed him nothing, apart from what she had already agreed to, and this…well, this was far more than either he or his Knights Fortitude brethren had expected. Yet he could not help but feel disconcerted by how things had transpired.

He pinned her with his gaze, unable to say anything for a moment.

Eventually, Warin de Talmont broke the silence by coughing and clearing his throat. 'So what you are saying, Mistress Eva, is that you now can recall what you put to memory—the contents of the missive?'

'Yes, I believe that I can. Most of it at least.' Her eyes did not stray from his, even when she was addressing de Talmont.

Nicholas could see that she was finding this difficult. He could see in the depths of her eyes that they were tinged with guilt, remorse and even regret. He could also see that she was uncomfortable with having to use the information for gain. But then this was what the streets of London had taught her, after all. To plan, scheme and look ahead, using any means that she could get her hands on to profit by it. And he could hardly blame her, not when it might earn her a measure of security. And, in truth, how different was it from the way in which the Knights Fortitude gathered information for Hubert de Burgh or the Crown?

'What is that you want, Eva?' he asked.

She did not answer for a moment but eventually she said softly, quietly, 'Silver. Fifty marks.'

Warin slumped back and whistled, while Nicholas kept his eyes fixed on Eva Siward's. 'That is a huge sum, mistress, but my question is this.' He leant forward. 'Is the information you have worth the value you have placed on it?'

The woman shrugged. 'That is something I

cannot answer directly. You will obviously have to judge for yourself.'

'How on earth can we possibly assess whether this information is even worth a sum of that size when we have yet to ascertain what it might contain?'

'I would suggest that you might put your faith and trust in the information I provide being of some use to you.'

'You would have me gamble on faith and trust?' Nicholas was incredulous. 'When we do not even know what the hell this damn information is?'

Eva Siward also leant forward, her face a mere fraction away from Nicholas's.

'That is not in any way my concern,' she murmured.

'Is it not?'

'No, Sir Nicholas.' She was so close now their noses were almost touching. So close he could see directly into her eyes and the swirling emotions in their depths. So close that her scent wrapped around his senses. 'Its value is for you to determine, not me.'

'Yet you put a value on its worth, Eva. You put this value on it almost the moment you knew we sought information from you.'

Again that insouciant shrug. 'And what if I

did? I have to protect myself and my interests. You can understand that, can you not?' Her eyes were earnest, as though pleading with him to comprehend her situation. He did. Yet he hated that he did.

'I can, but after saving your life I thought that mayhap you did not think of me as someone who would mean you harm.'

She flinched at that. 'I… I do not think of you that way,' she whispered.

'Well, that is a blessing.'

'But I must think on what might happen to me, and to Marguerite, after we are no longer of use to you. Afterwards, when we have to make our own way in the world again.'

'I would have seen you settled, Eva. With or without this new information.'

She opened her mouth to speak and then closed it again. They continued to stare at one another for a long lingering moment that extended into an even longer silence, until Warin de Talmont coughed again, clearing his throat. Nicholas had all but forgotten that his friend was even there. In the midst of all the irritation and annoyance that had risen within him, he had even forgotten the reason why they were all there in the first place.

'Very well, you shall have your fifty marks

of silver.' Nicholas nodded as his friend snapped his head around in his direction with a look of alarm. 'But on one condition. Once we have this information that you claim you have put to memory, we may have further need of your aid. And if that is the case, then you will give it without any complaint and regardless of the length of time we might need your assistance.' Well, two could play at this game. 'What say you?'

She frowned and shook her head in disbelief. 'How on earth can I promise such a thing, when you have not specified what this aid, should you need it, might consist of?'

He gave her a slow satisfied smile. 'I would suggest that you might also put your *faith* and *trust* in this scheme. After all, you seem rather fond of such stakes.'

Eva Siward narrowed her gaze, her jaw clenched, her spine rigid. But she eventually nodded and expelled an irritated sigh. 'Very well, Sir Nicholas, Sir Warin. I accept your terms.'

'Good. I shall see to fetching some vellum or parchment and you can put down everything that you remember from the missive.' Warin de Talmont rose, seemingly wanting an end to this awkward parley. 'But first I shall see to my wife. Until later, Mistress Eva. D'Amberly.'

'Yes, of course, Sir Warin. And thank you for your…consideration. And for agreeing to the terms.' With matters concluded, Eva rose too and smiled at Warin as he left the dwelling, unable to bring herself to meet Nicholas's eyes. Just as she moved in an attempt to make a hasty departure, Nicholas grabbed her arm.

'Just one moment, if you please.'

'No, Sir Nicholas, it would not please me to continue with this discourse any further.'

'I am sure you do not after getting exactly what you want.'

'I believe we will both gain what we seek.'

'Even so, I feel there is still much to discuss.'

'Mayhap later, once I have had my fill of this clean air and even a walk. Now, if you will excuse me.'

'Gladly, mistress, and what an excellent idea. I shall join you anon.' He smiled broadly at her, and her nostrils flared before she strode out of the dwelling, her skirts flapping around her inelegantly.

Nicholas watched Eva Siward for a moment before rushing to catch up with her. 'I see that you have the right of it, Eva. This is indeed quite a pleasant diversion.'

She quickened her pace. 'Hell's teeth!' she ground out.

'Such language from a maid.'

'As you have already discovered, I am not a usual…maid.'

'No, you are not.'

'Devil take you, Nicholas D'Amberly!' She marched through the grassy terrain, swinging her arms in exasperation. 'Has anyone ever told you, sir, that you are the most vexing man?'

'Yes, often.' He lengthened his stride to keep up with the woman. 'And has anyone ever told you that you are shrewd, canny and even sly?'

She gave an indignant huff. 'No, never.'

'Well, now, that is also most unusual. And unexpected. I was certain that a maid of your prodigious talents would have had such epithets bestowed on her.'

'Well, you are wrong. No one has ever spoken of me in such terms.' She continued to march on along the winding pathway that led to the woods.

'Not even Simon the Rook?'

She stopped her progress abruptly and turned to face him. 'You mean to mock me?'

'Not in the least.'

'How dare you speak of Simon, when you know nothing about him?'

He wondered whether there would be any point in withholding the truth.

'On the contrary, Eva, I knew the Rook quite well.'

'What did you say?' Her eyes widened in surprise as she swung around to face him.

'I believe that you heard me,' he drawled.

'That cannot be possible.'

'Oh, but it is.'

'You?' she muttered. 'You knew Simon?'

'Yes, I knew him well. Despite his many transgressions, Simon the Rook was an extremely clever, shrewd man. We made a bargain of sorts with him. We continued to keep his many…er…criminal interests from scrutiny and, in return, he worked with us for coin.'

'I cannot believe this.'

'Nevertheless, it is true.' He sighed, dragging his fingers through his hair. 'We had a mutual agreement between us. We knew of his many… er…activities but would look the other way, in exchange for anything that he deemed would be of interest to us. I was sad to hear of his demise, he was a useful ally.'

'But I do not understand,' she mumbled, shaking her head. 'I was told that it was a Crown Knight who had brought about his downfall.'

Nicholas frowned. This in itself was of

great interest. It seemed that the real killer of Simon the Rook had made a significant effort to blame a Crown Knight, which Nicholas and his Knights Fortitude brethren were also part of. 'Who informed you of this?'

'No one especially. It is what was heard on the streets and believed by those who knew and worked with him.'

'Well, you were misinformed, Eva. Knights of the Crown were not involved with the Rook's murder. They are not permitted to kill a man in cold blood without good reason or unless they perceive there to be a threat to the Crown.'

'This is all so much to take in.'

'I can see that.'

'And you say you knew him?' She lifted her head, her eyes searching his.

'I did, yes.' Nicholas wondered whether he should disclose more. 'In truth, he worked for us, Eva.'

'But he never said anything about any of this.'

'Then it seems we all have our secrets.' He took a deep breath. 'And no one more so than the Rook.'

'I do not believe it. He hated Knights of the Crown.' She assessed him for a moment before speaking again. 'But you are not just a Crown

Knight, are you, Sir Nicholas? That is what has been niggling at me since the very first. And it has something to do with Hubert de Burgh, has it not?'

No. He was not just a mere Crown Knight. As a member of the secret group, The Knights Fortitude of the Order of the Sword, they put King and country at the heart of everything they held sacred, unlike many other religious orders. This they did foremost by working tire- lessly to uncover and quash plots against the Crown of England. And they lived and breathed their motto: *Pro Rex. Pro deus. Pro fide. Pro honoris.*

In truth, it was inevitable that Eva Siward would discover and understand more about them. Indeed the fifty marks of silver that she would eventually get was not just for the in- formation she provided but also as a means to buy her silence.

'You are very astute, Eva.'

'But you will not say more.'

'No.' He shook his head. 'Not today.'

'And what of Simon? I cannot see how he would have ever been your ally. Or even work for you.'

'Yet he did.'

'How?' She stopped walking and rubbed her

brow. 'In what capacity? I cannot comprehend anything that you have disclosed.'

'Does it matter that you cannot understand his alliance with us?' Nicholas also stopped, turning to face her. He did not want this. He did not want this woman's inquisitiveness. 'The man worked for us—that is all there is to comprehend. And mayhap now you can leave the matter be.'

'I am afraid that will not do. I need to know more.'

'Are you certain, Eva, because the Rook's proclivities were not entirely known by many. And the confidential work he did for us formed the basis of that.'

Her brows furrowed. 'What is it that you are trying to convey?'

Nicholas sighed deeply. 'Simon the Rook did not just steal worldly goods and silver. He also stole secrets, Eva. And he traded in them…with us.'

She swallowed, almost as though anticipating what might be said presently but needing to hear it confirmed anyway. 'What kind of secrets?'

'Secrets that no man would want to come out in the open. Secrets of the flesh, of sin, of lust and corruption. Dangerous secrets that the

Rook exploited, but he was exceptionally useful to us.'

'But how? How would he gain secrets of this nature? Who on earth would entrust those to him in the first instance?'

It was remarkable that Eva Siward, astute, talented and intelligent as she was, who had run away to London and had been taken in by London's most notorious thief, could not have known about this. It showed the extent that Simon the Rook had cared for this young woman, to shelter and protect her from the darker side of his many dealings.

'Tell me, Sir Nicholas,' she asked softly. 'I would like to know.'

'Very well, if you are certain.' God, how he wished he did not have to disclose this about the man who had obviously meant a great deal to her. But there was nothing for it. 'The Rook knew of these secrets because…well, he was involved in such activities, Eva.'

'You mean he…he…with other men?'

How was such a conversation to be had with a woman? A woman who evidently mourned the loss of her friend.

'Answer me, please.'

'It seems obvious to me that the man protected you from this knowledge. Just allow it to rest, Eva,' he muttered gently.

She gave a determined shake of the head. 'I would still like to know. Tell me.'

He sighed. 'He sold the secrets of bishops, monks, barons and other prominent men to me.'

'So you could bribe them?'

'Just so, yes.' Nicholas dragged his fingers through his hair, assessing what he was able to disclose and what he could not. 'There were treasonous whispers abound in London, Eva, ones we needed to uncover and still do. Many months ago, on the eventide of the feast of the Epiphany, the Rook found his way to us with a proposition. You see, he had information that he believed that Hubert de Burgh would be interested in and, once we paid him coin for his trouble, he came back again for more. And so we made the bargain that I spoke of earlier.'

'So you would pay for these secrets that he gathered and then assess whether they were of use to you?' She wrapped her arms around her waist, the pallor of her cheeks decidedly ashen. 'And do you believe that this might have been the reason for Simon's murder?'

'The answer is probably yes. That is what I deemed to be the reason when I learnt of his demise. Regardless of this, mistress, he must have cared for you.'

'He did, Sir Nicholas, as I cared for him. Whatever his secrets and the exploits he was involved with as you put it, they matter not to me. He looked after me and many others. In truth, I had always suspected his leaning…that he… with other men. Not that I cared. But I am surprised of his involvement with Knights of the Crown, as he never breathed a word about it to me or anyone else, for that matter.'

'He must have realised that it would be prudent to keep his involvement a secret. The fewer people knew, the more assured he was of his own safety and those he cared about.'

'Yet he was found out anyway,' she muttered, her voice barely suppressing an undercurrent of anger. 'When I think that without him I would not have survived the streets. Without him, my life would have been so very different. I must find out who murdered him. I must avenge him. Simon was more of a guardian to me, a father-figure, than my damnable uncle, who was given that obligation and failed in his duty.

'I am sorry for your loss, mistress' He moved closer and wiped away a stray tear that had spilled onto her cheek. 'I did not mean to distress you.'

'You have not.' She lifted her head, her eyes filled with unshed tears, her lips pinched and her face weary. 'But it seems, from what you have conveyed, that his association with *you* did cost him his life in the end.'

Nicholas stilled. 'What are you saying, mistress?'

'What I am saying, sir,' she said coldly, 'is that, despite your assurances, Simon the Rook died seemingly because he was in your employ. Thus he died needlessly because of a Crown Knight, after all.'

Chapter Eight

Eva was still weary and discomposed after the revelations about Simon the Rook. Her head was reeling. Her eyes stung. Her throat was raw. Nothing, in truth, had prepared her for what Nicholas D'Amberly had disclosed. It had been surprising that the Crown Knight had known Simon at all, but to learn that they had been allies of sorts, with Simon selling sordid secrets—well, that had been something entirely different. Stunned, baffled and feeling decidedly uneasy about these new findings, she had much to ponder on.

The first was that she had been unfair to blame Nicholas D'Amberly for Simon's death, when the Rook had approached the Knights of the Crown himself with his proposition. After all, he had engaged in many dangerous pursuits and activities, and had taken great steps to shield those who were connected to him from ever finding out of his involvement. Yet in the end they had. It had cost him his life, anyway. Gut-wrenching though it was. The second realisation was that someone had gone to great lengths to implicate a Crown Knight in his death, which now seemed very strange, since it begged the question why anyone would do such a thing. Eva now wondered whether his death might have had something to do with the man who had hired her to steal from Nicholas D'Amberly in the first instance. It might all be a coincidence and mayhap she might never find out, but she would do all she could to uncover more.

The one thing that astounded Eva was that, despite everything, despite all these revelations about Simon, her love, respect and loyalty to him remained intact.

It made her heart ache that he had felt he needed to protect her from this dark side of his dealings, as he had always done since the moment she had met him as a young maid until he had breathed his last breath. He had been an unusual, complicated man, but he had cared for her and protected her in his own inimitable way. The life she had led with him had indeed been dangerous, but he had kept her safe.

* * *

'There, I think this is to be the last of it.' She gazed down at the letters and shapes she had scribed in the sequence she had remembered from the stolen missive onto a sheet of parchment.

'Well done. That is most impressive.' Joan had been keeping her company while Eva had painstakingly copied everything she could from memory as they sat in the main chamber of the small dwelling. 'Shall I fetch Nicholas or mayhap Warin would oblige, if you would rather not see that dashing scoundrel of a knight?'

She felt herself flush. 'I really do not believe that it matters either way.'

'My mistake. I had wondered whether there was discord between you and Nicholas.'

Eva shrugged. 'Why should there be? It is not as though we are friends.'

Her heart pounded in her chest as she hoped that her true feelings were not revealed to this young woman whose senses seemed far sharper than one would suppose, especially one with diminishing sight.

'Of course, my apology. I always seem to blurt out what I happen to be pondering on before giving it due consideration.'

Warin de Talmont stepped inside the chamber and nodded at both women.

'You will be happy to know that I have now completed it all, sir. This is all I remember.'

'My thanks, mistress. I shall take a look, if you wouldn't mind.' The man moved around the table, kissed his wife's cheek and turned to peer down at the shapes and letters that Eva had scribed. 'This is going to take a little time for me to unravel and decipher.'

Joan squeezed her husband's hand affectionately. 'Ah, but if anyone can do it, it is you, my love. My husband is exceptionally good at what he does, Eva.'

Her husband turned to her and shook his head in dismay at yet another example of his wife blurting out information, making Eva smile. It was difficult not to warm to these two souls. But at that moment it was another who occupied her mind.

'I shall inform Sir Nicholas that my task is finally complete. Would you happen to know where he might be, sir?'

'Indeed, mistress, he is by the stream, attempting to catch another freshwater fish for the evening's meal. He always finds that particular task gratifying when he needs time for contemplation.'

'Then I should leave him to his reflections.'

'Nonsense, I am sure he would be happy of your company.' Joan smiled at her. 'And mayhap he would also welcome a repast, since I doubt he has had anything much since he broke his fast this morn.'

'In that case, I shall take a basket.' Eva was relieved to have reason to converse with him after her outburst earlier that day.

She placed a few rolls of wheaten bread, a few apples and wrapped what they had left of the round of cheese in some linen and placed them all carefully in a basket before moving to the door. She nodded at the married couple and left the dwelling in search of Nicholas D'Amberly.

She followed the path around the stables at the back, and continued along until she reached the dense coppices and thickets that hugged the pathway, ambling through the trees, bushes and boulders dotted haphazardly. The pathway meandered around and sloped down suddenly. Then Eva heard it—the ebb and flow of the running stream. She followed the sound until she came upon the running water gushing through, hugged by a grassy bank, and there, in the middle of the stream, was the man she sought, holding a spear over his head in one hand and a knotted rope in another. He had his back to her, his legs submerged up to his knees. She watched Nicholas D'Amberly in rapt fascination as he stood motionless for a long moment before he pounced, hurling the spear down into the water, panting and splashing. He used the rope to grab the fish he had impaled, writhing and wriggling in his arms before he threw it to the side of the bank.

'Well done, that was very efficiently done,' she murmured, making the man turn around abruptly in the water.

'Ah, Eva, I did not see you there. Is everything well?'

'Of course. I thought to bring you some sustenance, Sir Nicholas.' She held up the basket of food. 'And to inform you that I have just recently completed the first part of our bargain. I have written down the shapes, letters and motifs that I remembered from the missive and have left them with Sir Warin.'

'Good,' he murmured as he waded through the water. 'Warin's expertise is in deciphering. He'll be riveted for the rest of the day as well as the eventide.'

'Then I am glad to have given him the challenge.' She watched the man come out of the stream and walk towards her. She stood there with her hands at her waist. 'Tell me then, if that is Sir Warin's forte then what is yours?'

'Finding things—people, objects, anything really. It does not matter where, what or how, I will track and find my mark.'

Oh, yes, she could attest to that, since the man had managed to find her the very night she had stolen from him. In truth, it had been astounding how he had followed her so breathtakingly easily.

'And yours, Eva, seems to be far more than just the thievery.' He smiled at her. 'I must say that your skill in memorizing and recalling information, as you did with the contents of the missive, is unlike anything I have ever seen before.'

She could feel heat suffuse her cheeks. 'Thank you.'

'Have you always been in possession of such talent?'

She shrugged. 'Ever since I was a child. And once Simon was made aware of this skill he made me harness and use it, incorporating it in his organisation.'

'I can imagine he did.'

'Well, anyway, here—you might be in want of this.' The moment she had uttered 'want' his eyes had dropped to her lips before looking away.

'My thanks.' He coughed, clearing the low gruff tone to his voice. After a long moment he spoke again. 'And, as well as my thanks, I would also wish to convey my apology to you.'

Nicholas D'Amberly could not have surprised her more by that admission. An apology? To someone like her—a thief? It seemed unthinkable. The man was not at all what she had ever imagined.

'An apology? Whatever for?'

He threw the net and spear on the bank and got out of the water. 'For the murder of the Rook.'

'I do not understand.' She frowned, her eyes riveted to his hose, drenched with drops of water clinging to his well-defined sculpted legs. 'But you were not the one responsible for his murder...'

'Ah, but I was. You were right, of course, to say that in some way I was responsible for Simon's death.' He sighed deeply. 'Had he not got himself involved with the work he did, then he might still be alive today.'

'You cannot know that.'

'Even so, I never contemplated that a man

such as the Rook would have dependants who would mourn his loss, but I should have known.'

Eva blinked. 'And what would you have done with that knowledge, sir?'

'I do not know how I could have prevented his death, but I should have looked out for those who worked for me. For too long the need to find what needs to be found, seek what needs to be sought and accomplish what I must has been my dogged aim, without a care or thought of any consequences. But, of course, there are always consequences.'

'True. But in this case the outcome would always have been the same.' She dropped her gaze for a moment before lifting it to meet his. 'And you must know that the fault of Simon's death does not lie with you, Sir Nicholas. I was wrong to imply that it did.'

'That relieves my conscience.' He gave her a faint smile. 'In truth, it was easy to assume that a man such as the Rook—lowborn, thief, criminal—to be someone devoid of integrity but, in a strange way, he was one of the most principled men that I had ever known. He looked after his own. I cannot help but admire him for that alone.'

She was bewildered by Nicholas D'Amberly. It almost seemed that Simon's ability to protect 'his own' was something that this proud, strong knight had not experienced for himself and as a result had gained his admiration.

'I am sorry for your loss, mistress,' he muttered eventually, breaking the silence.

'My thanks, but you know I cannot help thinking that with Simon this would always have been his inevitable ending, one way or another.'

'Is it not for us all? It claims us all in the end.' His voice had become pensive, devoid of his usual charm. Real and utterly raw.

'True, but when someone gambles on his life as many times as Simon did, the stakes become too high to overcome in the end.'

'At least he protected those who mattered to him.'

She nodded, frowning. 'Yes, I suppose he did.'

Eva had not realised that she had come towards him, drawing closer with every step. The moment she could see clearly into his eyes, she could tell that he was lost in his own thoughts. What was it that haunted such a man? There was something more here, something that made her want to know more about him—his past and what led him to be a Knight of the Crown.

'You sound as though you did not have such attention.'

'No.' His lips twisted into a smile but his eyes remained glazed and hard. 'That I did not, mistress.'

Nicholas D'Amberly did not divulge more and Eva knew better than to press the man. She watched him as he bent down and washed his hands in the water before stretching to his full height, looking out into the distance. Yet still he said nothing.

'My father is a great ennobled baron from a distinguished family, with all the usual requisite honour and valour, adhering to all courtly pretensions,' he said bitterly, exhaling through his teeth. 'Yet he had none of the integrity and fortitude that Simon the Rook seemingly had. And, unlike your protector, whom you once described to have been a father-figure to you, the man who sired *me* from his own loins did not do his duty. In truth, he failed at the essentials.'

'How?' She sucked in her breath. 'How did your father fail you?'

He did not respond and Eva wished she could take back the question that had readily tripped off her tongue. Instead, he grabbed linen cloth that he'd brought to dry himself and moved to peer inside the basket that she had placed on the ground. Grabbing an apple, he threw it in the air, caught it and took a large bite of the juicy flesh.

'Sadly, by something so futile as *love,* I am afraid.' He shook his head. 'My father chose his desire for a woman half his age over his duty. I had always known that his obligations were somewhat conflicting, especially since the man held no real fondness for me. Nevertheless, I wrongly believed that, as his only son, I should have counted for something... Something, at the very least.'

'I hope you do not mind me asking what happened?' she asked softly.

'No, I don't. However, I think it best to leave this pitiful tale in the dung heap where it belongs.' His eyes softened as he turned towards her. 'Let me just say that the Rook, with all of his trickery, duplicity and thievery, had the right of it. He must have cared for you, Eva Siward, as if you were his own, for him to protect you and shield you as he did.'

Stunned and unable to move, she lifted her head to find him gazing at her with such longing and such intensity it fairly took her breath away. She raised her head, anticipating what was about to come, as he bent his head and kissed her softly.

* * *

The kiss was meant to stop her curiosity. It was meant to stop the anger and bitterness that always consumed Nicholas whenever he thought of his father's betrayal. It was supposed to be a brief kiss. It was supposed to be many things, yet the moment his lips touched hers he was lost in the wonder and warmth of her lips. She smelled of flowers, honey and woman.

He wanted to explore her then, and discover whether the sweetness extended to her taste. Pulling her closer, he slid his fingers behind the elegant curve of her neck, while his other hand cradled her head, moving slowly down her neck, along her spine. He opened her mouth with his, his tongue meeting hers, tasting her as his blood turned to liquid fire, pooling down to his groin.

Nicholas suddenly felt consumed in an entirely different manner. With heat, hunger and want. He wanted her. And with her hands plunged into his hair, holding him in place, she evidently wanted him just as ardently. He caught the moan at the back of her throat and pulled her closer, her breasts pressing against his chest. His hand travelled the length of her spine, along the curves and dips, and settled on her backside, giving it a squeeze. He tore his lips away and kissed, nipped and licked his way down from her jaw, down the column of her neck and the vein pulsating at her throat as she writhed against him. He moved back to her mouth, slanting his lips across hers, when he suddenly heard someone walking towards them as they stopped and cleared their throat from behind somewhere.

Slowly he pulled away from Eva, watching her flushed face, her swollen lips and her eyes, still dazed and filled with the dying sparks of desire, slowly turning to embers. God, how in heaven had this caught and blazed between them so quickly? It made little sense. He took a big breath and turned around, making sure that he stood in front of Eva, hiding her from view, knowing precisely who would be there— Warin de Talmont.

The man had the decency to refrain from speaking for a moment as Nicholas collected himself but the slow smile that curled around his lips revealed his bemusement at finding his friend not only wrapped around the woman now behind him but that he was hard as flint... everywhere.

Hell's teeth!

'Ah, D'Amberly, there you are. I have been looking for you, my friend.'

'And here I am, precisely where I said I would be,' he muttered through gritted teeth. 'Yet you came here, anyway, of course.'

'Of course. It has been an age since you came to these parts. I would hate for you to take the wrong turn and go down the wrong path…' de Talmont said, still smiling. 'And I wanted to make certain that Mistress Eva found you, which I can see quite clearly that…er…she did.'

Eva came around from behind him, crouched down to the ground, collecting the basket, and rushed past both of them. 'Yes, I did. Now, if there is nothing else, I believe I will make my way back to the cottage.'

The two men stood facing each other and waited until Eva had left the clearing before Warin de Talmont's smile slipped from his lips and he frowned.

'Now, would you care to explain what in God's name you are doing?'

Chapter Nine

The two men stared at each other, neither one moving or speaking. Nicholas knew that, although his friend's interference in his affairs was unwelcome, he was glad that he had interrupted them all the same. Where in heaven would either of them be if de Talmont had not arrived when he had? How had he lost sight of what he was doing and so quickly? It was staggering how they were both suddenly caught up in this ardent passion that crackled between them.

'I do not believe that this is anything to do with you, de Talmont.'

'Oh, quite the contrary, *this* has very much to do with me, since Eva Siward is part of *our* mission, D'Amberly, unless you have forgotten. She is currently working with us.'

'I do know that,' he ground out.

'Glad to hear it because you seem unable to remember that you cannot allow any indiscretion or amorous connection between yourself and the woman—until our association with her is over.'

'Do you think you are in any position to remind me of my duty after your own indiscretions and "amorous connection", as you call it, with Joan last year, nearly cost us our mission?'

De Talmont stepped forward towards him. 'You dare to bring Joan's name into this?'

'I do no such thing, least of all to Joan, so sheathe your talons, man. But I will not have you reminding me of my duty. Matters between Eva and I got carried away but it will not happen again. Not that I owe you any explanation.'

Nicholas had to ensure that he would keep to the promise, as it would do neither of them any good to give into the smouldering desire that blazed between them. Nothing good would ever come of *that*—it was a path to disaster. He should know that better than most after everything that had happened with his own father. And what in heaven's name had made him divulge much of that sorry tale to Eva? He had never spoken to anyone outside of his Knights Fortitude brethren, and even they were not aware of the entirety of it all between him and his father.

Yet after what had just occurred with Eva Siward Nicholas would be not be amiss in believing he was more like his father than he would acknowledge. After all, the man had proclaimed himself to be in love only a few scant months after his mother's death. God, but that had not even been the worst of it. His father's lack of faith in him and his desire and love for a woman he took to wife had clouded his judgement to such an extent that those familial ties were severed for good. No, Nicholas would never be like his father. He would never give into such a temptation that forced him to lose sight of himself as his father had.

His eyes caught Warin de Talmont's, who was watching him steadily.

'You are right, of course. And I'm glad you happened on us when you did, my friend.'

Remembering his mother made Nicholas think of the loss of her ring, claimed by the waters of the Thames. It had always been his talisman, his good luck charm and, just like his mother, it was now gone for ever.

'The only reason I came to find you is that the missive Mistress Eva scribed from memory is proving exceedingly interesting. It is something you might want to see.'

Thank goodness they were putting this strange interlude behind them and returning their attention back to the reason why they were all there in the first instance.

'Very well, lead the way.'

It was not long after they had all shared their evening meal when Joan de Talmont retired to bed, leaving Warin and Nicholas sitting around the small wooden table with Eva Siward, gazing at the looped markings, letters and motifs on the vellum that she had scribed earlier that day.

'I will go through the particulars later, Nick, but look at this here.' Warin pointed to a motif that looked like a flower. 'A repeat of this flower motif every so often. And this here looks to be a turret.'

'Mayhap that represents a castle then.' Nicholas rubbed his jaw.

'I thought so too. And what do you think on this?' The man pointed to another looped motif that looked similar yet was quite distinctively different.

'I would say that appears to look like a fort before each of the flowers that Eva has scribed.'

Warin de Talmont nodded, his brow furrowed in contemplation.

Eva lifted her head. 'I should mention that every one of those flower motifs was distinctly dyed in a golden hue, which I could hardly replicate. That struck me as strange as there are many colours of flowers, and yet the same was chosen every time. Do you think it might be relevant?'

'Possibly, yes,' Warin said, rubbing his head. 'Golden flowers…interesting.'

'Mayhap golden castle?' Nicholas muttered. 'No, I believe it to be more golden fort.'

'Yes, or possibly Golden ford—gold ford.'

Nicholas's eyes widened with the realisation of where it referred to. 'Of course, *Guildford*…'

'Then could it be referring to Guildford Castle?' Eva said excitedly.

Nicholas turned to her and nodded. 'Yes… yes, that is precisely what I thought… Wait. Warin, isn't the King and the court in residence at the castle at this very moment?'

'As is our liege lord, Hubert de Burgh.'

And also the Bishop of Winchester, Peter des Roches.

Dear God…

Guildford Castle, situated south-west of London, was surrounded by green demesne land, coppices and woodland—and it was also a particular favourite of the young King. He enjoyed its vast open spaces and the pleasures of hunting, falconry and courtly pursuits.

The missive had been easy to decipher, but then it had never been intended for it to be stolen by his informant. Which begged the question who it had been intended for and who had scribed it in the first instance. This was one thing that had puzzled Nicholas and his brethren from the first. And if the missive was intending to convey a plan that involved the castle when the King and his court were in residence at that very moment, then it would not be too outlandish to suppose that it could pertain to a treasonous act. Especially since the informant who had stolen the original missive had later been found dead. Which meant that King Henry, Hubert de Burgh or someone at court could also be in grave danger.

Nicholas felt the blood drain from his face as he met Warin de Talmont's perturbed eyes. It seemed that they had both come to the same understanding of their predicament. They were not at Guildford Castle so that they could warn Hubert de Burgh and King Henry of a possible threat, and neither was Savaric Fitz Leonard, who was still escorting Eva's friend in another

direction. There was nothing for it. They would
have to use all their determination and tenac-
ity to send outriders to the castle as well as
to Fitz Leonard, before leaving for Guildford
themselves.

'How soon?'

'As soon as I can arrange it.'

'Good. We need to get the horses saddled
and ready.'

'With necessary provisions.'

'Yes. But we shall go back by horse, so I can
warn the others en route,' Warin de Talmont
muttered. 'And I presume you will get there in
the way you came.'

Nicholas nodded. 'Yes, and then that last leg
on horseback. But we need to have most of it
decoded before we part ways, Warin.'

'I know. Consider it done.'

'When?'

'By tomorrow morn.'

'Good, because we cannot afford any mis-
haps.'

They both stood when Eva Siward drew attention to herself by tapping her hand on the
table a couple of times. 'Would either of you
care to explain what you are planning and de-
vising?'

'Certainly,' Nicholas said. 'We are leaving and at first sunlight tomorrow morn.'

'That soon?' She raised a brow.

'I shall explain properly on the way. But for now there is much to prepare.'

He moved to catch up with de Talmont, who nodded at Eva before leaving through the door. He could hardly wait to do the same.

'One moment, Sir Nicholas. I would like to ask a further question, if I may. I assume that it is to Guildford Castle you wish to rush to.'

'Yes.'

'And you shall be needing my assistance once more?'

It would have been for the best if that were not true, since Nicholas would be able to distance himself from Eva Siward and this inappropriate attraction for her. But, alas, he could not. He still needed her…to assist in their work.

'Yes,' he said again. 'I would.'

'Just as I thought. After all, I am the only person who could possibly recognise the man who hired me to steal from you in the first place, am I not?'

'Very perceptive, Eva.'

'I like to think so. And I do want to help you, quite aside from the fifty marks of silver.'

'That is good of you,' he muttered wryly.

'Especially if the bastard and the organisation he works for—the one with the two entwined snakes you showed me—are responsible for Simon's murder.'

Indeed, the young maid was far more perceptive than he would ever have imagined. For her to make the connection between the man who had hired her and the emblem he had briefly shown her was quite simply brilliant.

'I can understand your need for vengeance and retribution but take care that it doesn't consume you, Eva. It can be cold comfort.'

'No, it will give me great comfort to know that I have somehow helped punish them—if they are indeed responsible for his death. That and the fifty marks of silver will be enough. It will be enough to begin anew. Which brings me to what I propose, Sir Nicholas.'

He raised a brow. 'I should have known you would somehow use this to negotiate better terms.'

'Only fairer ones.' She smiled. 'I would like Sir Savaric to escort Marguerite to Guildford Castle as well. And after all matters are concluded we shall part ways, after all terms are met.'

'You seem to have forgotten our original bargain, mistress. That if we were to pay you the exorbitant sum that you demanded, you would continue to assist us in any manner we saw fit until we no longer needed your services.'

'I believe that these new findings, and the fact we have to travail to Guildford, have changed that original bargain, do you not think?'

'And how can I be certain that, once you are reunited with your friend, you will not just abscond, that all of this is not some elaborate ruse to flee the moment you can?'

'Believe me, Sir Nicholas, I do intend to gain the silver owed to me but, more importantly than that, I need to find out the truth regarding Simon's murder.'

It was somewhat heartening that the murder of the man Eva Siward had considered a father-figure was at the forefront of all her endeavours. It once again spoke of the deep sense of loyalty she had had for the man.

Nicholas nodded, understanding her. 'So you would give us this assistance we seek willingly then?'

'If the terms are met, then yes, you have my word.'

'The word of a thief?' he said, raising a brow.

'Which are as good as a knight's!' she retorted. 'Mine are, in any case.'

He didn't say anything, allowing the moment to stretch before a slow smile spread on his lips.

'Yes, I believe you, Eva Siward,' he drawled, nodding in approval. 'Very well, you have your bargain. I shall send a missive to Fitz Leonard to bring Mistress Marguerite to Guildford as well.'

She exhaled, the tension visibly falling away from her shoulders. 'I thank you. You shall not regret this.'

'There is one other thing that you must consider, Eva. You would have to dissemble once again, and not as before.'

She frowned, rubbing her brow. 'I believe I understand your meaning.'

'Precisely. You cannot use your previous disguise—as a boy—even though you do it remarkably well. Especially if the man who hired you is also present at Guildford Castle and might somehow recognise you, just as you would recognise him, even if you had been wearing your mask in your first meeting. It would be too much of a risk.'

'True.' She lifted her head. 'It would have to be entirely different.' Her brows furrowed in the middle, as they always seemed to when the maid was deep in thought. 'What about a woman of noble birth?'

'You?' Nicholas's brows shot up. 'A woman of noble birth?'

'And why not, sir?' She tilted her head imperiously, making her point. 'It would be the obvious solution since I can observe and survey without being encumbered. And it is entirely opposite to how I initially appeared before.'

He scratched his jaw, bemused at her suggestion. 'I am sure you can, with a few changes and adjustments here and there, certainly look the part. But for you to perform as a courtier convincingly, it would take more time than we currently have.'

'Ah, you don't believe I can do it?'

No...

'I did not say that. You have obviously perfected those mannerisms that are singularly associated with the...er...male sex,' he said tactfully, refraining from adding that Eva Siward walked, drank and ate just as she always did even when she was attired as a maid, which was exactly the reason why it would not work here. 'However, none of that could be used when acting the part of a noblewoman.'

'Do you believe that I would be unable to pull off such a ruse? For I can tell you, sir, that nothing piques my interest more than a challenge such as this.'

'I can well believe it.' He raised a brow. 'You have challenged me in more ways than one, ever since I first met you.'

'Is that why you stole a kiss by the river earlier?'

The moment she uttered those words, Eva wished she could take them back. Nicholas D'Amberly stared at her, evidently shocked by what she had said, before dropping his gaze to her lips.

Oh, dear. Had her head become so addled after their intimate kiss by the stream that she had lost all of her senses? Evidently so.

It had begun innocently enough, but soon descended into heat, need and so much want that she hardly knew what would have happened had Sir Warin not encountered them.

One moment Nicholas D'Amberly was divulging private and obviously painful matters regarding his own father and his lack of familial duty, the next she had raised her head in anticipation as he touched his lips to hers. It had been shocking how much she had lost herself. And how much she had wanted his kisses. Yet, in a strange way, she understood the need to push away his awkward revelation of bitter heartache and disappointment in the people who were supposed to care, to protect, and who had utterly failed.

And, more than that, Nicholas D'Amberly had posed a question in that kiss, one that she'd answered fervently, because she knew it all too well. Eva knew that the kiss was the perfect foil to forget that pain, and to leave those difficult memories behind. But then everything had changed, becoming far more heated and charged than either of them had anticipated. And that was what shocked her the most—that she had kissed Nicholas D'Amberly back with as much ardour as he had... And the awful truth was that she wanted more—more of his kisses, his touches. But it could never happen again. She could not lose sight of why she was even there. No matter how much she had enjoyed his attentions, and this impossible desire humming between them.

It was not something that a woman in her position could readily afford.

'No,' she murmured. 'Please do not answer that.'

He dropped his arms to his sides. 'As you wish, Eva, but allow me to say that the way in which you challenge me has more to do with how you provoke me to think differently about everything around me. Even what I hold to be true.'

She inhaled softly through her teeth. 'I don't quite comprehend.'

'We are taught that only men, especially those of high birth and in possession of valour, courage and fortitude, who are knighted by their lord, can possibly deign to have honour and loyalty to do what is right. Your desire for justice for Simon the Rook and the need to care and look out for others and even make a better life for yourself dispels that notion.'

Eva was speechless, a lump forming in her throat, as she took a step towards him. 'No one has ever said such words to me.'

'Mayhap no one sees you in the way I do.' His eyes held her gaze and for a moment they stared at one another, unable to move, unable to breathe.

He dropped his eyes, breaking the charged moment, and cleared his throat. 'And for this reason I will say that if you are confident that you can pull it off—if you believe you can do it—disguise yourself as a woman of nobility, then I will help you, just as you have agreed to help me.'

'Thank you. Indeed, I would need all your help and good advice to be able to do it.'

'Good, we can practice on the way to Guild-ford, so that in time you will be comfortable to play your part at court with the monarch in attendance.'

'I would not actually come to be in the same chamber as the King of England?' She frowned. 'Would I?'

Nicholas began to pack some of his belongings into his large saddlebag.

'Of course you would. Even as a pretend courtier you would be presented to King Henry.' He smiled. 'Come now, this was your idea in the first instance. And with the necessary guidance, tutorage and instruction, I am convinced you shall pass for a woman of noble birth.'

'But the King…'

'Will believe you to be whom we tell him. Have faith in your own ability, Eva. You have the voice and the manner in which you carry yourself. All you need now is to add polish, poise and to whittle away any of the mannerisms you usually employ, dissembled as a boy. And, with the correct attire, I am certain that no one will ever be any the wiser. So, do you think you are ready for such a challenge?'

'Yes,' she muttered unconvincingly, as doubt crept under her skin for the first time. Yet, in truth, it was too late to renege on the scheme that had, after all, been her idea, as Nicholas reminded her. God, but she hoped that she had the necessary skills to pull this scheme off.

'And remember that if you can make me and even the man who hired you believe that you were a young *male* thief—an apprentice to Simon the Rook, no less—then you can pass for such a woman. All you need is a little polish to walk, talk and move as such. The essentials you already possess in abundance.'

She could feel her cheeks getting warm but chose to ignore it.

'Yes,' she said again, but this time with more conviction. 'It might just work.'

'I am certain that it will. You will need to be amongst the throng of the assembled courtiers in the hall, Eva. And you will need to be my eyes and ears so that we can uncover whether that man who hired you to steal from me is even present at court and involved with treacherous activity.'

Once again the implication was there, that Nicholas D'Amberly was far more than just a Crown Knight. Not that he disclosed much more. But it mattered not. Eva would find out little by little who Nicholas D'Amberly was beneath the veneer and polish of his knightly armour. In the meantime, however, she would keep her end of the bargain.

'Very well, we have an agreement, Sir Nicholas.' She stuck out her hand.

He gazed at her hand, then back at her, and smiled, taking the proffered hand. 'Let us begin the lessons now.' He turned her hand around so that he was now clasping it gently in his and bowed, kissing the back of it, his eyes never leaving hers. 'My lady.'

That touch, those lips, the wicked gleam in his eyes. Oh, Lord, this was going to be far more difficult than Eva had anticipated.

Chapter Ten

The following morning their small group broke their fast together, organised their movements and stratagems before finally parting ways. Warin and Joan de Talmont took to the road, making their way west towards Guildford Castle by horse. They were to meet Joan's brother and gain his counsel, and then inform Savaric Fitz Leonard of their plans, before they would all gather together at Guildford Castle as expediently as possible.

Eva wondered whether Joan would comply with her husband's wishes and stay at her brother's manor house after having witnessed their heated discussion in surprised bemusement before they had departed. It had left her with no doubt that the couple cared deeply and passionately about one another and it gave her a twinge of wistfulness that she quickly dismissed.

And with all of these newly made plans underway, it meant that Eva would soon be reunited with Marguerite at Guildford Castle. And soon, very soon, God willing, they would be able to part ways and Eva and Marguerite could start a new life with a huge purse of silver. She just had to give a convincing performance as a lady—a lady of noble blood—and all would go as planned. That and being the requisite eyes and ears in the hope that she could recognise the man who had hired her to steal the missive from Nicholas D'Amberly.

Firstly, however, Eva needed to accompany the man to Guildford…alone. She had realised from the first that she really ought not spend too much time alone with Sir Nicholas. It posed a challenge with these strange inexplicable emotions that the man evoked in her, yet having to pretend indifference whenever he was close by.

And the choice in the manner of their travail to Guildford had surprised her—by skiff along the river until they once again reached London, then to change vessels and continue again along the river. Not that she comprehended the reason for this chosen mode of conveyance. But it had all been decided so swiftly that it was not long before Eva found herself onboard a skiff once more, returning back to the city.

Being aboard the vessel brought back many unpleasant memories of the turmoil she had felt only a few nights ago when she'd almost lost her life. Yet Nicholas must have understood these feelings of apprehension and had been careful and considerate enough to make the journey on the skiff as untroubled and pleasant as he could, which Eva was exceedingly grateful for. There were plenty of warm woollen blankets aboard for warmth and enough food and ale for the duration. Indeed she began to feel far more at ease as they moved up the river, the water dappled with sunlight through the bordering canopy of trees and bushes.

'You are very quiet today, Eva.' Nicholas raised a brow as he looked over at her as he helped navigate the vessel with his squire.

'I have been taking this time to contemplate my situation.'

'I see. Then I hope that your reflections are not as troublesome as they seem.'

She turned around in her seat. 'How could you possibly deduce that?'

A faint smile curled his lips. 'Your brows here, meet and crease every time you are deeply considering and pondering on something. Just as you are doing now.'

'I am glad to be so easy to read, if every feeling is etched on my face.'

He moved around the skiff as he took an oar and began to row. 'No, not so easy to read, mistress. You are actually good at masking your feelings, as I would assume you would need to, having lived on the streets as a thief for so long. But then, I am also known to be able to gauge those very feelings that people strive to hide.'

'I see.' Eva wondered once more about the mysterious work that Nicholas D'Amberly and the others were involved with. 'My thoughts and contemplations have obviously revealed my concerns, then.'

'They have. But I wonder whether I can ease your concerns, if you would care to share them with me.'

She sighed. 'Well, for one thing, we are travailing back to London, where I really have no wish to be, for reasons I am sure you can guess. I have no attire that could pass as belonging to a noblewoman and, since we have rushed off this morn to Guildford, I wonder when I am to be instructed as I should on how to behave and act as such.'

'Let me assure you and rest your mind at ease, Eva. To answer your questions. We shall not be in London long—a mere hour or two to gain supplies and change the mode of conveyance, so there is no need for you to worry on that front. Your attire shall be provided for the moment we get to Guildford and, finally, the lessons to turn you into a courtier—we shall fit and incorporate such instruction every time we stop. I very much doubt that it will take long to turn you into a graceful, refined lady.'

Eva snorted and shook her head. 'I may have been a little hasty with my belief that I would be able to impersonate such a lady, but thank you for your assurances all the same.'

'You do have all the necessary prerequisites to be a noblewoman. But you need to be diligent and have a certain belief in your abilities to perform. Starting now.'

'Now?' Eva blinked. 'What will you have me do?'

'I think we should start with your posture.'

Her brows furrowed in the middle. 'What is wrong with my posture?'

'Well, for one, you slouch, Eva.'

'I slouch no more than you do, Nicholas.'

'Yes, but I am a man and thus it is not believed to be as unseemly as it is for a lady.'

'Unseemly? For a noblewoman to slouch?'

'Apparently so.'

'That is preposterous.'

'I care not whether you slouch, snort or belch, Eva, nor do I make these courtly rules. I merely impart my wisdom on such matters' He smiled at her. 'And, by the by, I am glad that you are finally calling me by my given name.'

'Although I suppose now that I am to be a proper lady mayhap I should only call you *Sir Nicholas.*'

'I think Nicholas will do well enough.' He chuckled sofly. 'Now, roll your shoulders back. Like so, and straighten your spine. That's it. Chin up…there you are…and give me an imperious look.'

'Like this?'

'Come now, I know that you can do better than that. And I also know for certain you have such a "look" at your disposal. In truth, the time I followed you to your chambers at the inn, I recall your anger was mixed with a haughtiness that gave me pause for a moment or two.'

'I had no notion I possessed such a fierce look.' She tilted her head up even more and narrowed her eyes. 'Does this remind you of it?'

'Just so. You are a natural, Eva.'

'I am glad I pass muster.' She continued to look down at him with haughty disdain, perfecting the look. 'Tell me, Nicholas, as I am most intrigued—is this a look that is usually bestowed on you by all the ladies at court?'

'Indeed.' He laughed softly, making him look a lot younger than usual. 'How did you know such a thing?'

She gave him an impish smile in return. 'It was an assumption, since the look seems so familiar to you that I concluded it could not have been given solely by myself that time in my chamber.'

'I admit that it is very familiar—as are many others that the ladies at court bestow on me. I seem to bring about a wide range of responses to my person.'

'I wonder why.' She tapped her chin, enjoying the spark of mirth and levity that had risen between them.

'I have no notion to the reason why. And yet I have been told on occasion that I am the most vexatious of fellows.' He winked at her, reminding her of the times she had stated just that to him. 'However, if it helps you when regarding the men at court with that imperious look and tilt of the head, then by all means use me as your inspiration.'

A bark of laughter escaped from her as she could no longer hold it inside, making him grin. 'Oh, Lord, the things you say.'

'I am glad to be providing such amusement for you. Always at your service, my lady.' He clutched the oar and gave her an exaggerated bow. 'But mayhap you should attempt to avoid such a boisterous laugh when we are at court.'

Another bark of laughter escaped from Eva. 'I suppose it would be deemed unladylike,' she muttered as she wiped away a tear.

'Indeed, and I should remind you that it might be best to heed my advice.' He gave her a mock look of outrage. 'After all, it was you, mistress, who, only a few moments ago, sought my advice and demanded the necessary instructions to pass for a noblewoman. And yet you have resorted to roaring with laughter at my very first suggestion.'

'Yes, you are right, sir.' She held out her hands and pressed her lips together in an attempt to hold more laughter back. 'Please accept my apology for my lack of ladylike behaviour, especially my bellow of laughter.'

'I accept your apology, Eva.' He shook his head and he grinned at her. 'And would advise that when you are at court you check your… er…exuberance.'

Eva covered her mouth as she chuckled. 'Well, I must say that I did not know there was a limit on one's exuberance.'

'Ah, but there is a limit on many things at court. Especially raucous women bellowing and spluttering as much as the men.'

'I shall keep that in mind,' she giggled. 'I truly had no idea that there was an accepted mode of…laughter.'

He raised a brow. 'I think, in hindsight, I might have been a bit premature in my estimation of your abilities.'

She descended into another peal of noisy laughter. Oh, God, what was wrong with her? 'Indeed, we might need more lessons than you had originally thought, do you not think?'

'Mayhap we should.' He grinned, shaking his head. 'Or mayhap my student can be more diligent and take her lessons more earnestly.'

'I would if mayhap my tutor would refrain from being so entertaining.'

'Alas, he cannot help being so.' He winked at her again, his blue eyes twinkling with bemusement. 'Some might say that he was born an amusing, charming and dashing knight.'

'Ah, so you were always destined to be thus?'

'Just so.'

'And were you always destined to be a knight as well? A Crown Knight, that is?' Eva noticed the humour fading from his eyes, replaced by a little wistfulness.

Nicholas did not answer her at first, but after a long moment he glanced briefly at her before speaking. 'I suppose so, but in truth the journey to where I am now was not the usual one, Eva. I was not destined to become the man I am today and only certain circumstances determined it.'

All laughter faded as she turned her head to the side and gazed at the passing scenery, taking none of it in. God, but it was the truth for her as well. She had never been destined for a life on the streets—to become a thief. That was not supposed to have been her life. And yet it had been. The circumstances of her life to that point had all been unexpected, forcing her to survive by sheer will and determination. And, in a different manner, so it had been for Nicholas D'Amberly as well. She dropped her eyes before raising them to meet his.

'You refer to what happened with your father?'

'Yes.' His demeanour became far more rigid. 'But I must say that I am gratified that destiny had this—being a... Crown Knight intended for me. It has made me into the man I am today and I can only be grateful for that. Even if it did come about by such pitiful means.'

'In many ways I too can only be glad for how my life made me into the person I am today—

not that it was ever destined to be thus. I may not know any differently, but I can say unequivocally that my father would never have wanted this life for me.' She shrugged. 'Yet without it I would never have met Simon or Marguerite.' *Or you*, she had almost said. Eva swallowed and looked away, feeling a little discomposed. 'But, apart from the obvious difficulties and hardships on the streets, being under the protection of Simon meant that I never went hungry and was always cared for. In truth, it was the first time I felt safe since my family's death.' And since she had run away from her uncle's home.

'For myself I know that although I am content with how my life brought me to where I am now, I cannot say that it was without the undue hardship and difficulty.'

'Yes, that is true for me also,' Eva muttered, noting that the mouth of the Thames widened as they approached London. She closed her eyes for a moment, wondering how their amusement and laughter could quickly change to these pensive reflections. These shifting moods seemed to echo the mercurial weather and the gathering grey clouds in the sky. Her eyes opened as she felt the first drops of rain on her face. 'Sometimes I cannot even remember my family's faces—my father, my mother, and all of my siblings. I wonder at times if they ever existed, since I have nothing left of them.'

'Ah, but you do, Eva. You always carry their memory with you,' he murmured.

'*Vouloir, c'est pouvoir.* I do recall my mother saying that.'

'Yes. And you have willed yourself to survive, carrying your mother's language with you at all times. Why, your quick intelligence, your strength, fortitude and even the way you speak can be attributed to their legacy. Indeed, you carry both what your family instilled in you and also the very streets that shaped you. In some way, mayhap this was the woman you were always destined to be.'

'A thief?'

'No.' He shook his head. 'Someone who has endured much and withstood life's challenges, despite it all. *Vouloir c'est pouvoir en vérité.*'

For a moment she could not speak, for being so close to tears.

'Thank you.' Her breath caught at the back of her throat. 'That is one of the loveliest things anyone has ever said to me.'

'My pleasure, however it is true nevertheless.' He had stopped rowing and fixed his blue gaze on her, making Eva flush. She returned his smile and was thinking of a similar response when his squire's voice interrupted her musings.

'We're almost there, Sir Nicholas.' He pointed in the distance, breaking the charged moment between them. 'I can see London yonder.'

'Good, thank you, John.' He turned his attention back on manoeuvring the vessel. 'Let us quicken the pace, so that we might get there before noon.'

It was only a short time later that they were among many vessels of various sizes and shapes moving busily along the busy tideway on the Thames. They steadily made their way back to the embankment near London Bridge as Nicholas reflected on the unnecessarily overdone sentiment that he had uttered earlier. What a fool he had been, knowing that he ought to maintain some sort of distance with Eva, but every time he reminded himself of this he was somehow drawn back to her. He could not fathom it, nor comprehend how this woman had this strange hold on him. Still, he could not regret being the reason for her dazzling smile that had almost knocked the breath out of him, after he had delighted her with what he had said. It made him want to take her in his arms and keep her there for as long as he could. Thank God he had refrained from doing so.

They reached the quay on the south side of the bridge and hauled the skiff using the tow rope, with Nicholas yelling instructions to the quayside workers. And with the help of John, his squire, they secured the vessel before he assisted Eva to get out.

'Thank you.' She nodded. 'I have to say that, after this rather pleasant journey, I am no longer as apprehensive about travelling on the river as I was this morn.'

'Glad to hear it.' He let go of her hands once her feet were firmly on solid ground and dropped his own to his sides. 'Although I hope you know that I would not have allowed any harm to come to you.'

'Yes, I thank you. However, I wonder why we did not embark and disembark in the same manner on the outward journey. It might have saved a lot of the unpleasantness that followed.'

'You may wonder that and I am sorry about what happened, Eva, truly. But I could not risk you meeting with any possible associates or being recognised by any unknown men. Of course, at that time I was not aware that there were no such associates involved with the theft of the missive, bar the man who hired you. And I also did not know at the time of the theft that you had been disguised once again as a boy when you met him, so it was doubtful you would be recognised by him or anyone else now, dressed as you are.'

She sighed. 'And though I am dressed as a maid today, and would only be recognised by those who know me, I cannot, in good faith, pretend that I am glad that we will not tarry long in London.'

'No, we shan't and certainly not within the heart of the city.' He led the way to the gatehouse of the bridge. 'But first we shall stop for some repast. The Three Choughs awaits us, and this time we shall indulge in some of their hearty fare, which is surprisingly good for an inn.'

'I can hardly wait to sample this heartiness and hope it is much better than their ale, which I found rather lacking.'

He raised a brow and threw her a brief sideways glance. 'Did you, now? How interesting that you have such exacting tastes when it comes to the quality of ale. But then I suppose you did reside at an inn.'

'Precisely.' Her mouth quirked at the corners. 'Although there is a little more to it. You see, I actually rather enjoyed brewing the ale myself, changing and tweaking the recipe to a very distinctive flavour. Adding certain spices and secret ingredients that made it quite a popular brew.'

'You are making my mouth water, mistress,' he drawled, noting that her colour had risen again. 'I can hardly wait to sample it.'

'Mayhap one day you shall, Nicholas. My plan with the coin that I hope to gain is that I would be afforded the opportunity to open an inn for myself. A new life. Under a new guise.'

'Oh, and what would that be?'

'That of a widow.'

'Ah, a wealthy widow then. One who could take over the running of an inn.'

Her eyes glazed over as she looked out in the distance. 'I believe it could afford Marguerite and me a measure of peace, stability and contentment that has been lacking in both of our lives.'

'It is a good plan, Eva, and I wish you well in your endeavours.' His smile felt strained as he acknowledged with a pang that her plans did not include him, just as his could never include her. No, not when his life was consumed by the secret work he did for the Crown. Indeed, his association with Eva Siward would be fleeting. And before long they would go their separate ways.

They made their way inside The Three Choughs. 'For now we shall, unfortunately, have to make do with the inferior ale. Although I should add that my tastes have never been as exacting as yours,' he muttered in a low voice.

'Ah, but you have never sampled mine.'

He almost stumbled and lost his footing. Lord above, but had the woman even realised what she had just said?

'No.' He threw her a knowing look, making her blush deepen. 'I have not.'

He needed to cease teasing and flirting with Eva Siward and remember that this was a mission—an assignment—just like any other. He directed her towards the back of the inn, ambling past the rowdy revellers, merchants and pilgrims that made up the usual assortment of customers to a quiet secluded table. After helping Eva to her seat, he then went to order the food and a jug of the aforementioned ale, which came to their table soon enough, along with the food. God, it smelled delicious. Either that or he was hungry. He scooped a serving of the chicken cooked in mulberry pickle onto Eva's plate and a portion on his own before passing her a knife and spoon, and bread rolls with a small round of cheese. They tucked into their meal heartily.

It seemed that Nicholas was not the only one to have built up an appetite as he watched Eva devour her food. She took big bites of the chicken, licking her lips and interchanging this with glugs of ale.

Finally he cleared his throat, making Eva glance up and gaze at him in expectation. Well, now, he almost forgot what he was about to say. Ah, yes…advice…about something or other.

'Are you well, Sir Nicholas?'

No.

'Yes, of course.'

'Then is there something that you want or mayhap need?'

Yes.

'No.' He dragged his fingers through his hair. 'However, you put to mind that we should possibly resume our lessons.'

'Now?'

'I mentioned earlier that we should possibly use every opportunity to smooth out anything that we need to.'

'Yes.' She nodded, wagging a chicken leg back and forth as she continued to eat. 'I suppose we should.'

Nicholas gently removed the chicken from

her fingers and placed it back on the shared trencher. 'Let us begin with the proper way a lady should eat at court.'

'Ah, so this is yet another thing I must consider?'

'Indeed. I could not help but notice here, as well as back in the cottage, that your…er… hearty enjoyment of a meal is not in the manner of the ladies at court.'

Eva chewed her food, swallowed and then took a big gulp of ale before speaking. 'So now you do not approve of the way I eat?'

'I care not, Eva, as I said earlier. But mayhap I would advise a little refinement when attending a banquet at court when we're at Guildford.'

'So I take it that this…' she licked the sauce off every finger '…would not be acceptable?'

He lifted a brow and pressed his lips together, trying not to give into a bubble of laughter. 'No.'

'Where I come from, you need to grab the choice pieces of food and stuff it down as quickly as you can, lest someone steals it away from you.'

'Ah, but at court there is no need to *stuff* anything down, since there are plenty of choice pieces to go around, although the best is always served to the King's table first.' He picked up another piece of chicken and took small bites, chewing carefully. 'So there is no need to consume your meal with such exuberant haste. No one will make off with it there.'

Eva picked up the chicken leg that she had been eating but this time took small bites, copying Nicholas and bringing the food to her mouth, rather than slouching over her plate.

'Is this better?'

'Infinitely so.' He chuckled. 'And when drinking, remember to take delicate sips—ladies at court never wipe their mouths on the back of their hand either.'

'Ladies at court sound rather dull.'

'You would be surprised. And never forget your posture, Eva. Spine straight and shoulders back. That is it.'

'There is far too much to remember.'

'The main things being not to walk, talk or stand like a lad.'

'Or eat or drink like one either.'

'Just so.'

Eva took a small sip of ale and licked her lips and studied him. 'Tell me, how you are so knowledgeable about the way in which ladies at court should act?'

He gave her a slow smile. 'Are you certain that you want to know?'

'Ah, well, I forgot about the ladies who, you

once told me, desire your company so much that they seek a dalliance after taking many liberties with your person.'

He grimaced at being reminded of his flippant remark but gave no answer.

Her eyes widened. 'Please do not say that it is those women who inspire these lessons?'

He chuckled, shaking his head. 'God, no.'

'Then who?'

Nicholas did not need to think on the woman who had meant the most to him, above any other soul. There had only been one woman in his life who had ever shown him love, understanding, consideration and kindness. And he missed her still.

'My mother.' He smiled, thinking of her. 'She was the most kind-hearted, gentle, graceful woman you could ever have the pleasure to meet. And I've lamented her loss every single day since her passing.'

'I am so sorry.' Eva placed her hand on his, hardly covering it. 'It is never easy losing those we love.'

'No.' He sighed deeply, wondering why he had disclosed his feelings about his mother, who had been dead for over ten long summers. But it seemed he could not help himself. Mayhap it was because he connected with Eva, who knew what it was to lose those who had loved and cared for her. Or mayhap it was because he knew that Eva would soon be gone, after all this was settled. Yet he could not deny that it felt good to unburden himself to her. 'But, unlike you, Eva, I did have one lasting item left from my mother.'

Eva looked at him earnestly. 'What was it?'

'Her ring, which was so valuable to me that for sentimental reasons I always kept it with me. Until…its loss recently, that is.'

Chapter Eleven

Eva's eyes widened and her cheeks flushed with colour as she suddenly recalled the exquisite ring intricately made from hessonite entwined with droplets of freshwater pearl and wondered excitedly whether it could possibly be a coincidence. 'May I ask whether you possibly left this ring in the pouch that I stole?'

'Yes.' *Oh, God, it was not a coincidence.* 'Why?'

She dropped her spoon on her plate, making a loud clanging noise. 'I must show you something, Nicholas. I must show you now, at this very moment.'

He blinked at her in confusion. 'Can I enquire the reason for this urgency, especially since we do not have the time? And, judging from the inclement weather, it could also pose a problem for our travel.'

She stood and caught her lip with her teeth, trying to contain her excitement 'Never mind that. Come, I insist. Please.' She held out her hand. 'There is something I need to show you.'

He sighed as he stood and nodded in resignation. 'What is it?'

'A surprise.' She grabbed his hand and pulled her hood over her head. 'Come along, Nicholas.'

'Very well, but remember we cannot tarry long.'

They made their way back outside and strode to the southern exit of the bridge, passing the throngs of people making the crossing and out through the gatehouse before they wove their way through the narrow twists and turns of Southwark.

'Ah, I remember the last time you and I were here together, playing cat and mouse in the dead of night.'

'It was a game you seemed to revel in.'

He shrugged. 'Only because I am prodigiously good at it.'

'Yes, you told me how your skills lie in finding people and things with precision.' They turned into a narrow dirt track, and back along the deserted alleyway and through the wooden porch to her hideaway. 'I also recall being surprised to find you hiding in the shadows of my chamber, so I suppose I can attest to that.'

'It must be a gift,' he retorted wryly.

'As mine is to remember and memorize small details. But there is one thing I did forget, Nicholas, and I can only put it down to the strain and shock of falling into the Thames.'

Nicholas followed her down the alleyway, reaching the dead end, and raised a brow in surprise as she carefully removed the large stone from the wall and stuck her arm in as far as it would go, dragging out the leather saddlebag. 'You missed this place when you followed me that night after I stole the pouch,' she murmured. 'My secret hiding place.'

'Ah, then I am not so prodigiously good.'

'I would not say that. No one has ever known of this place.'

'What was it you wanted to show me?'

Eva placed her hand inside the bag and brought out his mother's ring and held it out to him. 'This here, Nicholas—my gift to you.'

He stared at the ring before lifting his head and giving her a half smile that made her stomach flip over itself. 'I thought I had lost it when the pouch was lost in the river.' He tilted his head to the side. 'I do not understand. Why did you leave this here, in your secret place?'

'I had no notion what would happen once I had met you at The Three Choughs that night. Once I discovered the ring's existence, I thought it might be of use, should I need more to bargain with you.'

'My God, Eva.' The corners of his mouth twitched and curled upwards. 'You never cease to astonish me.'

'I had all but forgotten it until you mentioned your mother's ring at the inn.'

'And why are you giving it to me now?'

'Because it belongs to you. Here, take it. It's yours.'

His hand wrapped around hers holding the ring, closed over it and gently pulled her towards him. 'This means more to me than you can imagine.'

Her heartbeat pounded in her chest as she took a shaky breath and lifted her head up to find that she was now standing so close to Nicholas that she could see every shade of blue in the depths of his eyes. From borage, slate and cornflower, his eyes bored into hers with such intensity, and so full of something that she could hardly fathom. His knuckle grazed softly down her cheek, making her shudder, as his hand moved around the back of her neck, pulling her closer still.

'A thousand times thank you, Eva.'

Eva lifted her head as Nicholas bent his and touched his lips to hers. He began to pull away when Eva stood on her toes and pressed her lips more firmly, grabbing him by his cloak and holding him to her. That was when everything changed. When a chaste kiss became wanton and heady.

A flame licked through her body as the rain began to pour, making her cold and wet. Not that Eva cared. She touched the seam of his lips with her tongue and felt his surprise before he growled into her mouth, kissing her with more fervour, his hunger matching hers. She parted her lips, allowing his tongue to lick into her mouth, exploring and sliding against hers. God, but she loved the taste of him. She wrapped her arms around his neck and pulled him even closer, her breasts pressed against the hardness of his chest. Her fingers tangled in his thick dark hair before sliding down his spine as their kiss became carnal, and desperate. His hands skimmed down her body and rested on her hips as he deepened the kiss.

The rain came down hard and fast but neither of them seemed to care. All that mattered was this. Being with him in this moment. Nicholas pulled away, slowly kissing her cheek, her jaw-line and moving around to her neck.

'Eva… We should stop.'

She tilted her head to give him better access to her neck as he used his fingers, his lips and tongue to explore her.

'Why?' she whispered as the rain began to soak through her clothing. 'It is nothing more than a little rain.'

She felt him smile against her neck before he took her mouth again, pressing one last hard kiss before pulling away. 'It is more than just a little, sweetheart. We need to get out of this del-uge. We could go back to The Three Choughs and wait there as the storm passes…'

Half dazed and giddy, she allowed Nicholas to lead her back before she suddenly stopped. 'Wait,' she murmured, her heart pounding, 'you implied there was an alternative.'

'It is nothing. Just forget I said anything.'

'Nevertheless, I would like to know.'

He muttered an oath under his breath before lifting his head. 'Do you propose we stand here and quarrel while getting soaked, or make our way back to the tavern?'

'No, I propose you tell me.' Her skin was get-ting cold, her clothing already wet and clinging tightly to her body. 'Nicholas?'

'I was going to suggest my lodgings, Eva. It is actually on this side of the bridge and far closer than going back to The Three Choughs. However, I see that would make you uncomfortable, so come let us get back to the tavern.'

It was ridiculous to be reticent about being in a chamber with Nicholas D'Amberly after spending the last few nights at the wooden cottage alone with him. Yet a thrill chased up her skin in anticipation. Anticipation of what? She really could not tell. Mayhap it was because they had only just shared such a passionate, intimate kiss and she could still feel the thrum of desire coursing through her. She damped this down and pulled her mind to the present and the question Nicholas had posed.

'No.' She shook her head, making little droplets fall from the ends of her hair. 'It is best, as you say, to go to your lodging, especially if it's nearby.'

'It is, but are you…are you certain?' He frowned.

'I am, very certain.'

He nodded before taking her hand and leading her back through the myriad of pathways and alleys that led to Foul Lane and around The Palace of the Bishop of Winchester before walking into a courtyard on the corner of the aptly named Maiden Lane. They ran the final part as they approached an archway and quickly climbed a stairway that led to Nicholas D'Amberly's lodgings. Eva absently wondered at the reason why the man would choose to reside so far away from the city and remembered that the Bishop of Winchester's name had been mentioned before in relation to Hubert de Burgh. Interesting. Could that be the reason?

They walked through the wooden door and into a dark chamber.

'Here, sit on the stool. I shall get a fire going anon. And we shall have to get out of these wet clothes.'

He strode into an ante-chamber and came back with a large linen cloth, which he wrapped around her shoulders before turning back towards the hearth that took up much space in the seemingly small chamber.

'My thanks,' she muttered, attempting to dry her hair with the cloth as Nicholas started a fire with kindling and then proceeded to light a few candles, adding light and warmth to the chamber.

'I have just come to the realisation that every time I venture to The Three Choughs with you, we somehow manage to get exceedingly wet.' He winked, making her stomach flutter.

'Ah, so now it seems that it is my fault that the heavens decided to open up and drench us to the skin.'

He smiled wryly and stalked towards her. 'It must be. Here, allow me.' His voice was a little hoarse as he took the cloth from her and helped dry her sopping-wet hair. 'You certainly seem to attract these…er…intense situations.'

'Of course it has nothing whatsoever to do with you.'

'No, never. Before you tumbled into my life, stealing and creating havoc, I led a very sedate life.'

Her lips twisted at the corners. 'Somehow I very much doubt that.'

'It is true.' He grinned. 'You have corrupted me.'

'I did no such thing. Indeed, I am a model of propriety and modest behaviour. Why, I am being instructed on posture and decorum, taking particular note of how I eat, drink and even the manner in which I laugh.'

'And how do you get on?'

She wrinkled her nose. 'I admit that I lapse now and again but as long as I continue to remember to do everything with a little less zeal, then my tutor might finally commend my progress. So, you see, it is quite futile to pretend that I might have somehow corrupted you.'

'My mistake. Tell me, are you a little warmer?'

She nodded. 'I am now, thank you.'

He rubbed the sides of her arms and stood. 'You will need to get out of those wet clothes, Eva. If we lay them out in front of the fire they'll dry soon enough. In the meantime, you can wear one of my tunics and hose. Here, you should feel snug, dry and quite at home in this clothing. It is a man's attire, after all.' He placed the garments on a wooden coffer before leaving the chamber so that they could both get out of their wet clothing and change in privacy.

'Yes.' She frowned. 'I thank you.'

Nicholas returned a few moments later, having donned a pair of grey hose and a dark blue tunic which brought out the glittering specks in his eyes. And really, must she continually notice such things about the man?

'Here, pass me your wet clothing and I shall put them to dry,' he said, taking her clothes and hanging them out near the hearth.

'Are you warm enough?' he asked again, the timbre of his voice penetrating her senses.

'Thank you, yes.' She pasted a smile on her face and nodded.

'I have very little here, but I do have some

ale, which I believe might be a little better than the swill they serve at The Three Choughs. Would you care for some?'

'That would be most welcome, thank you.' She took the proffered cup that he held out and gazed at it for a moment before taking a small ladylike sip in the way in which Nicholas D'Amberly had instructed, refraining from wiping her mouth on her hand. 'How was that?'

'Much better.' He smiled. 'You will do well enough, Eva. No one at court will be any the wiser.'

'Well, that is a relief.' She looked away, catching her lip between her teeth, and considered again the wisdom of this mad scheme and whether she would be able to convince courtiers that she was one of them.

Nicholas dragged his hand through his hair and sighed. 'Would you like to tell me what troubles you?'

'How on earth could you possibly tell that?'

He shrugged. 'I told you before, I am particularly good at finding and seeking anything and anyone. However, I do possess other skills. For one, I am also quite perceptive and a good listener, so will you not tell me what concerns you?'

'There is not much to tell, only that I... I find

that with these instructions I have been made aware how very lacking I am as…as a woman.'

'Come now, that is not true.'

'Ah, but it is.' She sighed, moving to the hearth with its roaring fire and held her hands out, warming them. 'You were not mistaken in the least in assuming that I am more at home in a man's attire.'

He ambled towards her. 'I was only teasing you, Eva.'

It was true that Eva felt far more comfortable and uninhibited when she was wearing clothing that was designed for the masculine sex. But recently she had wished that it was not so. It made her feel far more unfeminine and ungainly wearing clothes that were not cut for a woman's shape than having to contain peals of laughter or noisy slurping and slouching ever could.

'Nevertheless, you spoke the truth. Not that I believe that is what it means to be a woman. To be a docile noblewoman who seldom laughs, drinks or eats as she might want to.' She shrugged. 'That is not me, in any case. But it is something I wish to find out—to discover what it means to be *womanly*, which has far more to do with my life on the streets than dissembling as a lady at court, Nicholas.'

He bent down and pushed the wooden kindling in the fire with a metal prong.

'I see. And I presume that this *truth,* as you call it, has made you feel somehow lacking?'

She nodded. 'I have never known differently, as I was always made to act and behave like a lad—and I was even given a male name, Evrard. In truth, I was encouraged to hide who I was until very recently.'

He stood up and she found him beside her, staring at the fire. 'Yet you know that after all of this is over you will have the opportunity to live exactly how you wish, Eva, and be the person you were always destined to be.'

'Which I am eternally grateful for.'

'There is no need. I hope you realise that there is no need to hide who you are, Eva. Not any longer.' He caught her hand in his. 'You are a beautiful, unusual woman. And, trust me, you are more than womanly. In truth, it is not your attire or anything else, for that matter, that could determine that. Only you—and you are perfectly fine just as you are.'

She turned her head towards him and blinked in amazement. 'Truly?'

'Truly,' he murmured, squeezing her hand gently. 'You need not change to please anyone.'

She was taken aback by the man's frankness. 'Thank you. I am grateful for your esteem.'

Eva smiled, shaking her head. 'It is astounding how differently I now regard you, in comparison to that first encounter.'

'Then all I can say is thank you, and that I am also grateful for your esteem,' he murmured, repeating what she had said only moments ago.

It was strange how her feelings had altered entirely. Eva had considered the man a ruthless, dangerous, disreputable Crown Knight, but now he was someone who stirred her blood. And although she still believed that Nicholas D'Amberly was just as ruthless and dangerous when he needed to be, he was certainly not disreputable. No, never that. He was everything that was steadfast, resolute and honourable and he made her ache and feel far more than she should.

'So we both evidently esteem one another.'

'Evidently we do.' He turned around to face her, his fingers laced with hers, his chest rising and falling quickly. Nicholas seemed to be waging a battle with himself. One that she could only gauge by the rawness in his voice and the way his breath seemed to have caught.

'Good,' Eva whispered.

She lifted her head and met his eyes. Their

lips were almost touching, their breaths coming in short bursts.

There was only one thing for it. One thing that she could do, wanted desperately to do. One thing she needed...*oh, dear God*. And that was to be reckless.

She curled her arms around his neck and went up on her toes, meeting his lips, and rekindling the flare of desire between them. The kiss instantly became just as hungry and fevered as before, continuing from where they had left it, standing in the rain and storm. And it quickly became just as wild and intense as the elements outside.

Nicholas's head was spinning. The woman in his arms had inflamed his senses and there was little he could do about it. He knew somewhere deep inside that he should put a halt to all of this madness between them but he found that he was unable to. He craved more. Wanted more. Needed more. God help them both!

He swooped Eva up into his arms and carried her across the chamber, untangling the bed curtain ties and placing her down on the pallet. He hoped that this might propel the woman to reconsider matters between them. But it did not. His breathing was rasping, his chest rising and falling as his hand skimmed down her body, making her shudder. She dragged him down with her as the little moans and gasps that escaped from her lips made his blood rush through his veins. He wanted to taste her, touch her, devour her. She was ridiculously beautiful and alluring—this woman who believed herself to be somehow lacking.

He divested Eva of her—or, rather, *his*—clothing, revealing more silky skin, more dips and curves of her lush body, and replaced it with kisses, licks and nips, making her writhe and arch beneath him. In the stretch of silence he could somehow hear the crackle of the fire and the rumble of thunder outside, as the rain thrashed against the wooden shutters of the stone building. But nothing was as loud as his own heart beating madly in his chest.

He pulled away and stared at her as she trembled beneath him, knowing that he would always remember this. Always recall every small detail about this woman.

'We should stop, Eva,' he said, even as he moved over her, shifting his weight onto his elbows. He pressed his mouth to the throbbing pulse at her neck and sucked. 'We are edging towards dangerous ground here.'

'But what if…what if we both crave the dan-

ger?' she muttered as she reached out for him
and traced his mouth with her finger.

God's breath, but he needed to make her see
sense.

'What we are doing now would alter things,
when neither of us can afford such complica-
tions.'

'Yet I find that I simply cannot think on such
matters presently.'

Nicholas dropped his head and sighed through
his teeth, knowing that he must do the decent
thing here. He moved away from her and tried
to calm his violently beating heart. 'Then if you
cannot think about such matters, I really should,
sweetheart.'

Eva leant across, stroking his back, gently
pulling him back to her. 'You misunderstand,
Nicholas. There is no need for your consideration here. We agreed, did we not, that we
would suffer together—this want and need between us.'

'Are you certain?'

It was madness. Pure madness.

'Never more so,' she murmured as he
wrapped his arms around her and took her
mouth again in a deep kiss, long and languid.

He had to make her understand what was at

stake here. 'You realise it will change every-thing between us?' he muttered, panting.

Eva slid her arms around his neck and pulled him down to her, kissing him open-mouthed. 'No, I think not. It changes nothing. We are both seeking relief from the suffering of this want and need.' She pressed her mouth to his again. 'Nothing more and nothing less.'

'I do not agree. This is something that we must resist.'

'Can you? Can you resist this—what there is between us?'

'No.'

'Neither can I.' She cupped his jaw.

'What if I get you with child?' He dragged his fingers through his hair in frustration. 'What if this changes all of those plans you mentioned earlier?'

Nicholas wanted Eva. He wanted her more than she could possibly know. Yet he had to allow her the choice that might otherwise change the course of her future—as well as his.

'I know perfectly well what you are saying, Nicholas. but you forget that I am not an in-nocent maid but one who was shaped by the streets.' She brushed her lips along his jawline, making it difficult to think. Yet he had to. He had to make her understand. 'I also know perfectly well that there are ways in which you can prevent such a thing.'

'Yes,' he murmured. 'There are.'

'Which you are naturally proficient at.'

'Naturally.'

Nicholas stood beside the pallet, divesting himself of his tunic and hose, throwing them on the coffer before turning back to face her without a stitch of clothing on. He lay down beside Eva and looked across to find her shivering.

'You're cold. Come, let us get beneath this.' He pulled the coverlet and manoeuvred both of them underneath as he moved over her, and kissed her cheek. 'Better?'

'Yes.'

'Good.' He slanted his mouth over hers, kissing her again and again. He could do this. He could give her pleasure in a manner that would leave her with no doubt in her mind about his desire for her without actually giving in to it.

His hands skimmed over her body, touching and learning every sweeping rise, curve and dip of her. His mouth, tongue and teeth followed and teased where his finger left, licking, sucking, nipping and grazing the curve of her neck, the soft skin behind her ear, her chest, collarbone and underside of her breast, eliciting a desperate moan from Eva. God, but he loved the sounds that she made.

Her taste and her scent wrapped around him, making him fevered with desire. A palpable tension grew between them, shooting straight down to his groin.

It made his chest ache with need, watching her as he cupped her breast in his hand, licked around the rose-pink nipple, catching it between his teeth and taking it into his mouth. She arched beneath him, digging her fingernails into his back as he sucked and grazed her nipple before moving his attentions to her other breast. He moved further down, licking around her belly button, as her hands roamed around his back and shoulders, exploring him as he was exploring her.

Reason was slowly dissipating from his mind, replaced by need, want and hunger, yet Nicholas knew he would have to keep himself in check. He had to. His hand grazed the inside of her legs and moved to the apex of her femininity and gently unfolded her before he slid a finger inside, drawing out a surprised cry.

He paused and watched her beneath him in the throes of passion, her chest falling and rising, a sheen of moisture on her forehead and eyes closed tightly. Eva had never looked so wondrous, so glorious, so beautiful. It made his chest ache, thinking how vulnerable and unfettered she was in that moment. And to think she believed herself unwomanly, whatever the hell that was.

His finger brushed along her neck, skimming over her shoulders, making her eyes open suddenly. She smiled wordlessly, telling him so much. There were no words to describe this sensual carnal need. No words that could convey the depth of what he felt at that moment. Only mouth on mouth, hand on hand and skin against skin.

He pressed his mouth to hers in a long lingering open-mouthed kiss and moved over her, gently pulling her legs apart before he entered her in one long thrust, catching her gasp in his mouth as she arched her back, yielding her body to his.

Nicholas paused, allowing the moment to last, wanting to put to memory every small detail about her.

'Open your eyes,' he whispered. 'Look at me.'

Her eyes fluttered open and she smiled, reaching out for him as he held her gaze, wanting to watch every emotion swirling in her eyes. He bent down and kissed her, catching her bottom lip between his teeth before starting to move inside her, filling and stretching her, gradually quickening his speed.

His blood roared and blazed through every part of his body as she gripped his shoulders for dear life. Nothing, but nothing, had prepared him for this, yet he knew he could no longer hold off, even though he wanted it to last for eternity. It could not. He pulled away from her body just in time and used his hands and his mouth to pleasure her slowly and so completely instead, making her scream out his name.

God, but she was exquisite as she came apart in his arms, thrashing her head from side to side. This was unlike anything he had experienced with a woman. It was as though it had been his first time. And yet it was not just any woman who speared through him and had his head spinning in a daze—it was Eva Siward. A woman who had seemingly stolen far more than just a pouch from him. A woman who had somehow managed to get under his skin without even realising it. More potent than if he had been pierced through his damn heart. But he had never felt so alive, so vital, so whole.

Chapter Twelve

Eva felt as though she was about to shatter into a thousand tiny pieces. Every single part of her—her heart, her body, her soul. She had never experienced anything that made her feel this alive, this elated, this amazed. Indeed, she had lived her life in the squalor and dirt of London's streets and seen all kinds of evil, sin, vice and lasciviousness but this…with Nicholas D'Amberly was something else entirely—it had somehow felt true and good.

Yet she did not want to examine more, as the extent of this coil of emotion frightened her. It made her feel unsettled and this lingering feeling was something that she no longer wanted. Not when she was so close to getting what she had always wanted—a place where she felt safe, without constantly looking over her shoulder.

For most of her life she'd had a clear expectation and understanding of how matters in her life would unfold. She had learnt to become proficient at stealing everything from coin and valuables and had even taken on the identity of a stripling lad, apprentice to London's most notorious thief. And once again she would create another guise, one that would turn her from a thief to a lady. And from a lady she would change once more to a widow—a wealthy widow who could easily acquire her own inn.

Yet she had never felt more like her true self than in these past few days with Nicholas D'Amberly, discovering more and more about the woman she had been beneath the boy's attire. She was slowly finding out who she had always wanted to be. Someone courageous, loyal, caring and kind. Someone with a strong sense of purpose.

And yet she could not risk losing all that she was so close to gaining—a home and somewhere she could truly belong—for an attachment that neither she nor he actually wanted. Not that Eva had spoken of this with him. Besides, they were from two very different worlds that had come together unexpectedly and would soon drift apart once more.

And for all that Eva knew that this interlude would end, she would take the unbridled wonderment in the brief time she had left with Nicholas. After all, she was used to taking.

'Are you well, Eva?'

'Yes,' she murmured, touched by his concern.

'Good. I shall return anon.'

The man who had aroused so much confusion and contemplation stroked her arm before sitting up, pulling back the bed curtain and getting up from the pallet. He returned moments later with a bowl of water and a clean linen cloth that he tore into strips before holding them out to her.

'You might want this,' he murmured as she flushed, realising where he intended for her to use it.

'Thank you, I shall take that.' Her cheeks heated as she quickly took the bowl and cloth, turning away to clean herself under the coverlet. He waited until she had finished, then removed the bowl and re-emerged again on the other side, peeling back the bed curtain and getting into the pallet. He quickly gathered her to him, planting a kiss on her head.

They lay beside one another with Eva nestled against his chest, listening to the wind and rain outside, filling the silence. The day had all but given way to dusk and the hazy glimmer of the fire was making her feel sated and ridiculously sleepy.

'Why did you not tell me, Eva?' he whispered.

Her eyes fluttered open again. 'And what should I have told you?'

'That this was your first time.' He sighed. 'I assumed when you said you were not an innocent, and your life on the streets…well, I just assumed.'

She lifted a shoulder. 'I suppose it is an easy assumption to make. But, in truth, without Simon's protection, the streets might have claimed far more than just my innocence. My experiences would otherwise have been very different.'

'Then I am glad the Rook kept you safe. But tell me…why me, Eva?'

How to explain. How to answer, when she did not fully comprehend it herself? In the end Eva settled on simply responding the best that she could.

'I found that I wanted you, Nicholas. Immeasurably.' She took a deep breath and covered her face with her hand, her embarrassment growing.

He gently removed her hand and kissed the back of it. 'You honour me,' he whispered. 'In truth I felt the same.'

They lay together, wrapped in each other's arms, for a long moment before Nicholas broke the silence again. 'But you still should have told me, sweetheart.'

'It is not as though I am expecting anything from you.'

'Why? You should be demanding far more from me, Eva, in light of what has come to pass.'

'No, I believe I have made all the demands that I require—nothing more, nothing less. What happened between us was something else entirely.'

'Oh, and what was that?'

'You really need me to explain?' Eva chuckled softly. 'Besides, it makes very little difference either way.'

On the street such matters were not so important as they seemingly were at court. If two people wanted one another there was nothing that would hold them back. Still, she was glad that, despite it all, despite everything she had experienced, Eva was able to choose this for herself. She had chosen him—the man beside her.

Nicholas hooked his arm around her and, before she knew what had happened, flipped her around so that once again she was lying beneath him.

He kissed her and shook his head. 'Oh, I disagree, Eva Siward. It would have made all the difference.' He pressed a kiss on her nose. 'I could have taken more care of you.' He kissed her forehead. 'And would have been more considerate.' He kissed her lips again. 'And I would have seen to your needs.'

'Ah.' She reached up and cupped his jaw. 'But you did see to my every need, Nicholas,' she whispered with a small smile playing on her lips. 'However, if you feel in any way that you need to prove your manly expertise then we should, by all means, attempt it again.'

'You believe I should prove…' he rolled her around as she gave a squeak of laughter '…my manly expertise, eh?'

'Only if you feel the need.' She covered her mouth with the back of her hand. 'Not that you should, as it was all perfectly…*nice*.'

'Oho, so it is like that, is it? You want to dent a man's prowess and vigour.' He leant down and kissed her hard on the lips. 'Well, let me assure you that next time it won't be in any way "nice" but something altogether unexpected.'

'Is that so?' she mumbled as he cupped her

breast with his hand, his thumb grazing her nipple. 'What…what exactly are you alluding to?'

'Wickedness.' He bent down and caught her mouth in a long languid kiss, making her gasp. 'And when you least expect it.'

She drifted off to sleep curled up in his arms and was woken not once but twice in the middle of the night to be given, as promised, unbridled pleasure that went beyond any of her imaginings. Eva blushed when she later considered all the various parts of her body that had gained his undivided attention and how he had brought her to an unfettered peak of rapturous passion.

Wickedness indeed.

She had eventually fallen into a deep slumber in a tangled heap, completely exhausted after all of their endeavours, only to be woken a few short hours later by the streak of morning light piercing through the slats of the window shutters.

Eva opened her eyes to find that Nicholas had already risen, washed, changed and was ready for the day.

'Good morrow,' he drawled, pressing a cup of ale into her hands.

'Thank you and good morrow to you.' She

took a sip and frowned. 'Should you not have woken me earlier?'

'I believed you might want to rest after, well…in any case you can get ready now, Eva. My squire would have known to continue on last night. And if we make haste and start on the journey presently we should reach Guildford by nightfall.'

She nodded and stretched her arms out, stifling a yawn as her stomach gave a loud rumble, which made him smile.

'And we shall break our fast along the road, if that is amenable to you?'

She blinked and returned his smile. 'It is.'

The river had swollen its banks due to the turbulent weather the previous day and with the route no longer being a safe means to travel effectively they sought another way. Eva found that in no time they were riding on horseback out of the city and into the rolling countryside, and it surprised her that it had all been arranged so expediently. How Nicholas had managed to organise everything so efficiently Eva did not know, but comprehended far more about his standing and his position with the mysterious work that he did. Matters seemed to be accommodated at his request so easily and, although she had ascertained that the man was far more than a mere Crown Knight a few days earlier, she'd also realised that his connection with courtiers and the most powerful men in the land had to be a close one. Indeed, he was one of them, and even if Nicholas and his friends did inhabit the shadows they were still part of that world, unlike *her*. Not after the life she had led. And although she would have entrée into this world it would be of short duration, after all.

They rode through dense forest that opened out to verdant fields and gently rolling hills. Pushing their mounts further, they continued through ancient woodland with a running brook that was shallow enough for their horses to trot through. But after riding all morning long they were ready for a short rest, which had come at a good time since she was feeling increasingly tired, especially after last night's exertions.

Nicholas jumped down from his saddle with ease and came around her horse to help her.

'Thank you, but there really is no need. I have always seen to my own dismounting.'

'There is every need, Eva. You are about to act the noblewoman and it would be good to remember that, the closer we get to Guildford.' He wrapped his hands around her waist, helping her down.

'Not yet. I hardly look like one.' She was dressed in the clothing she had worn the previous day, which was now dry. A drab grey kirtle, threadbare and patched at the hem, with a cape and plain veil on her head.

'Even so, you soon shall.'

His fingers remained wrapped around her waist as he looked down at her, his hands firm, warm and strangely protective. It made her giddy just standing this close to him, reminding her of the night before. She flushed, just remembering how their bodies had been so intimately entwined, discovering every pleasure imaginable within each other. Yet it did surprise her that after such intimacies there was no uneasiness from him. She had expected a little awkwardness, if not embarrassment, which could not be helped, but it seemed that Nicholas D'Amberly was intent to be just as agreeable as before last night. If anything, he was more attentive and yet this made her feel a little uncertain.

'What is it?' He searched her eyes. 'Are you unwell, Eva?'

'No.' She forced a smile, shaking her head. 'I assure you I am quite well.

In truth, she did not know the reason why she felt this restless and apprehensive. Mayhap it was comprehending that everything would change once they reached Guildford. Or that her uncertainty was more about what would come to pass once they were there. Especially since Eva still felt a little unprepared, however much she corrected her posture or remembered to behave as a lady.

But it was more than that. Eva knew in her heart that it was far more to do with all her bewildering feelings regarding the man standing in front of her. She was beginning to care for him in a manner which was wholly inappropriate and unwanted. Nicholas did not belong in her world, despite his associations, and she did not belong in his. It would be prudent for Eva to remember that and not form any further attachment to the man. She did not regret sharing her body with him, but it would be ruinous to give her heart as well—that path could only spell disaster.

It would be best to remember that and enjoy this connection for what it was—fleeting.

'Are you certain that you are not too sore after…after last night?' Nicholas swore an oath under his breath as he studied her.

'No, of course not.' Eva shook her head. 'I believe that I'm just a little hungry, that is all.'

She took a step back from him and stumbled,

falling backwards. A pair of strong hands, the same ones that had, only moments ago, wrapped around her waist reached out and gripped hold of her, setting her back on firm ground.

'Very well then, let's eat.' He brushed his knuckle across her cheek, sending a shudder down her spine.

They meandered near the brook and laid out the blanket that Nicholas had fetched from his saddlebag, along with the parcels of food. She unfolded the small parcels of thin slices of cured beef, a few red apples, a small round cheese and freshly baked rolls.

'It is only simple fare but it should tide us over until we reach Guildford, where we shall dine on the finest of foods.'

She busied herself by passing some to Nicholas before tucking in herself, taking small delicate bites.

'Feeling better?' he asked.

'Much better, thank you. Despite this being simple fare, as you call it, it is delicious.'

Her gaze fell to the ring that she had given back to him yesterday, which was now threaded through a leather cord and tied around Nicholas's neck. 'I am glad to see that back where it belongs.'

'As am I.'

'How was it that it ended up in that pouch in the first place?'

He dragged his fingers through his hair. 'In truth, I usually have it on my person, but for some reason I believed it would be safer inside the pouch than visible around my neck at that damned inn.'

'Ah, so you believed it might be safe from someone like me?'

'Exactly,' he murmured, reaching out and curling one of her dark tendrils that had escaped from under her sheer veil around his finger. Eva leant into the touch, his whisper of a caress, before slowly moving away, knowing that it would be best to resist this temptation, even after what she had experienced last night.

She sat back and attempted to steer the conversation back onto safer ground. 'You professed that the reason the ring is of value to you is that it belonged to your late mother?'

'Yes.' He bit into a roll that he'd piled with a few slices of cured beef as well as some of the cheese. 'But it is just sentimental nonsense really. Nothing more.'

It seemed to Eva that it meant far more to Nicholas than he would have her believe. For one thing, it was always on his person, as he had explained earlier, and for another it was an item that evidently meant a great deal to him.

'And it is all that you have left from her?'

He grabbed his flagon, taking a swig before answering her. 'Much of her other possessions were either discarded or kept for another.'

'Oh, God.' She tilted her head to the side, frowning. 'That seems a rather heartless thing to do.' A long moment passed where the silence stretched and they both turned their attention back to their meal. Eva reached over and placed her hand on his. 'Apologies, I did not mean to talk out of turn, Nicholas.'

He stared at her small hand barely covering his and slowly turned it so that they were now palm to palm. 'There's no need to apologise. After all, my father was, as you said, a heartless bastard—a very apt description that.'

Her jaw dropped. 'I did not mean...'

'No, I know, Eva. But he was, nevertheless, as you described. In every sense.' He curled his fingers over hers, gaining warmth from this small tender touch. 'When my mother, who was everything that was kindness and benevolence, was ill, without hope of getting better, he thought only to seek his own comfort, his own contentment. This, when my mother needed his care, his love—when she constantly asked for him. But he refused to see her. Instead, the bastard had already found a replacement for her—before she was even in her grave. He paraded this woman under the very roof where my mother lay on her deathbed, instead of doing his duty by her.'

Eva squeezed his hand. 'I am so sorry.'

'As am I. And while my mother lay in her bed he allowed the scheming woman to make an inventory of everything that she either wanted to keep or get rid of—from my mother's precious loom, threads and other such stuff that she kept in her bower chambers. And if anyone, from retainers, maids to labourers, protested or complained about this treatment of my mother, who was loved and well respected, they found themselves turned away, and all this while she was still alive.'

'Dear God, how appalling.'

Nicholas gazed at Eva, who had only mere hours ago made his blood roar. 'Yes, it was,' he muttered absently.

This discourse was a timely reminder of the tacit reason why he had avowed that he would never get attached to another—not in the manner in which his father had done. He could never give his heart away, whatever that even meant.

He did not want that—someone who would turn him inside out and manipulate him, in the manner in which his father's wife had done to him.

'What happened, Nicholas?' Eva murmured beside him.

'Everything else that the woman wanted for herself she took. She stole, as though she had stripped my mother of her worldly possessions and her dignity. And do you know what my father did? He allowed it all to happen. If anything, the man encouraged the deplorable behaviour.'

Nicholas knew that he had shocked Eva by everything that he had disclosed. But then his mother's treatment at the hands of his father had been truly reprehensible. He could still recall watching the only woman he had ever loved being dishonoured in such a wretched manner.

Eva muttered, shaking her head, 'That is shameful.'

'Yes. Yes, it was.' He shook his head in revulsion. 'And, being only a lad myself at the time, I could do little about it. My mother must have realised what was happening and held onto one last possession before it could be taken from her.'

Her eyes widened. 'The ring.'

'Yes.' Nicholas nodded. 'Which she bestowed on me before she died.'

'That is awful. But I am glad that it is with you,' she said softly. 'And did he remarry after your mother's death?'

'Almost immediately,' he muttered bitterly. 'My father was besotted and infatuated with his young mistress and did everything he could to secure her hand.'

'So this is the betrayal you talked of?'

'Not quite.' He shook his head. 'After my mother's death I joined the retinue of Lord de Montford as a squire and after a few years was summoned by my father to visit and pay my respects to him. It was a disaster from the moment I returned. He was a changed man—harsh, unscrupulous and venal. And completely infatuated and under the influence of his vindictive wife. However, it was after one particular night that everything changed for the worse.'

'What happened?'

'His wife, Maud, came by my chamber one eventide, alone. And after I rejected and spurned her advances the viperous woman accused me of attempting to accost and compromise her.'

Eva covered her mouth with her hand. 'And your father believed her? He believed that you would do such a thing?'

'Oh, yes, with great ease,' Nicholas said with disgust, a muscle pulsing in his jaw. 'There was no question of his believing her word over mine. After all, I was only his son. He demanded retribution but settled for banishment from my home. I shall never forget when he declared that he had the hammer and anvil to make far better sons with his wife. In any case I left soon after, never to return.'

'I am truly sorry for the suffering that both your father and his wife caused you. It was unjust and contemptible of them.'

'Either way, I do not give them much consideration, Eva. Instead, I try to remember my mother, and have this to remind me of her.' He held out the ring dangling from his neck. 'And the fable she wove around it.'

She blinked. 'A fable?'

He nodded with a faint faraway smile. 'You see, she told me that this ring, which her own mother had given her, had magical qualities but only if it was worn by someone pure of heart. Which, of course, meant that it excluded every hale and hearty man. In truth, it could only be worn by a fair maid.'

'Yet she gave it to you.'

The metal glinted as it caught the light as he turned the ring around in his fingers. 'I have no sisters or other female relations. But I am only its keeper, Eva. My mother made me vow that I would one day present it to the one who could be entrusted with such a gift. And who was worthy of such an epithet.'

'Then I am glad you have it, so that you can one day fulfil your promise to her.' Eva smiled. 'But know this…none of it is sentimental hogwash.'

It was entirely sentimental but Nicholas was not going to argue with her. He was not going to tell her that he would never be able to honour the oath he had made to his mother. Not when he inhabited such a murky world, which did not just include the exalted assembly at court. No, the world he knew was dark, filled with misery, avarice and sin, where no one could ever lay claim to such nonsense.

He screwed up the empty food packaging and shoved it in the saddlebag before rising. 'Come, we should be making haste.'

Chapter Thirteen

Day had faded into dusk by the time they rode to the small hamlet of Guildford with its magnificent castle built high on a motte, a large sprawling bailey contained within the stone curtain wall around it. Eva could see from a distance the shadow of the great towering stone keep, which probably held the standard of King Henry on the battlement.

They entered through the heavily fortified gatehouse, with the King's garrison on patrol, making their way through an arched gate and onto the cobbled inner bailey, teeming with the hustle and bustle of having the royal court in residence.

After stabling their horses, Nicholas led Eva to the great hall, to seek both his Knights Fortitude brethren and also his lord liege, Hubert de Burgh. They hurried up to climb the stairs and reached the large wooden doorway, when Eva stilled him with her hand on his arm.

'Nicholas, wait.' She took a deep breath. 'Can we not go and ready ourselves first? We have been riding all of today and I have the day's dust and dirt on my kirtle and most likely my face as well. I would rather refresh myself before being presented to anyone here.'

'We will do just that, Eva, and there is no need to be nervous. I need to enquire where I am to take you, where you are to be situated here in the bailey during your stay.'

'You and I will not be staying together?' She swallowed uncomfortably.

'No.' He shook his head. 'It would be considered unseemly for an unmarried lady to be situated with a man who is unrelated to her.'

'Even after you and I have spent so many nights and days together?'

'Even then. And besides, no one at court knows about any of that.'

'Oh, yes, of course.' Yet Eva looked so unsure, so uncertain of this new situation and surroundings that he really needed to reassure her.

'All will be well, I promise.' He squeezed her hand gently. 'Your stay will be as comfortable as we can manage. But for now I need to find out about the arrangements.'

Much as Nicholas would love to spend more time with Eva, it was not prudent to pursue this path with her. In fact, the best course of action was to take a step back, put a little more distance between them and get on with what he had to do—find the man who had hired Eva to steal the missive and discover any possible link he had with the shadowy treasonous group The Duo Dracones. And hopefully then he would uncover what the bastard's intentions were here at Guildford, not that he could imagine them being good.

Once Eva had helped them he would see to it that she was settled and received the fifty silver marks he had promised. Nicholas would honour his promise, but that was all it could ever be. Nothing more, not that she had wanted any more from him, having made that perfectly clear at his lodgings. And their arrival at Guildford now provided the opportunity for both of them to maintain a more detached and professional stance with one another.

God, but he had been a selfish bastard to take her to his bed and a fool to disclose as much as he had about his woeful past. In truth, it had been wrong of him to get as close to her as he had, and it served neither of them well.

'Come, Eva.' It was time to put forth their plans. 'It begins.'

It had been many hours since Nicholas had left Eva with Joan de Talmont, and in that time he had changed and washed before hurrying for a privy meeting with Warin de Talmont and Savaric Fitz Leonard, who had arrived a short while ago, escorting Mistress Marguerite with him. The three men met their lord liege, Hubert de Burgh, in a hidden closet within the ante chamber attached to de Burgh's rooms.

'So you believe that this maid would be able to recognise the man responsible for killing our informant and stealing the missive?'

From what Warin de Talmont had deciphered from the missive that Eva had remembered, it was highly likely that the man who had hired her to steal from him was involved with The Duo Dracones. And they meant to threaten the Crown, and in particular Hubert de Burgh, here at the castle within the next few days. But they had to be stopped. It was high time that they made progress with this group that always managed to thwart their efforts to catch them. And though The Duo Dracones had failed to cause the mayhem, rebellion and dissent that they sought with their treachery, it was not through lack of effort. No, The Knights Fortitude worked tirelessly to frustrate and oppose them, but they needed more. They had to find out who they were, and who their leader was.

'That is the hope, my lord,' Nicholas muttered.

'Then you have pinned a great deal on a mere hope, D'Amberly.' The older man, who was still King Henry's trusted advisor and the most prominent lord in the land, paced the small narrow chamber.

'Oh, I believe that Mistress Eva would most certainly recognise the man if he was in attendance here at Guildford. She has the most remarkable memory.'

Warin de Talmont nodded. 'I can attest to that, my lord. She managed to put to memory the very missive she lost in the river. Which has been most interesting to decipher.'

'And what of Peter des Roches, the Bishop of Winchester? Can we link the blasted man to The Duo Dracones from what you deciphered in the missive?'

'Unfortunately, no, my liege. The Bishop is incredibly careful and seems beyond reproach.'

'Shame.' Hubert de Burgh rubbed his forehead impatiently. 'But is this young woman to be trusted? Do we know whether she is manipulating us into believing that she's no longer in league with the man who hired her?'

There was no question in Nicholas's mind about that.

'We can.' He nodded. 'Apart from anything else, the man who hired her, and who is likely to be involved with The Duo Dracones, may also be the one who had her protector killed, possibly because the work he had done for us put him in direct danger.'

'Ah, yes, I nearly forgot that she is also a thief, trained by Simon the Rook himself. And this is the person you would have me trust with our endeavours, D'Amberly? This woman?'

'Yes, my lord, on my honour. We can trust Eva Siward. After all, her involvement has always been based on the need to avenge the murder of her friend, since she believed that it was a Crown Knight who had brought about his demise. Now she knows differently.'

'Well, for your sake I hope you are right.' He grimaced. 'And what of her conduct at court? Will she be able to pass for a lady as you have instructed her? Are we able to pass her off as *my ward*?'

Nicholas was more uncertain about this than

anything else, but he had to have faith in Eva's ability to disguise herself and inhabit a character that was not her own. 'Yes, I believe so.'

'Make sure that you do.' The older man said tapping his fingers together. 'We need everyone ready and vigilant at the banquet. For once again, we know not what to expect.'

'We do know one thing, my liege.' Savaric Fitz Leonard pressed his lips into a thin line. 'We know that every time we get close to those suspected of being associated with The Duo Dracones they resort to damn well killing themselves before we can get anywhere near them.'

'Yes, they choose death above revealing anything about their organisation.'

Yet they also knew that the target of their vengeful malevolence was their liege—Hubert de Burgh.

'And it has always been *you* that they're after, my lord.' Nicholas rubbed his chin. 'Their aim has always been to undermine you and your standing with King Henry.'

'Indeed, from the very first, when we gained knowledge of their existence from Thomas Lovent in Wales to that business with the tanner merchants in London last year, they have always attempted to implicate you, condemn you or attempt to instigate your downfall from grace. Their threat was, and still is, very real.'

And it was a good thing that they had more knights, more guards protecting both de Burgh and the young King.

'There is one other thing we know. We do now know when the threat of this plot is likely to manifest itself,' Warin muttered grimly.

'What?' Nicholas stared at him in the shadowy room. 'When?'

'I managed to decipher the remainder of the missive en route to Guildford.' Warin crossed his arms over his chest. 'Mistress Eva had also drawn shapes that looked to me like a thorn rising up, with wings on either side.'

'Ascension Day!' Nicholas's eyes widened.

Warin nodded. 'Which is henceforth in two days from now.'

De Burgh rubbed his hands together, seemingly in thought. 'And let us not forget that Henry's father, King John, was crowned on Ascension Day, nearly thirty summers ago.'

Savaric Fitz Leonard grimaced, shaking his head. 'It cannot be a coincidence that the very day that the copied missive alludes to is when we come together to celebrate the ascension of Christ and commemorate the crowning of the old King in two days forth.'

'Mayhap we should postpone the celebration banquet then, my lord?' Warin suggested.

'No,' de Burgh retorted. 'We cannot do that. This man that you speak of would then be alerted to the fact that we know of his intentions, forcing him to abandon these plans and crawl back into whatever hovel he came from. No, we shall carry on as before, with more guards around the castle, the keep and the gatehouses. Is that understood?'

'Yes, my lord. We shall be ready.'

Nicholas frowned. 'Yet after all this time we still do not know who is involved with this group.'

The older man slammed his fist against the wall. 'Then we must catch them before they kill themselves or murder me.'

Warin dropped his head before raising it again. 'Which means that Eva Siward might be our only hope at finally identifying a possible member of The Duo Dracones. This is a chance that we cannot afford to squander.'

It made Nicholas apprehensive using Eva to draw the man out, but they had little choice with the success of this mission at stake. This was what they had planned after all. Yet Nicholas would have to ensure that she was not exposed to danger whilst under his care and protection.

He would never forgive himself if anything happened to her.

'Yes, it does, and if the bastard who hired her is here I have faith that she will do her part.'

Hubert de Burgh turned around, his eyes hard and grim. 'I hope you are right, D'Amberly, I hope you are right.'

Eva smiled at Joan de Talmont, who she was not surprised to find here at Guildford despite her husband's protestations a few days ago. And since her own arrival at the castle Eva had spent every day with Joan, her maid and Marguerite, who had arrived soon after with Sir Savaric.

They had conversed with other ladies, eaten a few times at the hall and Eva had even ridden on horseback with Joan and her husband in the demesne lands which hugged the periphery of the curtain wall of the castle. Marguerite, however, had been uncharacteristically pensive and distant, preferring to stay within the chamber, which made Eva concerned for her friend, despite her reassurances that all was well with her. Yet she refused to speak of it.

As for Eva, in the past couple of days she had yet to meet Nicholas D'Amberly. It was as though the man had purposely avoided her. Either that or he'd now acquired more responsibilities since his arrival here and could no longer give her any of his time, which Eva could not help but be a little disconcerted by.

The only time she had glimpsed the man was at the Ascension mass in the crowded chapel that morn and at vespers earlier. And to mark the occasion they were to celebrate with a banquet that very evening.

Eva gave a huge sigh as she sat on the pallet in the chamber that she had shared with Joan from the first night she had reached Guildford. It had been decided that this arrangement would afford Eva the necessary consequence and allow her to polish any of her unladylike quirks if needed. They had been lucky to secure such superior rooms in the keep, but then it probably had more to do with who Nicholas worked for rather than anything else, as most of the courtiers stayed either in the King's apartments or in tents dotted around the bailey if they were unable to find other accommodation.

The women were now assembling the final touches of both Joan and Eva's clothing for the court banquet that eventide. Thankfully, Joan had brought with her the appropriate attire needed for Eva and, with the help of her maid, they set about transforming her into a lady. They helped lace her into a fitted green velvet kirtle, the finest Eva had ever beheld, with swirls of silver-work embroidery around the square neckline and the wide hem of the bell-sleeves worn over the softest linen tunic. The sumptuous resplendent clothing at least gave her the confidence she needed for this night. And God only knew that she needed it.

She watched as Joan's hand fumbled on the coffer until her fingers felt the gauzy wisp of the most beautiful veil she had ever seen. The young woman brought it to her as she continued to explain how she had persuaded her husband to agree to bringing her along to Guildford with him.

'As it was, I managed to persuade Warin to allow me to accompany him here, telling him how much you would need my assistance, Eva. A load of nonsense, of course.' She handed the veil to her maid, who helped secure it on Eva's head. 'But I believe he accepted my argument. However, I could not make him bend from allowing our little Anais to accompany us as well. He can be so ridiculously protective.'

Eva sighed. 'You are lucky to have your husband's care and protection.'

'I believe we are.' The young woman nodded. 'But it is good for a man not to be too complacent, otherwise he would verge on being too high-handed and arrogant.'

'Ah, so is that the reason why you challenge Sir Warin as much as you do?' She chuckled.

'Oh, yes, my sister by marriage, Brida, informed me *that* to be the basis of a happy union. It would be prudent to keep a husband from always understanding his wife's mind. That way, he would always be seeking more inventive ways to keep her content.'

That brazen quip alongside Joan's impish grin earned her the most unladylike burst of laughter. But as the laughter subsided Eva pondered the reason why she had been so enlightened regarding the union of marriage. That particular state was one that she would never experience or have any hope of doing so for herself. A sudden pang rippled through her as she pushed the thought away. No, her plans lay in a very different direction altogether. She would use the silver she hoped to gain from Nicholas D'Amberly to start her life again. And, God willing, by being able produce and sell the ale that she took pride in.

'True.' She nodded at Joan. 'Although I have always thought that a woman, and indeed a man, should be careful not to pin their happiness or contentment completely on another.

They should endeavour to seek their own ful-filment, to avoid disappointment.'

Joan tilted her head and regarded her for a moment. 'I used to think just as you do, Eva, but I suppose life can sometimes throw up un-expected surprises. That was what happened to me.'

'And I am glad that it did. But it is worth knowing that sometimes it doesn't. Sometimes life does not unfurl the way in which one would hope.'

'True. But we can only grasp the opportuni-ties that come our way.'

Precisely. And Eva's one opportunity was this, here and now—to secure the silver that she had all but negotiated in her bargain with the man who constantly crept into her thoughts— Nicholas D'Amberly. She knew it was un-seemly, she knew it was futile and yet she could not help feeling these unwarranted emotions.

No matter, Eva would comply with what they had agreed, and only that. She would play her part and act the noblewoman and hope to find the man who had hired her—the man responsi-ble for a missive that had found its way to Nich-olas's hand, which had brought about the need for it to be stolen again. She would find him and she would avenge Simon's murder, once she knew who was culpable.

Yes, she would do everything in her power to bring about a favourable outcome. God, but when she considered how her endeavours might afford her the chance to finally have somewhere she truly belonged, somewhere that was home if she succeeded, she became impatient. Yes, Eva would do everything she could, that and more, for such an opportunity.

She turned to face Joan and smiled. 'I think I am ready.'

'You are. But just one last thing.' Joan clutched her walking stick and went back to the coffer set in the corner of the chamber and took out a circlet—an intricately beautiful silver head-piece. And as Joan secured it on her head over the veil she felt a flutter whisper down her arms, making her shudder. No, this would not do. Eva pushed the apprehension away and straightened her spine.

'Yes, I think it is time to venture to the hall. Are you certain you would not like to join us, Marguerite…? Marguerite?'

'I'm sorry—were you speaking to me?'

'Yes, dearest. I wondered whether you were ready to accompany us to the banquet this evening?'

'No, I thank you,' her friend muttered, shaking her head. 'I shall prefer to stay here and rest, if you do not mind.'

Eva frowned at Marguerite's stillness, wondering again whether anything untoward had occurred on her journey here with Sir Savaric. It would have to keep for later but she would have to get to the bottom of what had caused Marguerite such malaise.

'Very well, as you wish.'

Eva lent Joan her arm to help guide the young woman with diminished eyesight as they walked together down the stone spiral staircase, before grabbing a flaming torch from the metal sconce. Sir Warin met them at the bottom with a ready smile to escort the two women to the hall.

'My fair wife and Mistress Eva.' He made a bow. 'You both look exceptionally lovely on this auspicious evening. May I escort you both into the hall?'

'Of course.' Joan slipped her hand into his and smiled up at her husband. 'And thank you, my gallant knight.'

Sir Warin walked them in through the huge wooden doors and into the noisy hall, which had been decorated with crisp linen tablecloths stretched over the trestle tables that ran down the length of the hall and the top table on the dais, where the King and the most prominent men of the realm sat.

Green foliage and edible spring flowers and herbs were strewn on the tables as well as the newly clean stone floors. Flaming torches were held inside iron sconces set on the stone walls and candles were lit and took centre stage on all the tables, encased within pretty spring herbal wreaths. The entire chamber looked enchanting and smelt wonderful and yet Eva still felt the unfurling of butterflies within her stomach.

She fixed a serene smile on her face and scanned the chamber a few times before her gaze caught Nicholas D'Amberly's. He sat in the corner of a long table, his eyes fixed on hers. Exhaling a shaky breath, she moved closer as he stood and stared intensely at her with those penetrating blue eyes that matched his blue quilted gambeson. Oh, God, he was so ridiculously handsome. His hair had been combed and slicked back and his tall muscular form had been encased in his fine court attire. Her pulse tripped as they approached their end of the table and she noticed a smile tug at the corners of his lips.

A flash of unwavering heat and longing passed across his eyes before being masked as

Nicholas turned towards her and bowed. 'Good evening. It is delightful to make your acquaintance again, Mistress Eva. I think the last time I was honoured to have the pleasure of your company was in Poitiers two summers ago.'

She curtsied. 'Thank you, kind sir.'

'And you are as lovely now as you were then.'

'Is it necessary to state such falsity?' she whispered as she leant close to him.

'I believe I must,' he drawled in that low voice that always made her heart beat a little faster, holding out his hand to her.

A shot of awareness prickled up her arm as she slipped her hand in his, making her suddenly feel hot and unable to breathe. Nicholas inclined his head over her hand and helped her to her seat beside him.

'You are lovely, by the by. And look every bit a beautiful noblewoman,' he whispered in her ear as they both sat down.

'Thank you. You look very well yourself.' She threw him an impish smile and shrugged, deciding in that moment that she would endeavour to enjoy this evening as much as she could. If anything, it would help in giving off that air of the refined yet insouciant lady who she wanted to portray.

As she sat beside him their arms touched

briefly, sending a shock of awareness through her. Trenchers of succulent pork braised in plum sauce, spring lamb with crusts of mint and rosemary and fresh fish laden with a verjuice, borage and mace sauce were brought to the table. The delicious scent reminded Eva of the scant few days she had spent in the small timber cottage with Nicholas and his prodigious talent for preparing delicious food. She flicked a glance at him as he helped spoon some of the choicest cuts of meat onto her plate before serving himself.

'I hope that I finally pass muster, Sir Nicholas,' she whispered, 'and have improved my countenance as I sup with you here in this grand hall.'

'Most assuredly you have, Eva.' He smiled into his cup. 'But what I am surprised to encounter is that you are back to calling me "Sir Nicholas" once again.'

'I believe I must,' she said, repeating his words, making him smile. She took care to chew the small morsel of food that she had carefully popped into her mouth. 'After all, you were kind enough to remind me of the proper courtly conduct for an unmarried maid such as I.'

He raised a brow as he passed her a plate

of bread rolls. 'Only for the duration of our stay, Eva.'

'Either way—' she gave him her most serene smile '—I am glad that there is clarity in the difference in our station now that we have arrived at court.'

He frowned, turning to look at her. 'I am at a loss to comprehend you.' As was she. Eva had not meant to say it, yet the words seemed to spill from her lips. 'I hope I have not in any way given offence.'

'No, of course not.' Her smile softened. 'But surely it would be prudent to observe this difference while we are at court. After all, I am disguised as a noblewoman.'

'Indeed you are, mistress.' The brief appreciative look he threw at her made her stomach clench. She pushed away the simmering hum of tension and turned her mind to her task instead.

She took a sip of wine. 'And how am I getting on? Is my spine as straight as it should be? Are the bites of food small enough? And am I sampling this excellent wine in the manner I should?'

'Yes, you are as I would expect someone of your obvious talents to perform.' He dragged a finger to the corner of her lips and brushed away a drop of red wine, making her inhale sharply. 'There is not a gulp or slouch in sight, Eva.'

'I thank you.' Her voice sounded breathless and husky, even to her own ears. She instinctively licked her lips, watching his gaze drop to them before muttering an oath and tearing his eyes away.

'Would you care for more wine?' His gaze darted around the hall, allowing her a moment to calm her beating heart.

'No, thank you. I believe it might be best if I kept my wits about me on this night.' She sighed through her teeth. 'After all, I am here so that I might identify the man who hired me. We perceive that he would still attend, do we not?'

'We do.' He pressed his lips together. 'And have you, Eva? Have you managed to find him among the throng of people here at court?'

She scanned the chamber once more, taking her time to study every single person present. 'No—' she shook her head eventually '—he is not here, unfortunately.'

Nicholas exhaled in frustration. 'Hopefully he will be in attendance tonight. And all of this can finally be resolved.'

Eva nodded and turned her head back around as she took a sip of wine, noting the various groups of courtiers huddled together and those standing apart from others—surely that would be the more likely place to find him. It was then that she noticed a man who looked familiar, ambling into the hall with a beautiful young woman on his arm. He was not the man she sought, but something about him caught her eye.

'He is not here yet, but see, there by the doorway,' she whispered. 'That man does somehow look familiar, do you not think?'

It was only when Nicholas twisted his head around, his eyes widening in shock, that Eva realised who the man must be.

'Oh, yes, very familiar,' he muttered through gritted teeth. 'That man is my father, and he is seemingly here at court.'

Chapter Fourteen

Nicholas felt the blood drain from his face, with the earth beneath his feet seemingly shifting as he watched his damn father and his damn wife saunter towards him as though it were the most natural thing in the world to do.

His heart hammered in his chest fast and loud—so loud that Nicholas wondered whether the courtiers assembled in the hall could hear it, drowning out the din.

Hell's teeth, but what was the man even doing here? Why now? And why was he moving towards this end of the chamber—towards him, with that familiar sneer pasted on his face. Small beads of perspiration gathered on Nicholas's forehead as he breathed in and out, in and out to steady his racing pulse. Eva curled her hand over his, her gaze dropping fleetingly to his mother's ring dangling around his neck, reminding him that he had disclosed his sad, sordid family tale to her only a few days ago. And, just like a ghost from his worst nightmare, his father was here at court—with King Henry, Hubert de Burgh and even Peter des Roches, The Bishop of Winchester, all here in attendance. Could it get any worse than this?

God's breath, but Nicholas did not need this apparent reunion with the man who had sired him and his errant wife, who he had not seen nor heard of for the past ten years. He had far more important matters that needed his attention. Again, the question ran through his head—why now, after all this time? And on this night? He could not afford any unpleasantness with so much at stake. A muscle flickered in his jaw as they approached their end of the table.

'Good evening, Nicholas.' The man held out his hand to him. 'Do you not have a kiss of peace for your father?'

Nicholas stood and inclined his head a little but did not take his father's outstretched hand. 'Good evening, sir.' He turned and greeted the man's wife. 'Maud,' he said perfectly blandly, 'I must confess to being at a loss to find you at such an assembly.'

'I suppose you must, since you now move in such exalted circles.' The years had not been kind to his father, who had a ruddier pallor, with a paunch and a girth that he did not have the last time Nicholas had laid eyes on the man. 'But I have not come here to quarrel with you, son.'

Nicholas clenched his teeth at the man proclaiming such familial closeness when the truth was quite the opposite. 'Then why have you come?'

He chuckled, patting his stomach. 'Why, to be reunited with my only son, of course.'

Nicholas tilted his head to the side. 'Ah, so you were unable to make those better sons that you once claimed you would then?'

He knew it was beneath him to make such an acerbic comment but he could not help it. The man had been responsible for so much pain and yet he stood there as though nothing had happened. As though he had not denigrated his mother; as if he had not banished Nicholas from his home. The last time he had set eyes on either of them, many years ago, was when this woman, his father's wife, had accused him of assaulting her, when the truth was very much the other way around. It had been *she* who had come into his chamber. It had been *she* who had disrobed in front of him and begged for his touch. And after Nicholas had got over the shock of finding his father's wife in his chamber, after he had refused her, Nicholas had left the woman in his chamber and rode out of the castle. And on his return it was *she*, his father's wife, who had been so indignant, so resentful at his refusal to bed her that she had accused him instead and thus provoked his father's banishment. For the man who had sired him had naturally believed the poisonous lies that had dripped from that woman's mouth over his own son's word.

And now they were here at the banquet. At court. When Nicholas needed all his wits in order to capture a faceless, nameless adversary by using Eva Siward, a woman he was beginning to care for, as bait. He stilled a moment as realisation hit him. No, he was not beginning to care for her. He *did* care for Eva Siward.

'Well, are you going to introduce us to your fair companion?'

No...

'I asked whether you would grant us the introductions, son?'

Son...

God, but Nicholas wished his father would stop calling him *that*. It was no longer a term that belonged to him.

'Nicholas?'

None of this made much sense to him. Why?

Why the hell now? Was he wrong to doubt this man's intentions?

'I'm Eva… Eva de Courtney.' The woman beside him spoke up for him and even remembered the fabricated name they had given her. 'Delighted to make your acquaintance, sir.'

Nicholas's fists were clenched tightly, his knuckles white as Eva made the unnecessary introductions. He did want not her exposed to their malevolence and, thank God, she had the good sense not to introduce the rest of their party.

'As are we.' His father inclined his head a little. 'Sir Walter D'Amberly and my wife, Maud, at your service. I am glad to see at least you, my dear, have the necessary courtesy that my son seems to lack.'

He exhaled, knowing that he had to control his temper. He had to hold onto some semblance of restraint or the situation could quite quickly unravel around him, even though he wanted to roar at his father. How dared the man come here and insult him in front of his friends, in front of his woman?

His woman…?

Hell's teeth, but he must be losing his mind if he believed that to be true.

He felt Eva's hand squeeze his lightly as she

leaned a little closer to him. 'Oh, I do not know about such things, sir, but do know that Nicholas lacks for nothing. He is the very best of men.'

Nicholas blinked at her and smiled in surprise.

The best of men, was he?

God, but he wanted to kiss her then, for standing up against his father. For him. She had done it for him. And for one small moment he wished that it were true—he wished Eva was his woman. Even though their time together would soon come to an end and they would part ways, once all matters at court were resolved one way or another. For the first time since he had met Eva Siward he wished that he had not brought her here. He wished he had not made that damn bargain with her. He wished everything between them had been different. God, but if anything happened to her… No, he would keep her safe.

Without looking away, Nicholas pulled her gently to her feet and tucked her hand in the crook of his elbow.

'I believe I hear the first chords of the music, Eva. Would you care to dance with me?'

She blinked a couple of times before a smile

spread on her lips. 'I would be delighted,' she murmured.

'If you would excuse us, sir. Maud.' He kept his eyes on hers.

'Wait, Nicholas, before you run off with your friend, I believe you have something that belongs to me.' His father nodded at the ring—his mother's ring that was dangling down from around his neck. God, but was the man so heartless that he would demand the return of the only thing he had left of his mother? Evidently so.

He stared at the man who had sired him with unfettered loathing for a long moment before he untied the leather cord from around his neck and dropped the ring into his outstretched hand. It was just a ring—only a ring—and did not matter.

All that mattered at that moment was to get as far from his father's presence as soon as he could. His hand shook with barely disguised rage as he escorted Eva to the middle of the hall, where many others were assembling for a dance.

They lined up in two lines, the maids on one side, the men on the other. And then they came together. He reached for her hands and, gliding her around the room, took two steps forward and one behind as the melody wrapped around them. He came up from behind and held her hand in his and curled his other around her waist.

'Thank you,' he whispered in her ear as they swayed from side to side.

'Whatever for?'

'You know precisely, Eva Siward. You need not have done it but I am grateful for your intervention back there with my father. I have never had a woman speak out for me in the way you did.'

They crossed one another and took a step with another partner, moved in a circle, before returning back together again. He took her hand in his again and twirled her around and back to face him.

'I am happy to have helped. Is that not what friends do for one another?'

'Friends,' he murmured. Their arms entwined above their heads as they took a step right and then left. 'Is that what you and I are?'

'Yes,' she said in a whisper. 'But I wish your father had not taken your mother's ring.'

'Although she gifted it to me, in truth, everything she once owned does belong to *him.*'

'But it was unnecessarily cruel to take it from you.'

'Oh, sweetheart, that is the very least of his

cruelty.' Nicholas was touched by her concern. 'But the ring is just an object. It will never bring my mother back. It matters not.'

'I disagree, from everything you have told me, I believe it matters a great deal.'

No, it is you that matters a great deal.

He wanted to say it but instead grazed her face with his knuckles.

They had stopped in the middle of the hall with the other dancers giving them curious glances, but all that Nicholas could think was how he wanted to pull Eva into his arms and hold her for a while. They locked eyes for a long moment as Nicholas slid his fingers around the back of her neck. He wanted to lose himself in those warm brown eyes. He wanted to forget that his father was in the same chamber as him. He wanted to forget.

He knew this surge of emotion had much to do with seeing the man after all this time. It had unnerved and shaken him to his core and yet he had found solace in Eva's unstinting support. God, but the woman was fierce and loyal. There was something inherently good and true about her—a quality many did not have, despite her hardship in life, her loss of loved ones and the things she had done to survive the streets.

'Nicholas, people are staring at us,' she said in a hiss.

'Let them.'

'We cannot. This is not part of the plan.' She gently pulled away and blinked, flicking her gaze around the chamber. 'And you know the reason why I am here.'

'I do know, but I find that right at this very moment I do not care.'

'You do not mean that after everything you have done to get me here to court.' She leant forward and whispered in his ear, 'I realise it must be disconcerting to find him here, at this very time. But do not allow him to get in the way of what you need to achieve. Do not allow his presence here to matter.'

Nicholas closed his eyes and breathed in and out before making a single decisive nod. Eva was right, of course, the man should not matter any more and neither should his presence here. Let him and his damn wife eat, drink and be merry. He no longer cared. He needed to pull his mind back to the very reason why they were all here. To catch a devious, dangerous traitor who might be present at this very moment.

Eva watched Nicholas with concern, knowing that he had been shocked at seeing his father once again, and that had briefly clouded every thought and judgement. And he had justifiably been angry. God, but the man who had sired Nicholas was not fit to be called a father, and was just as abhorrent as she had imagined him to be, obviously enjoying the effect he had had on his long-forgotten son. Especially in taking the one possession he had of his late mother.

Eva was only glad that whatever emotion Nicholas had been suffering seemed to have passed.

They finished the dance, with the men bowing and the maidens dropping to a graceful curtsy. Thankfully Eva executed it well, judging by Nicholas's small nod of approval.

He came to claim her hand. 'Well, now that I have grown more accustomed to my father's presence, we can resume our plans.'

'I think that a wise decision.'

'Glad you approve.' He raised a brow. 'So, have you spotted the man who hired you amongst the revellers here tonight?'

'No, he is strangely absent.'

'Then continue to survey the hall and every person here present, from the chamberlain and steward to the squires, servers and other kitchen helpers. No one is exempt from scrutiny. He will be here, Eva, I am certain of it, in one guise or another.'

'Very well.' She nodded.

'In the meantime, come, *Eva de Courtney*. I shall reunite you with your ever-loving guardian, Hubert de Burgh, and mayhap even King Henry would like an introduction to a maid as lovely as you.'

She halted, colour seeping from her face. 'You are jesting. The King? Hubert de Burgh? It is one thing being in the same chamber as them, but entirely another to be presented to them.'

He shook his head and smiled. 'Come, they would be delighted to make your acquaintance, I promise.'

Eva could hardly believe it—from London's streets to being presented to the King of England. It was something that she would never have envisaged even a few days ago. Exhaling a shaky breath, she followed Nicholas towards the dais.

Many hours of revelry had passed and Eva felt the nerves and tension that had coiled in her stomach loosen in some respects but not in others. She had joined in the festivities and partook in the merriment but had not been able to identify the man who had met her in the inn and hired her to steal. Her eyes scanned the whole chamber as she clapped and cheered.

What if he was not going to be here tonight? What if they had made a mistake—or, rather, she had made a mistake in memorizing the original missive? What if the whole thing had been some elaborate ruse, and this night was not to be the night that the man had intended for the nefarious threat to take place? Her senses were alert and heightened to everything around her as she pretended not to have a care in the world. But the longer the evening wore on, the more apprehensive she felt.

A large group came together for another set of dancing and, before Eva knew what was happening, she had been coaxed to join them, finding herself in the middle of the hall, making a circle. It was livelier and far more engaged than the intimate dance she had shared with Nicholas. And soon she was paired up with one of the men, who stood behind her and led her around the hall as they stopped, clapped and continued to move briskly to the pace of the music. The man nodded and smiled at her but did not make much of an effort to speak.

'I hope you are enjoying yourself as much as I am, sir.'

'Who cannot but enjoy such festivities when one is paired with a partner as lovely as you, mistress?'

'I thank you.'

They parted ways again and joined the two circular rings of dancers, one inside the other, skipping to one side and the other before coming back together again.

'I confess that I have rarely known a night as enjoyable as this,' she said, chuckling.

'Nor I, mistress, but I fear that I am going to fall from sheer exhaustion.' He smiled warmly at her. 'Or mayhap it is having the privilege of dancing with the most handsome maid in the hall.'

'Oh, sir, you put me to the blush.' She smiled.

'I only speak the truth, mistress. But there is one thing I should wish to know, if you would oblige me.'

'Certainly sir.'

'How does it feel to be here at court—' they moved around one another and turned back to face each another '—when you were nothing but a filthy street thief?'

Eva gasped, stumbling as the man's arm shot out and clamped onto her wrist. 'I… I do not know what you mean, sir.'

'Oh, I think you do, Eva Siward.' The man's

lips curled into a sneer as he gripped her hand tightly. 'Now, let's finish this enjoyable dance, shall we?'

Chapter Fifteen

Eva's heart was beating fast, her breath coming in short bursts, but she had to maintain her composure as she considered every possibility, every eventuality. She racked her mind but came up with very little. He was tall, distinguished-looking, with black hair, dark eyes and dressed in all his finery, and she knew with certainty that she'd never met the man. Yet evidently he knew of her. Who was he, and how in heaven did he know her?

'I can see that I have confused you, mistress.' He followed the other couples, leading her down one side of the hall and then the other. 'Mayhap I should explain.'

'If you would be so kind, sir,' she muttered wryly. How she had managed to keep her voice level and disinterested she knew not. But her racing heartbeat betrayed her.

'Such pretty manners. No one would be any the wiser, knowing that you're nothing but a common thief.'

Was this stinging statement supposed to get a rise from her when she exactly knew what and who she was? Even so, what confounded her was that this man knew of her ruse.

'I do not know what you are talking of, sir. Mayhap you have mistaken me for another.'

He spun her around and held tightly onto her wrist as they gradually parted from the main group of dancers. 'I think not. And do not take that insolent tone with me, young woman,' he said softly, running his fingers down her arm. 'I am not a man you wish to cross.'

'I shall keep that in mind.' She tried to keep her voice even, understanding well the man's threatening warning. She had come across threats many times on the streets after all. 'Who are you, and what is it that you want?'

'Surely a woman as clever and conniving as you can guess who I might be and what I require from you.'

'I am evidently not as clever nor as conniving as you suppose, sir, as I am still at a loss to know what that may be.'

'Then let me enlighten you,' he whispered in her ear. They moved around a pillar and were now hidden away from any onlookers. 'You reneged on a bargain that we made, Eva Siward. And *we* do not take kindly to such trickery and deception.'

A chill went down her spine. This was not the man who had hired her, who evidently was not present tonight. But what Eva had not considered was that the man would have associates—such as the man standing beside her now. God, but that was a huge failing on her part.

'I do not know what you are alluding to.'

'Do not be coy, mistress, it does not suit you,' he hissed. 'You were contracted to steal a missive, as you well know, from Nicholas D'Amberly, a Crown Knight, with whom you seem to have formed a rather unfortunate attachment, judging by the manner in which you danced with him earlier.' He dropped his head, shaking it. 'As though a man such as he would ever want anything lasting from a whore like you,' he sneered. 'Oh, do not look surprised, mistress. We knew the moment that you failed to attend the meeting, following the theft, that you had backed out of our agreement. But can you imagine our shock, however, when we discovered afterwards that the old miser the Rook's apprentice was not who we believed him to be, but *you*—a maid with a penchant for pretence and deception, as well as pretending to be a boy?'

She exhaled slowly through her teeth, trying to think quickly so that she could remove herself from this situation, sensing the thrum of danger surrounding this man, whom she had never set eyes on before.

'Do not think for one moment that I will not expose you for who you are. I doubt the court will care too much about my humble background compared to having a traitor among their midst.'

The man tilted his head. 'Yes, it seems that there is much spirit in you, Eva Siward.' He smiled. 'Mayhap a little too much. And you will do no such thing, my dear. In fact, I believe that you shall make good the promise that you made, now that you have brought all of this mayhem onto yourself.'

Eva flicked her gaze around the pillar. Where was Nicholas? Why had he not wondered where she had got to? For now it seemed she was to deal with this situation on her own.

'He will not be coming to your aid. Not yet, anyway, as I believe Nicholas D'Amberly might have much to discuss with his father.'

Understanding dawned. 'You brought his father here.'

The man gave nothing away but did not refute her statement. 'God, but the things some men and even women do for coin. But then you know all about that, do you not?' He smirked. 'Either way, before Nicholas D'Amberly's friends wonder where you are, we shall conclude our business.'

'*We* shall do no such thing.' Eva attempted to pull free from his iron grip. 'If you do not let me go, I shall scream.'

'I think you might refrain from such histrionics, mistress. For you have not asked where my associate might be at this very moment. The one who met you at the inn in London.'

She felt the colour drain from her face. Oh, God she suddenly dreaded what he was about disclose.

'Shall I tell you?' he whispered, smiling. 'Why, he is making the acquaintance of someone you are well acquainted with and treat quite like a sister.'

Marguerite...

'How do I know you have even taken her? How do I know that this is not an elaborate scheme to ensnare me to do your bidding?'

'I wondered whether you would ask me this. But here, you can see for yourself, mistress.' The man dragged a leather cord hanging around his neck from beneath his gambeson, showing her a handful of cut red curling hair. 'Your friend Nicholas D'Amberly is not the only one who likes mementos and worthless trinkets.'

God, but how did he know all of this? She had to somehow discover a little more about him in return. Anything that might later help. 'So you are a collector?'

'How perceptive, mistress.' His brow arched.

'Very singular.'

He inclined his head, acknowledging it. Her eyes fell to the small knot of red hair that was tied to a plain silver medallion, which she had not initially seen.

'May I?' She nodded at the leather cord around his neck. 'To satisfy myself that it really is Marguerite's hair and no one else.'

'My, you do have a suspicious mind, mistress.' His lips curled unpleasantly. 'Very well, go ahead. Feel it if you must.'

Eva reached out with a shaky hand and pulled the cord towards herself, feeling the hair between her fingers and, just before she released it, brushed it to the side to get a better look at the medallion it was attached to. The medallion showed two snakes intertwined and above one was the word *'Renaisser'*.

'I hope you are satisfied, mistress.' He tucked

the leather cord back inside his tunic. 'And I will tell you that if you do not follow exactly as we decree it will be more than just some of the fair maiden's hair that I will have attached there.'

God, but the man was depraved.

Eva covered her mouth with her hand. 'You will not hurt her.'

'I have no desire to hurt the maid.' His smile faded and in its place was a thin cruel twist of his lips. 'But only if you now do our bidding, Eva Siward.'

She closed her eyes and took a breath before reopening them again. 'What will you have me do?'

'We need you to break into the chamber of your dear *guardian*, Hubert de Burgh, and steal an item that belongs to him—that recognisably belongs to him, mind.'

She frowned. 'You mean something like a signet ring?'

'Indeed, any such thing that can belong only to him.' And, just like that, this man had returned her to her old life. Once again she was relegated to being a common thief, as he had put it, but this time she was ordered to steal.

'What you ask is madness. Do you know how

well guarded his chamber, and the whole of the castle, currently is? It cannot be done.'

'It can and you will. And if you manage to accomplish this assignment then your friend will be returned to you. A substitute which would enable us to absolve you of the earlier debt you owe us and even overlook your betrayal.'

God, but Eva had had enough of Marguerite being used to coerce and manipulate her to do another's bidding. And it did not escape her that, by doing this, she would be deceiving Nicholas D'Amberly. Her heart sank. She was being forced to choose between her innocent young friend and the man who she cared about. The man, Eva realised, for whom she would do just about anything. The man who made her heart soar.

She exhaled in resignation. Of course there was no real question, however, about what she would have to do. She could not abandon Marguerite to this fate.

'Very well, I shall do it.' She clenched her teeth. 'But I want your assurance that you will let her go if I steal this for you.'

'Haven't I already given it?'

'No.'

'Very well, you have it. But you do this—

and do it alone. I warn you that if you inform Nicholas D'Amberly of any part of these plans then there will be no accounting for what we will do. Do you comprehend this?'

God, how reprehensible he was.

'I do.'

'Then you know what to do.' He let go of her wrist and began to move away. 'Meet us in the stables at the lower bailey at first light. Do not be late, Eva Siward.'

She instinctively rubbed the wrist that he had been clasping so tightly and by the time Eva looked back up the man had gone.

Dear God...

How in heaven had she got herself into this? And how was she going to get both herself and Marguerite away in one piece?

It was many hours later when Eva found herself dressed once again in dark male attire, her head covered beneath a hood. She moved between the shadows, knowing perfectly well that, although there were far fewer people milling about the castle at the witching hour, there were still many guards on patrol.

She had already stolen something earlier that night—a theft that had been far easier to accomplish than the one she was about to attempt. It had come to her—what she must do before she left Nicholas for good, after watching his despicable father torment his only son by taking the one remaining possession he had left of his mother. Well, no more.

Eva had easily walked into the chamber that Sir Walter D'Amberly shared with his wife earlier, dressed as a lowly kitchen servant, replenishing jugs of ale, sweeping and removing old rushes before exchanging them with new ones. And once the room had been cleared she had been left alone for a moment, giving her the opportunity to find Nicholas's mother's ring tossed aside, almost dismissively, on top of the plain wooden coffer. Eva had quickly dropped it inside her pouch, tying it to the inside of her skirts before leaving the chamber promptly. Buoyed by the success of this, she had changed her disguise again and was now onto her second theft of the night, which would be far trickier.

She moved stealthily around pillars and wooden dwellings and back inside the royal apartments. She climbed up the stone spiral staircase, taking care to make little noise as she took each step at a time. She reached the top and ambled towards the royal solar, knowing that Hubert de Burgh's chambers would be situated close to the King's, but as she turned the corner a hand reached out and grabbed her and pulled her around so fast she had no time to react.

'Nicholas?' she murmured in the dark. 'What are you doing?'

'I could very well ask you the same question.' His tone remained indifferent but even in this diminished light it was his eyes that betrayed his barely concealed hurt and disappointment. 'Were you going to tell me?'

'Tell you what?'

'Any of it?' he muttered, cupping the side of her shoulder with one hand and tipping her chin up with the other. 'Do you suppose I truly believed my father's visit to court to be a co-incidence, Eva? I knew he came with the sole purpose to provoke and aggravate. All that non-sense with my mother's ring was the sort of an-tagonistic ruse that made me suspicious as to why he was there in the first place.'

'Which was?'

He pulled open a door in the furthest cham-ber along the narrow empty corridor and ush-ered her in hurriedly.

'Me. I knew, Eva.' He took a flame from the nearby sconce and followed her inside, turn-ing around to face her. 'I knew the moment he walked with his wife towards me that everything was not quite as it should be. And when they attempted to engage me in discussion I went along with it, knowing that you, at least, might be able to uncover more. I kept my eye on you when you spoke with the man that you danced with, believing that finally we would be closing in on the one we sought. I waited and I waited more for you to come to me and tell me everything that had transpired. Instead, I gleaned nothing, despite the fact I vouchsafed you, giving my word to Hubert de Burgh that we could put our trust in you, Eva. But look at you now. Not only did you fail to inform me of any of it, but I find you dressed once again as a boy on the prowl, evidently to thieve once more.'

'Can you not think why?' Her eyes welled up as she wiped her face quickly with the back of her hand.

'No. How can I when you have failed to come to me, confide in me?' he whispered. 'We are supposed to work together, remember? We had a bargain. Can you imagine what would have happened if someone else had come upon you rather than me? Tell me that I have not been taken in by your wiles, Eva, because, as God is my witness, I am the greatest fool that ever lived if that were true.'

'You still cannot trust me?'

'Can you blame me?'

'Indeed you are a fool if you believe that, Nicholas D'Amberly,' she huffed. 'And to think that I would care for such a fool.'

His brows shot up. 'You care for me?'

'Please do not change the subject of our discourse.'

'I must if I am to comprehend you better.'

'I did not betray you,' she said through gritted teeth. 'Believe that or believe it not, but I do not have the time for this.'

'What is it? What has happened?'

'It is Marguerite. She has been taken.'

He expelled a frustrated breath and muttered an oath under his breath.

That seemingly had surprised him, which annoyed her all the more. It was intolerable and hurtful that Nicholas D'Amberly would believe she would so readily deceive him.

He dragged his fingers through his dark hair. 'Do you believe she has been taken by the man who assigned you the task to steal from me at the very beginning?'

'I do.' She nodded. 'But the man tonight, who I danced with… I have never met him before.'

'Why did you not tell me any of it?'

'I had little choice. He said they would hurt her if I did.'

His lips curled into a smile that did not quite reach his eyes. 'It seems that you also have little faith in me if you cannot trust me in this.'

'I had to think fast and I had to take care of this unexpected situation as it arose, which is what I have always done, Nicholas, even while I worked for the Rook. He never accepted anyone who could not look after and fend for themselves. As a result, I have never relied on anyone to do my bidding.'

'Well, naturally, you would never dream of seeking any possible help when it is freely given,' he muttered in clipped tones.

'No, I would not.' In truth, she did not know how to. She had learnt the hard way that she had to take care of herself in order to survive.

'Ah, then I believe we are at an impasse.' He crossed his arms over his chest and raised a brow. 'And, after everything that has happened between us, it seems a little unfortunate that you still think of me just as you did when we first met.'

Her brows furrowed in the middle. 'Which is what?'

A reprobate sinner hardly worth her loyalty. 'A Crown Knight.'

She gasped, resenting the sting of accusation. 'That is not true.'

'Is it not?' He shook his head at her. 'You should have come to me, Eva, the moment you were informed of whatever plan this man had devised for you. After all, I was led to believe we were *friends*.'

'You must comprehend that he said he would hurt Marguerite if I told you.'

'Even so, you could have come to me.'

'I could not risk it,' Eva whispered, frowning. 'My decision tonight was never about you or me, but preventing a young innocent maid from coming to harm.'

'I do comprehend it. But I thought that you might believe I would do everything in my power to help you. To protect you.'

'There is no certainty in that.'

'There is no certainty in anything, Eva—not on the battlefield nor in the work I do, other than having faith and belief that another person you might trust implicitly would be there for you.'

And, just like that, it dawned on her. 'That is what you have, with Sir Warin de Talmont and Savaric Fitz Leonard? That is what binds you together, beyond the ties of friendship?'

He did not answer her but the shift in his

manner and the change in his stance confirmed her suspicions. Either way, she did not want to consider his words, knowing the truth in them. Eva had never found it easy to trust another, and she had never had anyone willing to self-lessly do her bidding. What Nicholas had said felt as unfamiliar to her as those lessons to act the noblewoman.

'There's more,' she muttered, needing to change the direction of the discourse. 'The man had a small circular medallion around his neck with some of Marguerite's hair tied to it. It had two entwined snakes and above it, etched into the silver, was the word *Renaisser.*'

'Reborn…?' Nicholas frowned.

'Yes, I thought it strange.'

As was the sudden reappearance of the man who had sired Nicholas—his father. And he was certain that this timely reunion must have some-thing to do with The Duo Dracones. God, but when he thought about the man and his brand of betrayal and treachery, and the possibility that his father might be consorting with a trai-torous group or even be part of them—Nicho-las had trouble even imagining it. It made his head spin when he considered what his father had become.

'Do you believe it to be his name?' Eva muttered, pulling his attention back to their discourse.

There was no question that the man who had danced with Eva was part of The Duo Dracones, based on what she had described, but *Renaisser*? Indeed, this was a new development.

'I do. One that was probably bestowed on him. One that might determine who he is within their organisation.' He nodded grimly, deciding that he would entrust her with further information. 'There was another man who we discovered earlier this year, and on his demise we found that not only did he have links with the group but he also wore a similar medallion around his neck, etched with an equally strange name. In his case it was *Agneau*.'

Nicholas had wondered whether this marked some manner of hierarchy within The Duo Dracones organisation and with this new information from Eva it now seemed far more likely.

'Agneau?' she muttered. 'As in lamb?'

'Yes.' The man in question had ended his own life, just like every member of The Duo Dracones who they had caught, severing all ties and the possibility for Nicholas and his brethren to find out more about them.

Her eyes widened. 'Then mayhap it was a reference to being a sacrificial lamb?'

Clever. His Eva was always quick to grasp his meaning.

His Eva...?

Nicholas nearly stumbled as he quickly dismissed the notion. No, that could never be. She could never be his. And why did such a notion make his chest ache as much as it did?

Chapter Sixteen

Nicholas looked up to find Eva standing close by and studying him intently.

'Yes, I think that it could very well refer to the same sacrificial lamb you might hear in a priest's sermon.' Which meant those within The Duo Dracones who deigned to be lambs were probably expendable until they proved their worth. This, of course, begged the question what rank *Renaisser* alluded to, or what in fact he had been reborn to.

To think that the bastard—this *Renaisser*—had laid his hands on Eva, danced with her, conversed with her, before damn well threatening her, made Nicholas's blood roar.

None of this sat well with him. The difficult truth was that Eva Siward had not divulged the information she had gleaned about this threatening predicament, preferring, as always, to shoulder the burden alone. Always alone—and in this they were alike. But at least Nicholas had the friendship and fealty of his fellow Knights Fortitude brethren, just as she had rightly deduced. But what of Eva? Had the woman ever had anyone who fought for her? Protected her? Loved and cared for her?

No, Eva seemingly had no one, except for mayhap the Rook, who was now dead. Other than him, there was the young maid, Marguerite, who Eva felt responsible for, and who The Duo Dracones were using to do their bidding—not unlike Nicholas, he thought grimly. Lord, but they had all been guilty of using these two young women for their own ends, trapping them in the middle of this murky, dangerous world.

What a disaster.

And yet Nicholas had been a fool to believe that this connection with Eva was more than it was. But all it had been from the very first was a transaction—it could only be about the fifty marks of silver and nothing more.

Why had he forgotten that? Was it because he had got close to her? Because he had taken her to his bed? It had all been foolish beyond measure, when this arrangement would soon reach a resolution one way or another, forcing them to part ways. And why did such a thought hurt?

Nicholas had to stop this wave upon wave of emotion hitting him like a damn boulder. He was wholly unprepared for it and what it meant, knowing that all he wanted was to wrap his arms around her shoulders and protect her. Even if he also wanted to howl in frustration at the same time.

He took a deep breath and turned his attention to the woman who was tying him in all sorts of uncomfortable knots.

'What did the man, this *Renaisser,* want from you, Eva?' He frowned, taking a step back. 'What plan did you agree to?'

She worried her bottom lip. 'I cannot disclose it, Nicholas.'

'You cannot or will not?'

She closed her eyes and sighed before answering.

'He said he would hurt her if I spoke to you about it. And I cannot allow that.'

'Listen to me.' He grasped her shoulders as he looked down at her. 'I will not allow anything or anyone to endanger you, or Mistress Marguerite for that matter. Do you hear me?'

'Yes, but he said that…'

'Did you comprehend me?' He squared his shoulders. 'On my honour, I will protect you. Both of you.'

'Yes, I believe that you would.' She sent him the ghost of a smile and shrugged. 'I have never had anyone champion me in such a fierce manner.'

'Well, you do now.'

He wanted to kiss her—he wanted to convey that he would always be there should she need him, but Nicholas knew it would not do. It would not serve to confuse the situation more than he already had.

He took a deep breath, dropping his outstretched arms to his sides. 'Tell me, Eva. What have you agreed to do in exchange for your young friend?'

She lifted her head, meeting his gaze. 'I am to meet him at dawn, after stealing a personal belonging of Hubert de Burgh's.'

'To what end?'

'That I do not know, but I swear that is the extent of my part in it.'

Nicholas believed her. But that was not much of a plan. It revealed it to be far more of a cobbled-together desperate attempt to implicate his liege lord for a reason known only by The Duo Dracones themselves. Either way, their desperation made it all the more perilous, especially for Eva.

'I realise that and will do all that I can to facilitate anything you want.'

She blinked. 'You are going to help me steal from Hubert de Burgh?'

A slow smile spread across his lips. 'No, I am going to help you pretend to steal from Hubert de Burgh.'

She reached out and cupped his jaw. 'You and your penchant for pretending.'

He wanted desperately to cover her hand with his larger one, to pull her into his arms and erase the worry from her brow, but it would never do. He clenched and unclenched his hand. 'You and your penchant for stealing. And dressed as a boy, I might add.'

She nodded. 'Tell me what you would have me do.'

'Good, I am glad you have asked me that.' He walked her back towards the door.

'Where are you taking me?'

'To make a plan, but we are not going to accomplish this alone.' He raised a brow. 'I hope you understand me, Eva Siward. We are to do this together. As one.'

There was no other in Eva's life who made her feel the way that Nicholas D'Amberly did.

He cared for her, protected her and made her feel oh, so safe.

But she could not ponder on any of this now—that could wait for another time. For now, she had to consider the danger that Marguerite was in—and the precarious situation that she was in.

One thing was true; Eva now had every faith in Nicholas and his determination to do right, knowing that he would do everything he could to bring about a favourable outcome. Yet that did not mean that she was not apprehensive about what was required of her to secure Marguerite's release.

God give her strength.

What if it did not go to plan? What if it all unravelled around her? What then?

Eva might be used to the danger of getting caught when she had used to thieve for Simon the Rook, but never anything like this, where another's life depended on her skill and ability. No, she must not give in to these doubts.

'Are you ready?' Nicholas gave her an encouraging smile as he escorted her out of Hubert de Burgh's ante-chamber after their privy meeting planning exactly what each member of their group would do.

Eva had noticed every detail in which Nicholas, Warin de Talmont and Savaric Fitz Leonard exchanged views, discussed ideas, disagreed and planned everything with surprised interest. Their accord obvious. Their friendship close. Their bond extremely strong. It was more their affinity and rapport, which was strikingly more like brothers than she would otherwise have envisaged. Even the usually laconic Savaric Fitz Leonard seemed subdued and far more ashen of face, with a sombre outlook. Eva had not been sure whether he was brooding for Marguerite or concerned for his friend.

Either way, she was glad that Nicholas had these men in his life who clearly looked out for him, and would still be there once she had left. Their fealty to one another had not escaped her notice as they huddled in a circle and placed a hand on one another's shoulder. Or how they had quietly recounted a motto: *'Pro Rex. Pro Deus. Pro fide. Pro honoris.'*

They said this together as though it were chant when soldiers rallied, raising their spirits before going into battle. Then, one by one, each man left quietly, leaving just Nicholas and Eva.

Well, if these men were prepared for what was to come, then so was she.

'Indeed.' Eva nodded, her heart tripping over itself. 'I am ready.'

'Good.' Nicholas took her hand in his and guided her back through the narrow, cold hall and turned the corner, leading them to the spiral staircase. 'You remember everything that was discussed and everything we agreed to?'

'I do.'

Nicholas grabbed a flaming torch as they started down the steps. 'Do not forget that I, along with the others, will be close by, Eva. You shall not be alone, sweetheart.'

'Yes. That is most comforting.' And it was.

They continued to make their way down the cold stone stairwell but now a palpable silence had descended on them, with an uneasiness that began to seep into Eva's bones. How she hated this—the unknown—and although she had encountered this anticipation and even thrill before she would ready herself for thievery on London's streets, this was wholly different. Another's life had not been at stake, which made this predicament far more tense and dangerous.

By the time they reached the bottom her hand began to shake uncontrollably.

'All will be well, I promise.' He caught her hand, squeezing it encouragingly.

'How can you be so certain?'

'Faith, Eva.' He tucked a stray lock of her hair behind her ear, his touch sending a ripple of awareness through her. 'Faith that you will do your part with aplomb, which I believe you shall. Faith that I shall be there when you need me. And faith that you know I will come to you.'

'I hope you are right.'

'Listen to me. I know you shall prevail,' he murmured. 'Now, do you have Hubert de Burgh's gold chain and insignia?'

'Yes.' She dangled a leather pouch in front of him. 'I have my trusty pouch.'

He sent her a flash of a smile before frowning. 'You will take care, and remember that we will not be far behind you. In fact, I shall be making my way out of the castle through the many underground passages here, shortly.'

She nodded. 'Yes.'

'It's time then. Ready?'

'I believe so.'

'Then Godspeed, Eva.'

Unable to respond, she nodded again, sinking her teeth into her bottom lip before turning around to face the entrance of the keep. Glancing around one more time over her shoulder, she noticed that Nicholas was no longer there. It was time indeed.

Taking a big gulp of air, Eva stepped outside and exhaled, noticing the hues of light pinks and coral bursting through the inky sky and heralding the arrival of a new day. A day that might change everything. A day which might usher in the unexpected. Eva hoped that whatever that was would be of good. Still dressed in a boy's attire, she closed her eyes, taking a moment before reopening them again and climbing down the steps, making her way to the inner bailey.

She passed by the blacksmith, busy hammering away a long piece of metal. He glanced up and gave her a small nod as she followed the path leading to the gatehouse. Here she passed two carpenters who were carrying a large plank of wood. They too stopped and acknowledged her, as Nicholas had promised they would do. Not that Eva knew whether these men served under Nicholas and the others or they had been recruited for this very purpose. But, either way, she was glad that they were there to keep an eye on her as she made her progress through the castle. It made the butterflies in her stomach ease a little, knowing she was being protected in this small way.

She made her way through the stone gatehouse and followed the pathway to the side of the curtain wall that led to the royal stables. Something here, however, did not feel as it should. She could feel it in her bones, making the fine hairs on the back of her neck rise. It was an unnerving quietness, reminding her of the stillness before a storm broke.

A breeze gently fluttered the hem of her cloak as she took tentative steps towards the entrance but again no, the only sounds she could hear were the shuffling noises of the horses within.

Strange. She gulped, swallowing down her concern as she stepped inside the large timber-framed stables.

'Is anyone here?' She raised her voice and it echoed around the space.

She blinked as her eyes adjusted to the darkness, noting that, apart from the horses stabled along the sides of the long structure, there seemed to be no one else present.

'I have come from the keep,' she said inanely, hoping that she might gain a response. 'Where... where are you?' Her breath hitched in her throat as she slowly realised that the man who had danced with her, the man *Renaisser*, who had made his demands, and had to be part of the nefarious group that Nicholas had spoken of, did not seem to be here—and nor did Marguerite.

Where in heaven's name were the stable hands? A chill rippled down her spine as the swish of an arrow flew past her and lodged itself in the wooden door. It was no ordinary arrow either but a flaming torch arrow which impaled the wooden beam, before one after the other flew past, haphazardly striking different parts of the timber-clad stables and hayloft at the top of the wood-beamed roof.

It was a trap! Eva was in no doubt that the perpetrators were intent on starting a fire in the hope of leaving destruction and death in their wake. After all, the stables housed some of the most valuable destriers, palfreys and coursers in the land. And if these majestic animals perished then it would halt the progress of the royal party and even weaken it for a while, forcing the court to be stranded in Guildford.

The horses tethered inside began to become agitated and skittish as they jumped and made distressed noises. Eva had to get them out of there, especially as there seemed to be no one nearby to help her. And she had no time to fetch anyone else, as the fire would soon spread far too rapidly. Her hope was that once the locals working in the bailey would see the fire they would rush and help her, damp it down before it spread everywhere.

She quickly opened every wooden gate of every stall housing groups of horses together and slapped their rumps, encouraging the animals to gallop out of the building.

'Come on, go. Leave!' She continued to release the horses as she began to feel the effects of a fire that was spreading in various pockets around the stables. It would not take long for it all to go up in an inferno. She would need to get out of there soon.

'Eva!' a voice belonging to Nicholas D'Amberly bellowed from the furthest end of the stables as he rushed towards her. 'Watch out!'

Watch out? What on earth did he mean? Eva did not have to wait long to find out. She snapped her head back round to find a man with a black hooded cloak flapping behind him riding a horse that was hurtling towards her.

Eva scrambled backwards, just about avoiding the rider as he continued past her and galloped towards Nicholas instead. Oh, Lord, it was Nicholas D'Amberly that the black-cloaked rider was after now, not her. She had merely been used to lure him to the stables. Why? None of this made sense. Unless, of course, he was after both of them. In which case it would be the two of them against a lone rider.

Eva took a deep breath and chased after them, watching as Nicholas pulled the rider off his saddle and punched him in the jaw. She sprinted towards the entrance of the stable as Nicholas became engaged in hand-to-hand combat with the rider—or, rather, the man who had threatened her the previous night—*Renaisser*.

The fire in the stables began to spread, making the horses still trapped in their stalls draw out high-pitched whinnies, kicking out in distress. She stopped to unbolt the last few gates, allowing the animals to leap and rush out of the burning building.

'Watch out, Nicholas!' she yelled as a bale of smouldering hay fell from the loft above and just about missed the two men. Eva turned and sprinted towards them as Nicholas threw a heavy punch, knocking the other man to the ground. He unsheathed his sword and pointed it at *Renaisser* when his young squire, John, opened the gates and ran to his side.

A sense of relief washed through her but as Eva continued to make her way towards them at the far end of the stable house, this turned to horror as she watched the young lad strike his master with the metal hilt of his sword, catching him off-guard. Nicholas lost his footing, dropping the sword to his side, allowing *Renaisser* to scramble to his feet, grab the weapon and point it now at Nicholas.

'No!' Eva screamed, just as the man was

about to thrust the blade into Nicholas's chest.
She drew her dagger from the inside of her
boot and clasped it tightly. 'No! You touch him
and you shall find this dagger wedged in your
heart!' Eva approached them cautiously, holding the hilt at shoulder height, ready to hurl it
at the man.

'You're bluffing, Eva Siward.' She was, but
Renaisser did not know that.

'Shall we put that to the test?' This had to be
the most convincing performance she had ever
given for the man to believe her false bravado.
'If you let Nicholas go, then you can have me.'

'*What?* No, Eva!' Nicholas bellowed as the
fire spread around them.

Eva ignored Nicholas as she homed in on
Renaisser, aiming the dagger at his chest. 'What
is it to be? Choose now or find out how good I
really am with a dagger.'

'Very well.' The man dropped the sword to
his side and rushed towards her.

'No, Eva!' Nicholas roared as he elbowed
John, winding his traitorous squire, and rushed
towards them. But Eva took no heed—she could
not risk him getting hurt.

Renaisser grabbed the reins of the last
courser making its way out of the stables and
mounted the animal. He pulled the reins, allow-

ing him to scoop Eva up in his arms and gallop through the stables, kicking Nicholas in his stomach before breaking through, out onto the bailey, as more and more of the locals rushed towards the stables with buckets. The horse reared up before galloping at speed through the castle gates and out into the demesne lands. Eva was held tightly as they rode out at breakneck speed, making their way out to the vast green pastures and gently sloping hills.

'Well played, mistress,' *Renaisser* sneered. 'And if you hope to survive this horse ride, then I would advise you not to jostle too much, lest you might find yourself thrown off this magnificent animal. Not that I care too much, but we do have unfinished business, you and I.'

She clung on for dear life as she adjusted her position on the saddle. 'Where is Marguerite?' she muttered, trying to catch her breath. 'You reneged on the agreement we made.'

'And I told you that any agreement would be forfeited if you involved Nicholas D'Amberly and the Knights of the Crown, which you did not take heed of, just as I knew you would not,' he said coldly. 'The fault of this lies with you, not I.'

'No, I think that you always planned to set fire to those stables, in an attempt to cause a diversion. And I think you meant to draw Nicholas to the stables, so that you could hope to dispatch him there.'

'Is that so?'

'Yes. And in the ensuing mayhem you could leave the castle without further difficulty. As you just have.'

'You are far too astute for your own good, Eva Siward,' he said in a clipped tone. 'Rather like that fool Simon the Rook, who similarly tried to deceive me, but found, rather to his cost, that anyone who attempts such a feat always comes to an unfortunate end.'

Dear God...

'You were the one responsible for his downfall. You killed him.'

The man's lack of response spoke of his culpability. And when she considered that she had mistakenly believed that the responsibility of the Rook's murder had lain elsewhere. But then, Eva had been mistaken on many things in the past and knew that regrets, however, were futile.

'You are going to kill me too, is that it?' She released a shaky breath, knowing that his answer was unnecessary. His intentions were evident and she did not have long to think of a way to extricate herself from this predicament.

'Where is Marguerite?' she asked again. 'What have you done to her?'

'You shall soon be reunited with your friend, as soon as I lose these belligerent knights.'

Eva exhaled in relief, knowing, even before she turned around to confirm it, that the man she had lost her heart to, the man whom she now knew for certain she loved, had come after her, along with his Knights of the Crown.

Chapter Seventeen

Nicholas had never felt as angry and frustrated as he had when the man, this *Renaisser*, had whisked Eva from the burning remains of the stables. Stables which the bastard had set ablaze after she had saved his life! And naturally in the commotion, with the skittish horses jumping and stampeding to get out, and many from both the castle and within the bailey rushing to the centre of the mayhem and confusion, he had been too late to catch up with them.

Damn, but Nicholas had been caught wanting when he had sworn on his honour to Eva that he would keep her safe. Indeed, it had been the other way around. It had been Eva who had come to his rescue and he'd never been more surprised. No one, outside of his Knights Fortitude brethren, had ever done that for him—and especially not a woman. God, but she had been magnificent. And he would do right by her. He would give his life to get her out of the dangerous situation she now found herself in.

Nicholas had managed to catch a grey courser in the bailey and had followed Eva and *Renaisser* on horseback, signalling to his brethren to follow suit. They had galloped on the cobbled path through the stone gatehouse and gained on them as they rode to the open fields of the demesne land of the castle.

Nicholas leant forward, gripping the reins as he heard the hooves pounding the ground behind him, knowing that Warin de Talmont and Savaric Fitz Leonard were nearby. They would do it—they would be upon them soon.

He pondered on his squire's betrayal, unable to come to terms with John's part in all this. How had it come to this? What had made the lad turn against him?

He growled, pushing the animal forward as they sped beside Eva and the man who had snatched her.

'You are surrounded, *Renaisser*.' He gained satisfaction knowing the bastard had not realised they knew his alias. 'Indeed we know your given name.'

The man remained silent and whipped his horse to race ahead even faster, pulling the animal to go right and then left, trying to put them off course. They continued to ride south at high speed, recklessly flying across the open fields, pastures and woodland that opened to the small hamlet of Eashing. The man pushed his horse further until he reached the grassy banks of the River Wey.

In the distance Nicholas could see that the man had dismounted with a jump and dragged Eva with him, taking her along the pathway.

Damn…

Nicholas and the others followed them on foot, leaving their horses beside the riverbank.

'You are never going to get away from us. There are more of us than you,' Nicholas bellowed from behind. 'Why not be done with this and put a stop to all of it now?'

Yet again, the man did not respond, yanking Eva with him, along the pathway that ran along the sloping riverbank, narrowing on one side with the dense coppices and shrubbery. It opened out to a dirt track that led to a double-arched stone bridge.

Nicholas noted another two figures standing by the bridge. One was a man, seemingly his associate—the *ordinary* one with the strange pale eyes who Eva had initially met at the inn—

and the other was a young frightened-looking woman with fiery red hair.

'Marguerite!' Eva cried ahead, struggling in vain to free herself from the man's grip. 'Let go of me.'

Nicholas, along with his two friends, drew closer as Eva twisted in her assailant's clutches, managing somehow to bend her knees and draw her elbows up and then ram them backwards into the man's stomach, winding him. The man's tight grip fell away and in the small time she had gained for herself Eva scrambled away. He tried to catch her again and failed, and she managed to run to Nicholas's side.

He clasped either side of her shoulders, his eyes raking her from the top of her head all the way down to her boots.

'Are you well? Are you unharmed?' The words tumbled out in a panicked rush.

'Yes…but…' She gave him a pleading look. 'Marguerite…'

They both looked back around and watched *Renaisser* and his accomplice draw out their swords from their scabbards and point them at them, while still clutching the maid, who looked as though she had been drained of every drop of blood.

His friends, Warin de Talmont and Savaric

Fitz Leonard, stepped to stand either side of him and in unison they all slowly drew their swords as well, taking a step forward together, pushing the two men back, making them retreat onto the bridge.

He knew Eva was standing a little apart from them but prayed that she would continue to stay back and not throw herself into the fray.

'Let the maid go,' Nicholas said evenly. 'She has nothing to do with any of this.'

Beside him, Savaric Fitz Leonard bristled with barely contained anger. God, but Nicholas had no time to wonder at his friend's strange behaviour today or even at the banquet yesterday.

'I think not.' *Renaisser* shook his head as he clamped a hand around the maid's wrist. 'This woman might prove useful, especially since you valiant and brave Knights of the Crown seem so invested in her.'

Nicholas, Warin and Savaric advanced slowly towards them onto the bridge, each one of them knowing that any rash move could prove disastrous.

'Come now, what need do you have with the maid?'

'Ah, but the question is—what is it that *you* want with her?' he sneered. 'After all, she is only just a maid, even if she is fair. And such beauty can tempt a man into damnation.'

He heard Savaric mutter an oath under his breath, his rage emanating from him in waves.

Hell's teeth, what was wrong with the man? He knew the code by which they lived, and knew how perilous it was to expose any kind of emotion. It was a soldier's rule, a knight's tenet. And at such a moment it was a weakness they could hardly afford.

'She means nothing to us.' Nicholas's voice remained steady and even nonchalant, although he could feel Eva's outrage at hearing him utter such words. 'But I will not have the maid used as a bargaining tool.'

'Tell me, as you will know better than I, but what price would such beauty fetch?' The man grazed a finger down Marguerite's face as she tried to pull away. 'If she means nothing to you then you will not mind if we do this.' He nodded at his associate, who pulled the young maid in front of him and clutched one ugly hand around her neck, with the other he groped the maid along her shoulder, down her curves, making the poor maid tremble in shock.

God's blood.

He sensed Savaric's anger, his temper hanging by a thread, and yet his huge brooding friend remained silent, even though the situation could hardly continue to endure as it was.

'Take your hand off her,' his friend growled.

'Or you would do what, exactly?'

'Oh, allow me to consider for a moment,' Savaric drawled with a shrug, giving a disinterested impression. 'Tear you from limb to limb.' Yet the hard glint in his eyes gave him away.

The other man simply smirked.

'What is it that you want?' Nicholas muttered through gritted teeth, ignoring the provocation, and took another step closer towards them.

'Her...' Renaisser pointed at Eva with the blade of his sword. 'I shall exchange this maid with one who does matter—who does seem to have a lot to do with all of this and who exchanged her life for yours, Sir Nicholas.'

He heard Eva gasp from behind. 'And what exactly would you want with her?'

'Eva Siward knows that a debt is owed from when she was hired by us.'

'I did precisely what you hired me to do,' Eva muttered.

'But was then thwarted by us—*me*, to be precise,' Nicholas growled.

'Felicitations, Sir Nicholas,' the man said sardonically. 'Nevertheless, a debt must be paid and paid this instant, especially since this woman you are protecting not only reneged on an agreement but became a turncoat. That is something quite unacceptable to us.'

Warin de Talmont raised a brow. 'Ah, I presume you talk of The Duo Dracones?'

A spark of surprised anger flickered in the man's eyes but he did not respond. Clearly, the bastard had not expected that.

'What will it be, Knights of the Crown?' He spoke evenly, nodding at Eva. 'An exchange—one maid for another. Neither of whom clearly matter to you good sirs.'

A muscle leapt in his jaw. 'No. That is not acceptable to us. We would only accept the release of the maid, along with your total surrender.'

'Would you?' The man's hand tightened around Marguerite's throat, making her squeal. 'It is a disappointment when one cannot quite gain what one truly wants, eh, Sir Nicholas. For we wanted that pouch clutched in Eva Siward's hand, which she was supposed to bring to us alone, in exchange for her friend. But alas she brought you—all of you—and once again reneged on an agreement we made.'

Eva threw the pouch and it landed on the dirt track on the bridge. 'Here, take it. It's yours, but let her go.' He was proud of Eva, who was standing up to these dangerous men and showing her steely resolve, even though Nicholas could only imagine the depth of her apprehension at this moment.

'No.' The man shook his head and looked at her coldly. 'That will not do. The content of the pouch is no longer pertinent to what we need or want, now that you have involved Knights of the Crown, Eva Siward.'

'Then what do you want?'

'I believe I have been perfectly clear.'

Nicholas pointed his sword at him. 'Then we are at an impasse, are we not, *Renaisser*?'

'If that is the path you wish to choose—one of unpredictability, mayhem and even death—then very well, so be it. And do not forget that death is something that we willingly choose rather than betraying our cause. Mayhap that is a virtue you could all benefit from learning.'

'Which is what, exactly? What is this cause that you would die for?'

The man shook his head. 'You would never understand, not when you have pledged yourself to a false boy king, spawned from the devil himself, and who now surrounds himself with false men, doing his false bidding.'

'You refer to Hubert de Burgh then?'

The man sneered instead of answering him.

'And who would be the rightful king, in your mind?'

Again, he was met with a stony silence. The man had seemingly said all he was prepared to…for now. They took in the measure of one another, just as Nicholas reminded himself of the need for caution, since the bastards still held onto Mistress Marguerite.

'No!' Eva bellowed. 'Wait!'

Nicholas snapped his head around to meet her gaze and gave her a small shake of the head. Surely she could not be considering acquiescing to these men's demands and sacrificing herself for the sake of her friend. Again, she would give her own life for another?

No. He would not allow it. There had to be another way to overcome these men that would not result in what the man had predicted. If anything, the man wanted mayhem and death. It was preferable to surrendering and being tried as traitors, as they would be. Eva gave him a nod as her shoulders sagged in resignation.

'No, Eva!' he said through gritted teeth. 'Stay back.'

She took no heed of his warning and without taking a moment to consider her actions she took a tentative step forward towards the men—members of The Duo Dracones.

God, but why did the woman have to be so honourable, so damn brave? Why did she believe that she should always be the one to bear any difficulties and hardship on her own? She needed to share her burden *with him*.

As she passed him her fingers brushed against his and, just as she took another step, he reached out quickly and grabbed hold of her wrist.

'Let me go, Nicholas,' she hissed, twisting around, trying to free herself from his tight grip.

'I cannot let you do this, Eva,' he whispered. 'They would otherwise hurt you.'

'As opposed to Marguerite? Who is completely innocent in all of this.' She let out a shaky breath.

'I know, but trust me, sweetheart,' he said in a low voice that only she could hear.

'What do you have in mind?'

His response was a wink and the smallest of smiles.

'Do hurry, will you, mistress.' *Renaisser*'s wry voice betrayed a hint of frustration. 'After you resolve your lovers' tiff, of course.'

The man holding onto Marguerite smirked. 'Aye, otherwise, this lovely piece might end up with a scar or two that might spoil her beautiful face.' He ran a finger across her cheek. 'And her lush, comely body.' His hand groped her curves again.

'Hell and damnation, I told you not to touch her, or was I not clear enough before?' Savaric Fitz Leonard roared.

The other man grinned inanely and had the audacity to repeat his repugnant actions.

This, of course, proved far too much for Savaric, who lunged at the man, catching him, without any due regard for anything or anyone around him. He was behaving out of character and the whole situation suddenly erupted, descending into the mayhem *Renaisser* had predicted. But then that was what the man had wanted. He had known that the odds were against him and this would be the only way out of this predicament.

Nicholas quickly exchanged a glance with Warin de Talmont and turned to face Eva. 'Stay here.'

'But I...'

'Please, sweetheart, allow me to do what I avowed. Let me do your bidding, Eva. Let me protect you, as you protected me earlier.'

She nodded as Nicholas motioned for her to stand back while he stepped into the fray.

Nicholas strode towards *Renaisser*, narrowing his eyes at him, his jaw clenched. This would end now. By God, the man had caused enough chaos and disorder.

He sensed his fellow Knights Fortitude brethren caught in a similar fight with the other assailant as he thrust his sword forward, crossing it with *Renaisser*, who struck back defensively. Stepping forward again, he lunged at the man, striking his sword with a powerful blow, changing the angle as he slashed back and forward, gauging the man's mettle. And though *Renaisser* had been trained in the art of sword fighting, it was soon clear to Nicholas that the man was no match for him. Being a bigger, taller and stronger man, his pace, agility and the weight of his strikes were all far superior to *Renaisser*'s.

'I hope you are not too overwhelmed by a mere Knight of the Crown, *Renaisser*.' His lip curled at one corner. 'I would not wish for this to end so soon when I would much prefer to give you the thrashing you so deserve, especially after what happened in the stables.'

'I wonder, do you always bestow such concern for your opponents D'Amberly?' The man raised a brow. 'Or is it just me?'

Nicholas struck out and caught the man's cheek, drawing a small slash. 'Only you.'

'Then I am honoured,' the man bit out, rubbing the newly made scar on his face.

'I very much doubt that.' Nicholas spun around and bent his knees so quickly he nicked the man's knee, tearing his hose. 'Honour is something that you very much lack. Which reminds me, how did you manage to get to my squire, by the by?'

'Nothing easier. However, I am not the one to claim it but your dear mama—Maud D'Amberly.'

'What?' he muttered, faltering.

Nicholas had known from the moment that his father had arrived at the banquet the previous night it had not been a mere coincidence, but this was more than he had expected. He had never envisaged that Maud could seemingly be involved with The Duo Dracones. Which meant that his father was also involved—and, if not, the man could very well be in danger.

'I do not believe you.'

'Believe what you wish, but it did not take her long to convince your squire to become a turncoat, Sir Nicholas. After all, you might know of Maud D'Amberly's penchant for young lads well enough.' How the hell did the man know of this? 'Although it helped that we have the boy's mother and sisters in our care.'

'You mean that you have them hostage? In which case, the boy's loyalty to his family makes me understand his actions more.'

Yet Nicholas wished that John had come to him with this. He could have helped him.

Renaisser lunged forward. 'How touching, and you must be averse to that, Sir Nicholas, since you lack the familial fealty that a father must surely expect his son and heir to possess.'

Nicholas stilled for just a blink of an eye, unable to grasp the man's implication. 'What did you say?'

'I believe you heard me.' *Renaisser* used this moment of weakness to attack, strike and parry, forcing Nicholas to retreat into a defensive stance. The man's smile twisted into a sneer. 'But to take one's mother-by-marriage to bed must be even more dishonourable, do you not think? Some might say it to be a greater sin.'

'You know nothing of it.' His nostrils flared, his shoulders squared as Nicholas damped down the surge of outrage. He knew the man was goading him. 'In truth, the sin that you speak of belongs to another. Not that I give a damn about what a bastard like you thinks.'

'You might not give a damn, as you say, then to know that convincing your father to betray you was surprisingly easy. The man detests you, Sir Nicholas, with every part of his being. Strange for a man to loathe his heir as much as he does you.'

And there it was. Confirmation of all of his suspicions—unless the man was bluffing.

'I care nothing for that.'

Renaisser raised his sword arm to lunge forward, but Nicholas was expecting the move. 'Do you not? Then you would not care to know that the worthless man kneels at the hem of his wife—worships the very ground she walks on. Such weakness in a man can only inspire disaster.' He flicked his chin at Eva. 'And in that you are far more like your reprobate father than you realise.'

Nicholas leant back against the wooden railing of the bridge for leverage, before kicking *Renaisser* in the stomach when he came at him with another attacking thrust. He rose his sword and roared at him, before swiping it at him in a fluid move again and again, until he fell backwards on the ground, putting his hands up in surrender. He would not need to explain his feelings to this man. Eva Siward was nothing like his father's wife.

'No, you are wrong. We are nothing alike.' Nicholas stood over the man, crouched at the edge of the bridge, the blade of his sword pointing at him, and shook his head slowly. 'Now do you yield and submit or do you want to continue because I can assure you that I can keep going like this. I haven't even broken into a sweat!'

Renaisser gave him a baleful, malevolent glare but nodded as he acquiesced.

Breathing a sigh of relief, Nicholas turned his head to find that the other man had also submitted to Savaric Fitz Leonard, who held him by the scruff of his neck and was shouting at him, 'You will never touch her, do you hear?'

'Yes, yes, just don't hurt me.' The man cowered. 'Please.'

'God give me strength! You are nothing but a pathetic miscreant, picking on a woman half your size.' Savaric grimaced in disgust. 'And the only reason I will let you continue to breathe is so that you would furnish me with more information regarding The Duo Dracones.' He pulled the man to his feet. 'Now speak!'

The man opened his mouth but, instead of doing as he was bid, he started to chant, with *Renaisser* joining in, their voices getting louder and more impassioned.

'Stop it! Stop this incessant noise.'

If anything, the strange chanting became more and more raucous and it was then, in the commotion, that the man somehow pushed himself into the blade of the dagger that Savaric Fitz Leonard had been holding, preferring to have a blade pierce through his chest than answer any questions.

Nicholas quickly glanced back around to *Renaisser*, but in the short interlude the man had stepped on the wooden barrier and thrown himself into the moving river below, and was swimming away before long.

Damn, damn, damn.

'Please tell me the man is not dead,' Nicholas muttered, rubbing his forehead in frustration.

Warin de Talmont felt for a pulse, closed the man's eyes and stood, giving his head a shake. 'I wish I could, my friend, but unfortunately the bastard is indeed dead.'

'While that might be a relief, we have once again found our investigation stalled. Once again we have failed in apprehending members of The Duo Dracones or learning more about them,' he said bitterly.

Warin shook his head. 'Not quite. At least this time we have met with one of their members who remains alive and is too high up in the organisation to be expendable, unlike this man.'

'*Renaisser.*' Nicholas clenched his jaw. 'And next time he will not get away so easily.'

'We shall be ready. And do not forget we also have your father, his wife and your squire.'

'As if I could ever forget their treachery. God, but John…' He shook his head, reflecting on his squire in dismay. 'That is another matter altogether.'

Warin nodded. 'Come. There's nothing for it today, however. Let's get back to the castle and give our report to de Burgh, not that the man will be happy. We need to inform him that these bastards are still intent on treason and on removing King Henry from power as well as the men who serve him and whom they consider to be false.'

Men such as Hubert de Burgh himself. 'But they will not prevail.'

'No, they shall not and at least we have foiled their attempts here at Guildford. Come, let us head back.'

At that moment Nicholas wanted to extinguish the feelings that were coursing through his blood, from fury to relief. He turned around and locked eyes with the woman who had been at the centre of all of this— Eva, who looked weary, exhausted, if not a little frightened.

'Not yet, Warin. Give me a moment, if you will.'

Chapter Eighteen

Eva stood, unable to move after what had come to pass. She had watched Nicholas's extraordinary stealth and skill, fighting sword against sword with *Renaisser*, and showing his mettle as he easily overwhelmed the man. But what no one had expected was how *Renaisser* had managed to get away, while his accomplice—the man who had hired her to steal from the outset—threw himself onto a dagger, all so that he would not reveal anything further regarding their organisation. The whole incident had been shocking to witness.

Yet as *Renaisser* made his escape and the inevitable disappointment that Nicholas must have felt sank in, Eva could not help but feel relief that, for her and for Marguerite, it was over. The danger that they had faced had been averted. She would have her life back and be able to have the relative freedom and autonomy that she had always dreamed of. What she had always longed for from the start.

Yet why was it at the very moment that this reprieve had occurred and the possibility of fortune was within her grasp, Eva felt hollow and so wretched? She could not fathom it. Mayhap it was because the pent-up emotion and apprehension had simply dissipated now that it was all over, leaving her only with a sense of relief and nothing more.

Her eyes darted in every direction before settling on Nicholas as he strode towards her with purpose. She had not realised that she had been holding her breath all that time, but as he walked towards her she could finally breathe again.

He reached out his hand to touch her but decided to curl it into a fist and drop it to his side. 'Are you well?'

'Yes, I thank you.'

'Are you certain?'

'Of course.'

'He did not hurt you?'

'No.'

'Because if he hurt you I would…'

'He did not.'

'If he hurt you Eva…'

'I assure you, he did not hurt me.' She gave him what she hoped was a decisive nod. 'Truly.'

He stared at her for a long moment before he smiled, relief emanating from him.

'You saved my life, Eva Siward.'

'As you saved mine, Nicholas D'Amberly.'

'Thank you.'

She nodded again, unable to say more, and fixed her gaze on her friend, who was slumped on the ground, close to the body of the man who had abducted her.

'I must go to her.'

'Wait.' Nicholas stilled her. 'Just a moment.'

They both watched as Savaric Fitz Leonard moved towards Marguerite, who was trembling uncontrollably. He picked her up as though she weighed nary a thing and took her away from the ugliness on the bridge. He muttered softly to her, reassuring, soothing and comforting, while gently caressing her with the back of his hand.

It was achingly tender and endearing. And once he set Marguerite down he lingered for a moment as though they two were quite alone, before he bowed and, without saying another word, he left her to address his friends.

'I shall venture south, following the river

upstream in the vain hope that I might catch *Renaisser*.'

'I shall come with you.' Nicholas nodded but his friend stalled him.

'You are better served escorting the maids back, D'Amberly, and seeing what has come about with your father and his wife. Besides, I am not hopeful of gaining on *Renaisser*, but at least it gives me something to do.'

'Very well, we shall see you back at the castle later.'

They clasped one another's arm, and with one brief glance at Marguerite the man walked away. It was then that her friend covered her mouth and burst into tears. Eva ran to her, almost stumbling as she wrapped her friend into a tight embrace.

'Oh, Marguerite,' she mumbled, kissing her forehead. 'What you must have endured. It is over, my dearest friend. Did you hear me, it is all quite over now.'

Marguerite did not respond, only looked away before they all removed themselves from the scene and made their way back to Guildford Castle.

Eva rode back with Nicholas while Marguerite was escorted by Sir Warin de Talmont. She felt ragged and tense after the events on the old stone bridge but it was more than that. It was both hearteningly reassuring as well as agonisingly painful being once again this close, this aware of being in Nicholas's arms and having her back pressed against the hard wall of his chest. She did not want this awareness. She did not want any reminder of the strong attraction she felt and attempted instead to ignore the feeling of being this close to him. It amazed her that although Nicholas was a strong capable warrior, he was only a man. A man with flaws—a man of flesh, blood, sinew and heart and she wanted desperately to comfort him after his perceived failure with *Renaisser*. He might not have apprehended him but he had saved both her life and Marguerite's—and for that she would be eternally grateful.

By the time they were upon the castle wall, dusk was beginning to descend. The air still carried the faint acrid burning smell from the fire earlier that day but at least it had been reduced to ash and soot and no longer posed any real danger.

'What will you do now, Nicholas?' She broke the silence.

'Give our report to Hubert de Burgh, regarding what happened today and how our carefully laid plans still went awry despite our very best intentions.'

'Yes, I can imagine that would be difficult to do.' She sighed deeply. 'However, what I meant was what you intended regarding your father.'

'Nothing at all, if I had my way. But, unfortunately, he as well as Maud and my squire are the only links we have left to The Duo Dracones, so I will do my duty and face them.'

She chewed the inside of her cheek, regarding his answer. 'I cannot imagine that it would be an easy feat.'

They meandered over a grassy hill that opened out to a glorious vista on an unusually temperate eventide. The setting sun in the distance cast orange and pink hues in the inky sky. 'No, but very few things in life are, Eva.'

'Would it not be better if Sir Warin or Sir Savaric were to do the interrogation, rather than you?'

He shook his head. 'I have never been one to shirk my responsibilities and, although it will be yet another unpleasant encounter with the man, I will do my duty.'

She turned her head and glanced over her shoulder, taking in his stiff posture and clenched jaw, knowing that, whatever he said, the meeting would be far more than merely unpleasant.

'I can just imagine what you are thinking, Eva.'

'Can you?'

'You must be considering the kind of man I must be, that I would so ruthlessly condemn my sire. This being a rather fitting revenge after the man so faithlessly betrayed me,' he said bitterly.

'That is not what I was thinking at all,' she murmured. 'I was just considering how distressing and onerous it would be for you to be the one to interrogate your own father.'

'It might surprise you to know how shockingly easy it would be for me to do this task. How my complete fealty lies only with Hubert de Burgh, and the ragtag group of men he brought together to work as one. To be as one. They are my family, Eva. No one else but them.'

If Eva had been in any doubt about not only where Nicholas D'Amberly's loyalty and trust lay but also the unbreakable bonds of friendship that only existed among those he called his true family, his true friends, then this was a timely reminder. She had known all along that while they had also been friends—lovers in truth—their lives were far too different, their stations far too disparate to ever be reconciled into anything more meaningful. And soon, sooner than she could ever imagine, her time with Nicholas was coming to an end.

Mayhap this was the real reason why she had felt so hollow earlier. The fact that she would soon leave and never see him again. She closed her eyes and straightened her spine. God, but did she have to feel so wretched about parting with him? It made her feel helpless, as though she was no longer in control of her head. That her heart had full command of her. And her heart felt as though it were being torn, piece by piece. It could not be so. She would get over this—she would. Eva opened her eyes and looked out in the distance and at Marguerite, riding ahead with Sir Warin. She let out a deep sigh.

'I should also add that de Burgh has been more like a father-figure than the man who sired me,' Nicholas added quietly, pulling her back to the thread of his words—his father's betrayal and the unpleasantness that would surely be caused by the manner in which he would then have to resolve matters.

But then it was not simply about the enmity that existed between Nicholas and his father but also the pain and dishonour that his father had bestowed on his wife, Nicholas's mother.

'I am glad to hear it.'

'You need not worry about de Burgh, Eva,' he muttered behind her. 'I shall make him aware that your part of the bargain was met and you did it admirably. You shall receive the fifty marks of silver that you are owed, as we agreed.'

She turned her head to the side sharply. 'Do you really believe that the coin is the only thing that matters to me? Do you think it is all I care about?'

A crease appeared between his brows as he halted the horse and gazed down at her.

'Eva?'

Oh, dear, she had not meant for that outburst to spill from her lips in the manner it had, but then it had been a long, trying day.

'Eva?' he murmured again, his breath close to her ears. 'Look at me.'

She slowly twisted around in his arms and lifted her head to meet his narrowed gaze. 'What exactly do you mean by that? What is it that you do care about?'

You... was the word Eva wanted to say. She drew in a shaky breath, her pulse tripping over itself, knowing it was not prudent to do so.

She loved him. She realised the truth in that. She loved him, body and soul. Mayhap she had begun to know it, understanding that it would only serve to cause her even more heartache than she could imagine possible. After all, it was not for someone like her to have the kind of happiness she longed for with Nicholas D'Amberly. That was never part of the plan. It was never what she had bargained with him, when she had negotiated the silver. To fall in love. To lose her heart. Nothing good would ever come of loving or getting too close to someone. Had she not learnt that? Even if it was something she only dared to dream when she was alone with only her thoughts, and the darkness, to keep her secrets.

No, it would be best to forget all this foolishness. To leave these futile feelings behind, once she departed from the castle.

'What is it? What is wrong?'

'Nothing.'

'Eva?'

'There is nothing wrong.' Eva caught her voice from cracking. 'It is just the events of the day, which have been rather trying.' She knew in that moment that she was also saying her farewell, here, now, without uttering the difficult words. It would prevent the inevitable heartache that would come. It might be considered cowardly to leave like a thief in the night but then that was what she was, in truth. And all she could ever be to someone like Nicholas D'Amberly. A thief who had stolen from him. A thief who had kissed him. A thief who had lost her heart…to him.

'Very well,' he said from behind her. 'Come, we had better get back to the castle.'

Nicholas had spent his time pacing the antechamber after a brief yet troubled slumber, waiting to be summoned into Hubert de Burgh's chamber for a parley, but all he could think about was Eva Siward. He pondered on the look of despair and sadness that had flickered in her eyes the night before. Not that he felt any differently. It had been an impossibly difficult day, which had roused far too many emotions. Yet the knowledge that his time with Eva was drawing to a close was making him frustrated. It forced him to reconsider his options and examine his life in a manner he had seldom done before.

He desperately wanted to somehow keep Eva by his side. In his life. Together. But how? There was much to overcome, much for Nicholas to face, with everything unravelling in his life presently. And in truth they were very different from one another and destined to take very separate paths. Had Eva not made that perfectly clear after their night together?

The wooden door finally opened and Hubert de Burgh ushered him inside. Nicholas followed him inside the chamber and turned to close the door.

'No, leave it open. De Talmont should join us in a moment,' the older man said. 'But I asked him to give you and I a little time…alone, Nicholas.'

His heart raced to hear his liege use his given name at such a time as this. He wondered what it could mean.

'Oh, and what would you need to say to me privately, that you cannot say without the presence of the others?' It was a redundant question since he knew exactly what the man wished to discuss—*his father*.

'You must know why.'

'Ah, then I take it that you have already spoken to him.'

Hubert de Burgh studied him for a long moment and then nodded. 'We have. Yes.'

'Why, my liege? Why would you not have waited until I could also be present?' He felt a sudden surge of annoyance. Was this somehow a test? Did he have to constantly prove himself over and over again? 'You must know that my fealty is to *you*, my lord, and the Knights Fortitude alone.'

The man held up his hand. 'Calm yourself, your loyalty is not in question.'

'Then what?'

Hubert de Burgh stood in front of the small arched window, his back to him, the wooden shutters open, allowing the first rays of dawn to stream through and lighten the stifling atmosphere inside.

He turned and sighed deeply. 'I did it so that I could spare you the task, Nicholas.'

'I see.' A muscle pulsed in his jaw. 'Did you believe that I might not be up to it? Because I can assure you that I would not have failed you.'

'Not at all.' The man shook his head. 'I knew that you would have done it splendidly. However, I did not wish to put you in that position in the first instance, Nicholas. No man should stand before his sire and condemn him, as you would have had to do.'

Nicholas exhaled on a sigh and rubbed his jaw, feeling detached and dispirited. 'So you gained a confession from him?'

'As much as one can with a man such as your father. Walter D'Amberly knew that he had been forced into a corner—one that he could not escape. Anything he would have otherwise said would have incriminated him further.' The older man took a sip of ale. 'His allegiance to The Duo Dracones was just as you had gathered but he had nothing of material value that linked him to them.'

'Then what convinced you of his allegiance?'

He rubbed his hands together in front of the fire in the hearth, taking a moment before answering.

'Your father, along with all members of The Duo Dracones, have, it seems, a small motif of two entwined serpents branded into their skin, at the base of their neck. In truth, it looks quite like a large mole.'

Nicholas frowned. 'How could we have missed this?'

'All the members we caught before killed themselves quickly soon after, the mark becoming undistinguishable.' The man shrugged. 'In any case, your father was, as I said, forced into a corner—once we made it known that by giving us information he might gain a measure of leniency, he relented.'

Which meant that he had been offered very little. God, what a mess. 'And was the information he provided any use to us?'

'A little, and most of which we already knew. Their organisation is such that they only report to one or two others and if discovered they choose death rather than expose anything of value, meaning that when one is cut off, they rise again from the ashes, reborn again. This is why it has been so difficult to get to the heart of the damn traitorous group.'

'But we shall, my liege. By God, we shall.' Nicholas turned away for a moment as he gathered himself together. 'Thank you, my lord.'

'Whatever for?'

'For sparing me, as you said, although mayhap I should still speak with him.'

Hubert de Burgh's head dropped and it was all he needed to confirm his suspicion. 'It is not possible, is it?'

'No…no, I am afraid not.'

'I take it that he is dead.'

De Burgh nodded.

'How?'

'The same as all the others.'

Nicholas suddenly felt a numb coldness sweep through him. 'He was a coward then. A coward and a traitor to the end.'

'He was. And the very opposite to his only son.'

'And what of his wife? What of Maud?'

'She has disappeared, as has your squire.'

Nicholas nodded, taking it all in before his

eyes flicked to meet the older man's steady gaze. 'Did he…did he ask about me?'

God, but did it matter? The man had never been a father to him.

'Yes. He asked for your forgiveness.' The man placed his hand on his shoulder. 'I am sorry.'

'As am I.' He needed to leave, only for a moment to process all that he had learned. 'Thank you, my lord, and if there is not anything else, I should like to take my leave.'

'Just one thing. The girl came to see me before you did, Nicholas.'

The hairs at the back of his neck rose. 'She did?'

'Indeed, and you will be glad to know that I have settled everything on your behalf.'

He stilled. 'You have settled it all?'

'Yes. The matter is now closed.'

Oh, God, no!

He took one step back and then another and turned. Heart racing, his breath caught at the back of his throat, Nicholas threw the doors open and rushed out, running along the narrow hallway and down the spiral staircase. He strode out onto the bailey, crossing the path to another building, where Eva, Marguerite and Joan had all shared a large chamber together. Opening the wooden door, he hurried inside, hoping that he might be wrong in what he would find there.

He was not.

She had gone.

The chamber was empty, packed up, containing nothing now apart from a few pieces of furniture.

He heard footsteps and the swish of skirts, coming to a stop behind him.

'She has left, has she not?' he muttered without turning around.

'Yes.' Joan de Talmont placed her hand on his, squeezing it gently. 'I tried to make her stay, Nicholas, I really did. But in the end she believed that it was time to leave.'

'Without saying *adieu*?' He shook his head. 'Without at least giving me that courtesy?'

He heard Joan sigh. 'Mayhap she believed it would be better to sever your…your association this way. Mayhap she believed that it would cause less heartache, without the *adieus* and tears that might have come.'

'What in heaven do you mean, Joan?' He spun around on his heel and searched her eyes. 'Heartache? That cannot be so.'

'Are you certain?' she murmured with a small knowing smile. 'Because sometimes we do not comprehend exactly what is staring us in the face.'

'And pray, what could that be?'

'Matters of the heart, Nicholas.' Her smile deepened, her eyes seemed far away. 'Love.'

'Love?' His chest clenched tightly, just uttering a word so foreign to him. 'That was not what was agreed between us.'

'It seldom is and always catches one unawares.' Joan caught his hand, her eyes not quite meeting his. 'But if I may, Nicholas, let me advise you not to spurn the chance of happiness, of contentment, and the love of another. It is rare, uncommon as it is surprising. And, as such, its value can never be truly measured. Do not give up.'

He opened his mouth to respond but the words would not form. Instead, he watched Joan fumble around her skirts, untying a couple of strings and grabbing a leather pouch and holding it out to him.

'Eva asked me to give you this.'

He reached out, opened the pouch, and found to his amazement his mother's ring buried inside. He bit back a smile at Eva Siward's audacity, realising that she must have stolen it back from his father the night he had caught her prowling outside Hubert de Burgh's chambers.

'Well?' Joan asked, raising a brow. 'What is it?'

'Something she once took from me.' He smiled. 'But might very well belong to her now, anyway.'

'So you are going after her then?' Joan clasped her hands together, sounding far too hopeful.

'No.'

'Why?'

He shook his head. 'Because I shall honour what Eva Siward wants.'

'Piffle. She may not know what that might be.'

'Then you do not know Eva.'

Joan's shoulders slumped. 'So you are going to let her go?'

He crossed his arms and sighed. 'You know, Joan, I can truly appreciate why Warin might find you exasperating from time to time.'

'Never mind that.' She waved her hand dismissively. 'Well, are you?'

'Am I what?'

'Cease being so obtuse.' She glared at him. 'Are you going to let Eva Siward get away?'

A smile curled around his lips. 'I do not believe I said that.'

Chapter Nineteen

It had been over three months since Eva, along with Marguerite, had left Guildford Castle to start their new lives, aided by the great man himself, Hubert de Burgh. He had agreed to her terms and paid the silver that she had negotiated with Nicholas, on the proviso that she would continue to work for him, albeit surreptitiously.

She had seized the opportunity, understanding well that having the protection of the most important lord in the land would allow her freedom that she had always wanted, bringing with it a sense of belonging. Finally, she would have a place she could call home, where she could put down roots, where she could have a quiet restful place to get over her heartache.

In truth, these past few months since she had taken over the busy thriving inn outside Dover Castle, where de Burgh held the office as its constable, she had still not felt as she really ought. Oh, Eva enjoyed administering and preparing her much-loved ale immensely and was content to witness its success. She was also much relieved that Marguerite was recovering from her ordeal, although there was still a change to her that she could not fathom. No doubt she needed more time. As did Eva…

When all was said and done, they had endured and she was content, living peaceably within the busy castle walls and close enough to its environs, the bustling port and the sea. It provided Eva with the means to keep her end of the bargain and report any strange goings-on, if she were to encounter them. But most of all it gave her the small, albeit significant link to *him*—to Nicholas D'Amberly, without the man even being aware.

There had not been a day since Eva had left him that she had not missed him. Her heart, her head, in truth, every other part of her ached for him. Yet she could not regret the manner in which she had left Guildford without a parting farewell. It had been for the best, and in time the pain would lessen to being just bearable. That was what she hoped for, but at least her inn, the hub of the village, kept her too busy to think on anything else.

She lifted her eyes, scanning the busy room, with long wooden trestle tables and stools for patrons and a long wooden counter where jugs of ale were topped up and pretty pots of herbs were dotted across. The hearth provided the necessary warmth in such a large, draughty chamber and in the back room she had installed a small kitchen that prepared food and served hearty pottage.

'Is everything well, Marguerite?'

Her friend approached her as she was wiping down the counter with small strips of cloth.

'Yes, the table by the door needs a jug for a group of five and a lone stranger in the far corner has declared that he has travelled a long distance to sample our famous ale.'

She stopped and turned, frowning. 'He used those words, "our famous ale"?'

Marguerite shrugged and began to top up the jug, placing it on her wooden tray, along with five mugs. 'I'll serve the group, if you see to the traveller.'

'Very well.'

Eva topped up a smaller jug and, along with a mug, carried it to the corner of the room, where the traveller seemingly sat in the shadows.

Anticipation chased down her arms as she

approached the table, just as he raised his head and tipped his hat up.

Dear God…

Her eyes widened in shock as she let out a shaky breath.

'Nicholas?' She blinked, unable to believe that he was really here at her inn. 'What are you doing here?'

'Well, good morrow to you too, Eva Siward.' He smiled, inclining his head. 'I could ask you the very same question.'

'I… I live here.'

'Do you, now?' He gave her a slow smile that made her stomach flip over itself. 'And how fortuitous that you have been here in Dover, of all places, under my very nose.'

She could not meet those intense blue eyes. 'Indeed, I have been here, overseeing this inn.'

'So it would seem. However, I do wish that someone had enlightened me of your where-abouts, so that it would have spared me scour-ing up and down the kingdom looking for you.'

'You…you looked for me?'

'Did you not think that I would?' He raised a brow. 'I did tell you that I would always find you, Eva Siward, however long it took.'

'But why, Nicholas? Everything had been settled between us.'

'Had it?' His eyes bored into her, as though they were penetrating into her very soul. 'And after the manner in which you left, without so much as a farewell.'

'So you have been looking for me all this time because I was lacking once again in re-fined courtly behaviour? Because I forgot to say a proper *adieu*?'

'No, Eva, I looked for you because I was concerned about you, because I care for you and thought that mayhap you might have also shared those feelings.'

Oh, Lord...

She closed her eyes, and rubbed her brow. 'I am sorry, I truly am. But I thought it for the best.'

'Did you?'

'Yes.'

'You were wrong.'

Her heart hammered in her chest as she took a deep breath, hoping it might settle her. 'What is it that you want, Nicholas? Why are you here?'

'Is it not obvious?'

'No.'

He gazed at her for a moment before answer-ing.

'Why, your superlative ale, of course.' His

mouth curved at the corners. 'I have heard much about it, after all.'

She poured a measure into his mug, noticing that his eyes never left hers, even when he took the mug to his lips and sipped the drink.

'Delicious.'

'I am glad. Now, if there is anything else, as I really should be getting to my other tasks.' Eva really needed to find a quiet place to still her beating her heart and quieten her scattered thoughts. Only then could she face him with a measure of her usual composure restored.

'There is just one other matter, Eva. In your haste, you forgot something.'

Her brows furrowed in the middle. 'I cannot think what you might mean.'

He reached under his cloak and pulled out a leather pouch, undoing the ties. She allowed him to gently clasp her wrist and turn her palm upwards, into which he dropped the contents of the pouch.

His mother's ring.

She gasped softly, her eyes flicking from Nicholas to the ring and then back again. 'What…what does this signify?'

His smile widened, his eyes softened, and her pulse tripped over itself.

'It signifies that it belongs to you, if you

would have it. It signifies that my mother had the right of it, after all. That the ring should be given only to one who was worthy of it. You, Eva, it has always been you. And it signifies that I missed you these past few months.'

'Oh, Nicholas.'

'And it signifies that I love you, Eva Siward.'

'You…you love me?'

'Yes.'

'How can that be so, Nicholas? We are from different backgrounds—not alike in any way. Opposites, in truth.'

'What does that matter?' He tugged her hand gently, making her lose her footing, landing her straight in his lap and into his arms. 'I love your spirit, Eva, your courage, that clever head of yours, but most of all I love that you slouch when you walk, roar with great big belly laughs and feel the weight of responsibility for those you care for. I love how you drink and eat in that ungainly manner.'

'I am outraged and I do no such thing.' She sat primly, with her back straight. 'I'll have you know that I have a tutor in such things and he is the very best there is.'

'Is that so?'

'Indeed, and I am particularly fond of him.'

'Fond of him, are you?'

'Well, mayhap I adore him.'

He grinned, pressing a brief kiss on her lips. 'Ah, that is infinitely better.'

'Mayhap I should confess the whole of it.'

'Mayhap you should.'

Eva took a deep breath and wrapped her arms around his neck. 'I love you, Nicholas D'Amberly.'

'Thank God for that.'

She pulled back slightly. 'Thank God? Is that all you can say?'

'I have declared my love for you already, have I not?' He winked.

Eva chuckled. 'When such a declaration has been made, and just the once, on such an occasion I suppose it really must suffice.'

'Then allow me to make another.' He reached out and grazed her cheek with the back of his fingers. 'I declare that I would like nothing better than to be wed to you, Eva Siward—if you would have me. Let me care for you, let me love you. You have quite stolen my heart.'

'I… I do not know what to say.' She was stunned, unable to take it all in. 'You would take me to be your wife?'

'As you would take me to be your husband.' He curled a stray tendril of hair behind her ear.

'It will not be easy, Eva. The life I lead is unpredictable, unsettling—in truth, it is all the things you wanted to leave behind in pursuit of a more quiet existence. And dangerous too, as well you know. But then I suspect you might have developed a taste for it.' He frowned. 'That is, I hope you have developed a taste for it.'

She desperately wanted to take the next step into the unknown with Nicholas, and although it was true that she would not have chosen a life as unpredictable as the one he described, Eva knew there was nowhere else she would rather be. It was Nicholas D'Amberly who gave her a sense of belonging...of a home.

'And what of your mother's ring? I cannot be what she envisaged for her only son.'

'She would have wanted her only son to have what she never had, Eva. She would have wanted him to be loved and love in return.'

'But I am not pure of heart.'

'You are close enough.' He grinned. 'So will you have me?' He pressed a kiss to her lips. 'Will you wed me and agree to be bound to me forever, Eva Siward—' he kissed her again '—until the ends of time?'

She knew that this was what she had always yearned for, but had believed it to be an impossibility for someone like her. With Nicholas she would finally have what she had always longed for—love, a home and a chance of happiness. Her heart soared as she uttered the next words, knowing how they would change their lives together.

'I believe I shall.' Eva smiled and stole a kiss. 'I shall like that very well.'

He slid the ring on her third finger and cupped her face. 'Then you make me the happiest of men,' he murmured before kissing her once more, stealing her breath, her very heart. But then it belonged to him now, for always.

* * * * *

COMING SOON!

We really hope you enjoyed reading this book.
If you're looking for more romance, be sure to
head to the shops when new books are
available on

Thursday 24th
November

To see which titles are coming soon, please visit

millsandboon.co.uk/nextmonth